The Thompson Gunner

NICK EARLS

VIKING
an imprint of
PENGUIN BOOKS

Viking

Penguin Group (Australia)
250 Camberwell Road, Camberwell, Victoria 3124, Australia
Penguin Books Ltd
80 Strand, London WC2R 0RL, England
Penguin Group (USA) Inc.
375 Hudson Street, New York, New York 10014, USA
Penguin Books, a division of Pearson Canada
10 Alcorn Avenue, Toronto, Ontario, Canada M4V 3B2
Penguin Group (NZ)
Cnr Airborne and Rosedale Roads, Albany, Auckland 1310, New Zealand
Penguin Books (South Africa) (Pty) Ltd
24 Sturdee Avenue, Rosebank, Johannesburg 2196, South Africa
Penguin Books India (P) Ltd
11, Community Centre, Panchsheel Park, New Delhi 110 017, India

First published by Penguin Group (Australia),
a division of Pearson Australia Group Pty Ltd, 2004

10 9 8 7 6 5 4 3 2 1

Copyright © Nick Earls 2004

The moral right of the author has been asserted

All rights reserved. Without limiting the rights under copyright reserved
above, no part of this publication may be reproduced, stored in or
introduced into a retrieval system, or transmitted, in any form or by any
means (electronic, mechanical, photocopying, recording or otherwise),
without the prior written permission of both the copyright owner and the
above publisher of this book.

Design by Miriam Rosenbloom © Penguin Group (Australia)
Cover photograph by Paul Wakefield/Getty Images
Author photograph by Ben Glezer
Typeset in 11.5/15.5pt Granjon by Post Pre-press Group, Brisbane
Printed in Australia by McPherson's Printing Group,
Maryborough, Victoria

National Library of Australia
Cataloguing-in-Publication data:

Earls, Nick, 1963– .
  The Thompson gunner.

  ISBN 0 670 04178 5.

  I. Title

A823.3

www.penguin.com.au

The Thompson Gunner

BY THE SAME AUTHOR

Passion
After January
Zigzag Street
Bachelor Kisses
Headgames
48 Shades of Brown
Perfect Skin
World of Chickens
Making Laws for Clouds

It's the same dream.

A man standing over me in a hood, spraying arc after arc of bullets before him, the gun bucking in his hands and he's shouting, mouthfuls of jumbled slogans coming out like the bullets and I can't quite hear. I *can* hear but the words don't make sense. And he leans back, braces himself against the gun and fires and fires, and I'm too sick to think and gunfire echoes in the middle of the city as if every street is rising up and fighting. Nowhere's safe, nowhere in the world.

And I lie at his feet on the hard cold road, looking right up at him with one eye, and he doesn't see me. I must be invisible. I lie very small, very still. It's hard to breathe and my head hurts, and my hand. My hand really hurts.

I've been sleeping on my hand. Thirty-five thousand feet over the Nullarbor Plain and the Great Australian Bight, somewhere between Sydney and Perth at the end of the longest and stupidest of days, I've twisted in my seat, slept on my hand, tangled myself in the headset cord and dreamed myself into this dream I could well do without.

I fell asleep, I'm sure, during a boring tourist video about wild flowers in Western Australia. That's the last thing I remember. Perfect for dreams, endless wild fields of flowers, but is that what I get? No. We had a news update as well, most of it news I was seeing for the second time today. A suicide bomber in the Middle East, then a tank in Bethlehem, its barrel swivelling around as if it could see fear, or smell it.

It's not good to think that way, as though tanks are creatures or people.

There's blood in my mouth. Worse than that, there's bloody drool on my shoulder. But the cabin lights are down now, the evening's caught up with us. I take a tissue to the drool, delicately, as though it'll leave no mark that way, pick up all the blood. That's not how it works, of course, but no one seems to notice. Across the aisle, a man in his forties dressed for business twitches and shudders in a messy dream of his own.

I broke a tooth today, smashed it to gravel and swallowed the wreckage, in a city that until three days ago wasn't even on my itinerary.

I started this morning in Christchurch. I ran in the gardens there in air too brisk to carry much of the smell of the flowers. Or maybe it's just all the time I've spent in air-conditioning lately, and the way it blocks you up. It was cool in the gardens, but not particularly cold. I ran laps, in a disorganised way – past flowering shrubs, over bridges, sending ducks onto the water, each one chased by the V of its own ripples. I looked at the trees and read their signs – temperate trees familiar from long ago, other trees I didn't know.

I got taken to the airport after breakfast, had a brief and unsuccessful fight with someone there about departure taxes and whether or not they were included in the ticket price, and I boarded the plane for Australia.

I was settling into my seat and connecting my headset when the flight attendant came up to me and asked if she could check my boarding pass. She called me 'Madam' and began the request with 'Do you mind . . .', but then she read my name and laughed and said 'I knew it was you' and she slugged me in the shoulder, without ever knowing she'd done it. Alexis, her name was, and she looked a bit like Naomi Watts, but with dark hair.

I was on my way home, and that's when I knew it. Home after the strangest time away, but not quite home yet. Not Brisbane. Perth via Sydney first, but back in the country where I don't do much in secret.

'You're my favourite comedian,' Alexis said. 'I hope you don't mind me saying that.'

And I didn't at all, because I don't see why you would. She said it as though she meant it, and this was a plane – a relatively public place – not my backyard. When your face has been on TV enough times, and in the papers, you reach a point where it's best to assume that nothing in public is private – plane flights, groceries, every kickboxing class you take, your worst hair day.

'Let me know if you want me to leave you alone,' Alexis

said, and I said, 'Don't leave me alone. I've been alone for weeks.'

Which is true, largely. Or at least it feels that way.

'Don't let them keep you inside.' That's what Paul Newman told George Clooney who told Matt Damon who said it on TV once while I was watching. And I realised I'd got into the habit of leaving home by the back gate and the quiet lane, just to keep home private. And my life isn't a movie star's – I'm not deluded, and that's not what I'm thinking – but it's not as completely unlike it as I'd expected.

'Our in-flight entertainment is about to commence,' Alexis's voice said throughout the cabin. 'First we have the news, followed by the sitcom *Everybody Loves Raymond*.' And she stopped at that, but held the stop like a pause, not like the end of the announcement, and then she went on, 'Not as funny as Meg Riddoch, I know, but it's the best we can do for you this morning. The sound will come through on channel one.'

People laughed, enough of them that I knew my place on the flight was no secret. In Canada last week I'd been anonymous, and that had been good sometimes.

There are always updates to the itinerary, and my agent tracks each one and keeps me sane – or at least functioning. Sydney, originally just a connecting flight, had become most of a day, and it complicated itself as it went along: a photo shoot with a designer, a long cab ride to a book megastore in Parramatta, the broken tooth – its corner, or in fact two thirds of it, snapped off clean by a piece of bone in a Cajun chicken filo. A bone, a stone, it hardly matters which – I swallowed it, and the pulverised chunk of tooth with it. And the people in the bookstore couldn't have been nicer, more horrified, more urgent in their wishing that it hadn't happened, more happy to pay for its fixing, wherever that might take place.

The fantasy ball-gown photo shoot was at a studio in Darlinghurst, and I turned up with my flight-addled brain having bought the fantasy. As I got out of the cab, I was imagining a rack of possibilities to choose from, all of them glamorous, and the entrance I would make from the change room to the studio and the sharp intake of breath it would provoke from everyone there. And the designer would say, 'Darling, it's yours. Keep it. I don't want to see it on anyone else.'

But no. There was no change room, no actual garment to change into and soon I was standing there, in a concrete-floored warehouse, wearing only my functional bottom-of-the-suitcase Kmart underwear, and the stick-thin assistant was frowning and I wanted to tell her it's a very practical bra. I have one or two better, but it couldn't be that kind of day. I've been on the road for weeks, and it gives excellent support. I've just flown from New Zealand, dammit.

But you lose with these people if you even think about coming up with a real-world context for your underwear, and it's best to pick your battles.

'Darl, I think we're going to have to lose the bra,' the designer said, and battle lines were drawn.

I told him I wanted to see some fantasy ball-gowns. I told him we could lose a couple of spare people who just seemed to be hanging around for no particular purpose. I told him I'd be keeping the bra on until and unless it was absolutely essential to remove it, and what did he mean by his surly 'You realise this is for charity?' remark anyway? Sure we might be promoting a fundraiser ball – one I might or might not be going to – but I never said I'd get my breasts out 'for the kids'. It just doesn't seem like it should be part of the deal. And, no, one of the spare people going to the kitchen and whipping us all up some daiquiris would not help.

He never liked me, not the whole time I was there, but I liked him far less. I kept my breasts to myself, so I was trouble, difficult, as far as he was concerned. Not that my breasts were of any interest to him – that was always clear – but he had definite issues with the bra. He found it aesthetically nauseating when it came to the clean, sculpted, ridiculous lines he wanted for the fantasy creation we were to pretend was a garment. Bras wouldn't work for it. Nor, it turned out, would my thighs.

And when they called the agency last week to line up the photo shoot, I'm sure they told Emma it would be fun, a bit of fun, and flattering and good exposure and very helpful. A big help 'for the kids'.

I stood there in my underwear as he took a deep breath, faked something like charm for a sentence or two and then kneeled down in front of me with a roll of Glad Wrap, 'Just to make the most of those lovely natural curves.' He practically grunted as he made the most – or in fact least – of my lovely natural thighs, wrapping them tight, and then he bound me to stop my lovely natural breathing and stapled me into a long spangly sheath of emerald fabric that turned me into some kind of mardi gras mermaid.

Then, when I thought things could only be made worse if he brought out a garland of seaweed and a buffed King Neptune, he got down on his knees again and tugged at the fabric around thigh level and said, in an annoyed kind of tone, 'Are you a cyclist? Or anything like that?'

To which I could only say, 'I don't know. What's like a cyclist?' because he seemed like the sort of person who would be flimsy enough to break if I hit him hard.

He looked at me blankly so I said, 'Other cyclists?' and the look turned blanker, if that's possible.

'Sorry, honey,' he said, 'but I really need to focus. So if I could have a bit of shoosh?'

Maybe just one slap to the cheek would have been good but, no, that's not me. I'll seethe, bitch to Emma, make sure I'm never back here, line up a couple of years of therapy to help me learn to love my thighs, and that'll be that. I left him to be slapped by someone else later in the day – someone without my grace. Or control.

I bumped into Susie O'Neill on the way out. She was sitting like a next victim, with a magazine rolled up in her hands, not reading it.

'Hi,' she said, remembering me, I think, from when we'd met at a couple of functions. 'What's it like in there? What do they do to you?'

I told her she'd be fine, but that she shouldn't expect a dress. And I sat in the cab on the way to Parramatta thinking I bet there'll be no Glad Wrap for Susie O'Neill. She looks as fit as she ever did, though leaner across the shoulders now than a butterfly gold-medallist.

We turned a corner and the sunlight came in my window and onto my cargo pants, and I looked at them and convinced myself they weren't bursting apart at the zips. These thighs run up hills when they get the chance. They do, occasionally, cycle. They've never been in better shape. They're as good as they're going to get, and that's the last time they'll be Glad Wrapped. And I haven't been asked for a bit of shoosh since I used to get terminally bored in geography in about grade nine. That designer had nothing to commend him, nothing at all.

At the shopping centre in Parramatta, a publicist was waiting to pay my cab fare.

'We're really glad you could make it,' she said as she signed the credit-card form and took her copy. 'Really glad.'

I never caught her name, but I knew she was a publicist by the way she treated me like a special idiot, someone who had some kind of gift but who could not be expected to show any sense or remember what they were there for. And I had little sense in me at that stage, and less memory, so she was on the money. The plane trips, the cab rides, the long, long time away – all that was catching up with me and leaving me a little woozy, and the air was already warm outside the cab at Parramatta while she paid. I couldn't in that minute remember much about the piece I'd written for the book, so I needed all the publicisting that was coming my way.

As we walked inside she handed me a copy, knowing I wouldn't have seen it. She told me a few new things about the charity it was raising funds for, briefed me on the people I'd be dealing with, checked I'd be okay to speak for a couple of minutes – never part of the plan until that moment, as we turned from the wide airconditioned arcade and into the crowded bookstore.

In a back room I met Jessica, one of the editors. I sat down, I drank a glass of water and it started to make sense.

I remember saying, 'Honestly, some days it's just one vacuous thing after another. It's a relief that this project's got some purpose.'

I turned the book over, and saw that all the contributors' names were arranged in mirror balls, and mine was directly above Boy George.

'How about that?' I said in a way that did no more than take up time as I worried that my use of the word vacuous might be misconstrued. 'After all those weeks when I watched 'Karma Chameleon' on *Countdown* . . . that's a clever idea, those mirror balls.'

Then the assistant manager came in with the Cajun chicken filo from the in-store cafe, since it was past lunchtime in Christchurch and I'd told them I couldn't see myself talking to the crowd unless I'd eaten something.

At the baggage carousel in Perth I practise their names in my head: Felicity and Adam, Felicity and Adam. Felicity the festival publicist, Adam her boyfriend. I can see that it's night outside. We're waiting for my suitcase – me, Felicity and Adam.

'It's Adam's car that we came in,' Felicity says. 'I don't drive. Well, not much. We'll be using cabs mainly, for the interviews, but I hope you're okay with the car. Adam was going to clean it, but . . .'

She's dressed better than I am, as though she's been out somewhere that required it. She's wearing a long navy jacket that makes her look thinner, and she's already thin. Her height exacerbates that. She's as tall as I am and Adam looks dumpy next to us. She swaps her phone from hand to hand and she's the first to notice any silence and make a move to fill it.

She asks about the flight, and where did I start the day exactly? And how was the food, and did I get a movie? She has freckles across her nose and thick wavy hair, a mixture of blondes, the kind of hair other women envy but that annoys its owner most mornings. Hair like mine, and that's how I know. Plenty of days you just end up grabbing it and shoving it into some kind of shape, planning to sort it out later.

Fortunately for Felicity, having been in primary school in the eighties, she should never know the need to try the perm I went for back then. Unless fashion turns on her, which it always might. I was eight feet tall with that perm, I'd swear it. And it was wide too. I was like a hedge on a stick.

My case arrives and I lift it from the carousel and click the handle up into place.

'Black with wheels?' Adam says, and he hasn't said much so far. 'I thought you had a green backpack. I thought I read that on a website.'

'Right, and now I'm supposed to just get into a car with

you people in an unfamiliar city and let you drive me off into the night? And there's nothing in the back but a big plastic garbage bag, a boning knife and a shovel . . .' Adam laughs at that, but Felicity doesn't. 'I did have a green backpack, but the Americans or the people at Heathrow busted every lock and every zip with the increased security they've got now. And I got back and I thought, bugger it, who am I kidding, I'm old enough for wheels.' We trundle towards the exit. 'It's nice to see websites don't know everything.'

'So, the partner called Murray,' Adam says, 'his daughter called Elli, you being Brisbane born and bred – does that all stack up?'

Felicity snaps at him. 'Adam. You are creeping Meg out. You are here because you have a car, remember, not to talk. I'm sorry, Meg.'

'It's okay. He was creeping me out until he got to Brisbane born and bred. Despite what most websites say, I was actually born in Northern Ireland.'

'It's his sense of humour. I'm sorry. Not the born-and-bred part but the creeping you out part. It's not funny, Adam. I knew I should have just used Cabcharge vouchers . . .'

'I don't think I was the one who mentioned the boning knife,' Adam says.

She snaps again. 'Don't say "boning knife" in an airport, you idiot.'

'But Meg . . .' He thinks better of it. 'I'm going to shut up now.'

Felicity says she'll sit in the back with me, if that's okay. There's festival business to talk through.

I take the seat behind Adam, Felicity fiddles with her phone, I find mine in my bag and turn it back on. My tongue finds the sharp edge of my broken tooth and can't leave it alone. It's the gap that's the most unsettling thing, the space where once there was good hard tooth. My tongue feels swollen back where the tooth has cut it, and the inside of my cheek is cut too.

There are trees on the way out of the airport, tall pale gum trees that seem almost white in the lights of Adam's car. He won't have hair when he's thirty. That's how it looks from where I'm sitting. But a shaved head would probably suit him. He's got a look that would work with it.

I ask him what he does and Felicity says, 'Adam's a writer, a novelist.'

'Well . . .' he says, as though a secret's out and he wasn't expecting it.

'He's writing his first novel while doing freelance web design on the side.'

'And,' he says, wanting to stop her, wanting his own turn at this. 'And working in a coffee shop in Northbridge a few days a week. That'd be on the other side. Freelance web design's a pretty competitive business.'

Felicity gives him a look, but only I get to see it. He clearly hasn't gone with her plan. I think, for the purposes of this drive from the airport, he was supposed to be a novelist. I want to pitch in and help him. Is this how their relationship works? Maybe it is, but I still want to pitch in and help him.

'Where would creativity be without the big silver coffee machine?' That's what I start with. 'It puts the Australia

Council in the shade when it comes to funding the arts. All you've got to add is a bit of dishwashing and you've got the perfect novelist CV in place.'

'I've done the dishwashing,' he says. 'It's the novel part that's holding me back.'

He checks if we'd be okay with music, and the CD he plays is Roger Sanchez. I heard it last week, driving through Calgary in a car at night, exactly this music, and I saw the video for the single days before leaving for the tour – a girl walking the streets of a cold city with a huge heart that gradually gets smaller, something sad being sung behind the beat, a chance encounter near the end, just before morning. The phone rang then, at home, and I don't know if the girl's chance encounter led anywhere. She looked lonely with that big heart, more lonely than foolish. Or maybe sentiment sucks me in all too easily.

I tell them that I heard the CD in Calgary, and that songs sometimes follow you on tour that way, and Felicity says, 'That was the PanCanadian Comedy Festival, wasn't it? That sounds big.'

'Well, yeah. It had its moments.' There's a fresh taste of blood in my mouth, and my tongue is trying to find where it's coming from.

'Oh, the tooth,' Felicity says. 'Sorry, I should have asked you about that by now. Emma called me about it.'

'Emma?'

'Emma from Big Talk – she's your agent, isn't she?'

'Yeah. I just didn't know she knew about the tooth yet.'

The weight of this settles on me. The weight of being

beaten here by the story of my day. I'm home, where everyone knows everything. This is my job and how it goes. Conversations are had about me – me and my tooth – people talking till they know each other and can mention one another like a third friend who's out of the room. I'm almost incidental to this, it feels, though if bits of me didn't break I guess these calls wouldn't be made.

This whole complicated thought seems horribly ungrateful.

'I don't have an appointment for you yet,' Felicity says. 'It's classified as not urgent since you aren't in any pain. Emma was reasonably sure you didn't have pain, so that's what I had to go with. I'm sorry if it's wrong. Tooth pain they were talking about. Like, if it's broken down to the nerve.'

I can still taste blood. It's from my cheek, I think.

'Oh, your itinerary,' Felicity says, and pulls some folded sheets of paper out of her bag. 'Emma told me you like an itinerary.'

'Yeah, um, my tooth. It's cutting my tongue. It's cutting the inside of my cheek, so I really think it needs to be fixed.'

'Oh, sorry. Yes, sure, sorry,' she says, as if she's let me down already. 'I'm sure they'll go for bleeding. As a reason, you know.'

'Or, just tell them there's pain. My mouth is sore, trust me. There's pain. All you need to do is get me in the door.' It's two or three in the morning in Christchurch, my hair is greasy, my mouth is sore and I can taste my own blood. 'If you could tell them whatever you need to, that'd be good. I know you couldn't have done anything before now, but if we could get it fixed I'd really appreciate it.'

She offers to take the itinerary back, since some interviews will probably need rescheduling. She says it's no trouble. She's feeling bad because I don't have a dental appointment; I'm feeling bad because I'm putting her neat itinerary into disarray in the minute she's handed it to me. I feel like someone who just made a colour-specific M&M demand, but who isn't cool enough or famous enough to do it. I come very close to switching the light on and opening my mouth wide to show her the damage.

Instead I tell her I'd like to keep the copy of the itinerary. Even though a few things might change, it'll still be useful for me to look through it tonight, to get some idea of what we're up for.

'Good,' she says. 'Good. I know you like to know what's going on.'

She takes another sheet of paper from her bag. It's a cream Oroton bag with a silver clasp, and she keeps adjusting it to different positions on her lap and next to her, as if she's not used to carrying anything like it.

The sheet of paper is an email from Emma, with questions for a magazine's Q&A column. I don't mind Q&A pieces, though if you don't keep it brief the sub-editors cut your answers in half, and each one ends up just intro and punchline and you have to rely on the reader to fill in the rest.

Felicity tells me Emma wants me to call her about 'the TV people', the ones I'm working on a show with, and it's only once the moment's passed that I realise a pause was left in there for me to elaborate. By then she's moved on to tell me there's a celebrity canoe race on Sunday, and she and

Emma were sure I'd want to say Yes so they've done it for me. And Emma said to tell me that there's a beer sponsor and a VIP marquee deal.

When Felicity mentions it's two to a canoe, I tell her I'll take anyone with a world record or an Olympic gold in butterfly or freestyle – anyone famous for their upper-body musculature.

It seems unfair that I should bump into Susie O'Neill at a photo shoot that was all about the stapling of spangly fabric, and yet I get dudded frequently at celebrity sporting events. I once played tunnel ball with an air-guitar champion, the state Health Minister, a hairdresser to the stars and Ronald McDonald, and there's a reason tunnel ball isn't usually played in huge plastic boots. Ronald was crap, frankly. The event was a fundraiser for cancer support, and we got caned by some ten-year-olds from Indooroopilly State School who, it has to be said, showed signs of considerable practice.

I tell Felicity not to expect much of me, that the moment I start hoping for a canoe partner with shoulders I'm pretty much guaranteed to end up with some fey boy interior designer from some crap TV show, who hardly has the upper-body strength to lift the Product to his own hair.

Felicity apologises, and I tell her I love these things, that's what I'm saying. This is all good. The race will be a happy debacle, we'll raise money for something that needs it, and there's a beer sponsor. Could a Sunday be better than that? I don't think so.

In the dark in the back of the car, this isn't all coming through the way I want it to. Maybe I should have mentioned

Ronald McDonald and the tunnel ball, instead of just drifting off into it as a hazy old thought. Maybe I should stop trying to play the role of the comedian just met at the airport. Most people expect you to behave like a chat-show guest, but perhaps Felicity doesn't. I should be glad of that.

We pass some shops and a park. She pulls a festival program out of her bag, and tells me there'll be a T-shirt but they come in two different styles and she thought it might be nice for me to choose. She says Elliott King and the TV people are looking at Saturday and they'll get back to Emma with the details. She goes through the last couple of minor items on her list, and seems to relax once they're all crossed off.

I ask her if there's a gap somewhere in the itinerary for me to have coffee with a friend and she says 'Sure' and she makes a note of it. 'Easy.'

So, that's business attended to for now, in a conversation that never quite worked the way it should. But that's probably just me, this day, these weeks. Roger Sanchez plays on. Adam taps the wheel sometimes. The Perth CBD appears ahead of us.

Calgary – two weeks ago

WHEN YOU ARRIVE at the PanCanadian Comedy Festival, it's the big gift-wrapped box with the plush bag and the genuine steel pen and pencil set that give it away – the festival's name comes from PanCanadian Petroleum, the principal sponsor.

The box was on the bed in my room at the Fremont Palliser Hotel, wrapped in gold paper, with a matching gold ribbon. It was the first thing I saw when I shut the door, my suitcase in tow and my other hand full of envelopes, a warm shower my only immediate plan.

I flew to Calgary from Melbourne via Los Angeles and Vancouver, and I was met by someone who said, 'You must be Meg Riddoch. I've seen your picture.'

She was holding a festival program above her head to rally the necessary passengers, and she kept it there while she spoke to me, her arm sticking straight up into the air. There were two other festival comedians on the flight, one from Vancouver who had flown only over the Rockies, one from New Zealand who looked in better shape than me. The Canadian was dark and wiry, the New Zealander looked like a dissolute Viking. He looked unstoppable, and it was only when I stood next to him at the baggage carousel that I could see how bloodshot his eyes were, and that the flight might have taken its toll.

'I met you in Melbourne, I think,' he said, and it might have been bourbon that I smelled on his breath. 'At the festival there, a couple of years ago.'

His name was Dave Stone, and his voice was quieter than I'd expected. I didn't remember him, but I covered well enough. He'd had a break from stand-up after that, after Melbourne, and he'd been getting back into it in the past couple of months. He told me he'd been filming *The Lord of the Rings*, not that I would have seen him. He ended up on the cutting room floor, every frame he was in.

'It pays, though,' he said. 'I had some lines, and lines pay. And they've brought me back for the director's cut on the DVD.'

We loaded our bags into the back of the brown station wagon, and I sat in the front passenger seat next to our driver, whose name I can't remember. She was a festival volunteer.

We'd flown over mountains, serious snow-capped Rockies, to get there, then circled Calgary over a dry brown plain that I supposed must be prairie. On the way into the city in the car, we passed low buildings built for snow, the Winter Olympic ski jump, dry leafless trees and people turned shapeless by the sheer volume of clothes they had to wear to walk outside.

'Winter must be cold here,' I said, as some drops of rain

hit the windscreen and the wipers shuddered and scraped them away noisily and the leaden sky seemed to go a long long way off into the distance.

Our driver turned to me, wanting to offer better news to a new visitor, and she told me brightly, 'Oh no, it's much worse in Winnipeg.'

She wasn't the last person to tell me that, or to explain the particular weather systems at work, the Chinook Arch you see sometimes in the clouds, the way winter operates in these parts when it's really set in.

I told her Brisbane city had never recorded a freezing temperature and she said, 'I can't believe that. How can it be? It must be strange for you. How do you know when the seasons change?'

Later, after my shower, I wanted good coffee but I had no idea where to get it. I went down to the festival office – in a suite on a lower floor – and kept myself awake by talking to the people there. They had coffee and it was offered to me I don't know how many times, but it was in a large pot kept warm on a table full of Danishes, and for quite a few years now I've had a serious attachment to the big silver machine and a fresh genuine skinny latte.

The time for the reception came, and my next Calgary fact came along with it. The reception was in a different building, but we never went close to outside to get to it.

'It's the fifteen-plus rule,' one of the staff said. 'All the downtown buildings are linked fifteen feet above the ground, so you don't have to go outside in winter.'

To me this sounded like a theme park idea, some kind of

urban maze, but they all seemed to think it was normal, passing from one building to another at altitude. It stopped me putting together a map of the place. I left Calgary without ever being quite certain where the PanCanadian building was, though I'm sure it's one of the big ones – it must be near the hotel and I ended up in it several times. But I have no compass indoors, it turns out, and each time I had to go to the PanCanadian building I needed help, and our arrival there took me quite by surprise.

There was food in abundance at the reception, stand-up canapé-style food, and my body decided it was a meal time though it can't have been later than five p.m.

I talked to a festival board member, an accountant called Tina, who worked for PanCanadian and who said, 'Oh, yeah, we're a big part of the community here, so we feel it's important to give something back.' She told me Calgary was often called the Houston of the north, that it started as a wheat town, that the company loved events like this. They were behind a few festivals throughout the year, and the writers' festival was just last month. 'There were Australians here for that, too,' she said. 'I think we get three of them, two or three. Your government helps. But I don't know the details of that, not as well as I should. We were gearing up for the comedy at that time also. I just love comedians. You're all just so darn . . . funny. Well, most of you. I've got to admit there's the occasional guest who remains a mystery to me. But it'd be no good if all our tastes were the same. I mean, what kind of world would that be?'

She had a severe fringe, and a glass of non-alcoholic

punch with an umbrella in it, and she chose only the neat canapés that were easy to handle. I drank wine and had tartare sauce sticking the fingers of my free hand together, and I'd already spilt soy on my boots. She seemed like the kind of person a festival such as this would find essential, but who would keep themselves determinedly low-key and who quite enjoyed it when jet-lagged comedians daubed themselves with food in front of her. That way, she could go home and tell the family something like, 'Hey, kids, quite a crop we've got this year. I met this Aussie . . .'

Dave Stone arrived at the door about then, and came over our way lifting an orange juice from a tray as he crossed the room.

'Goodness,' Tina said, '*two* of our international visitors. I can't keep you all to myself. I should leave you to mingle.'

She took two steps away before being caught by someone with festival business to discuss, and they walked off with their heads down.

Dave Stone had washed his hair and now it seemed to blow back from his head as though it was wind-tunnel affected. He still looked like a Viking.

He caught me noticing and said, 'Can't do a thing with it,' and he shrugged his shoulders theatrically.

He told me he'd had no idea where the reception was, and a volunteer had caught him in the doorway of the hotel as he'd been about to wander onto the street in search of it.

'Wrong, wrong, wrong,' he said. 'And she set me straight. "Comedians freeze till they snap out there." Apparently.'

I told him they say it's much worse in Winnipeg, and he laughed and said he'd heard that.

He clinked the ice cubes around in his glass, and took a mouthful. He shook his head to clear away the seediness of flight. He told me he only drank orange juice now, not even Coke, but that he'd flown from Hawaii smelling of the drink someone had spilled on him and it had been good to get his clothes on their way to the hotel laundry.

'How about the bloody gift on the bed?' he said, as he took a handful of prawns on sticks from a passing tray. 'Did you get that?'

'The gift from – how shall I put it – the naming-rights sponsor? Yes. Did you know about that?'

'No, I just thought it was going to be big, a big festival. Like, drawing people from all across Canada.'

'Sure, Pan-Canadian, from the Greek. Meaning "all across Canada".'

He laughed, and set his prawn sticks on the windowsill, all the prawns in his mouth already. The rain had stopped outside by then but there was a blustery wind blowing, trees bending, and not too many people out in it.

We agreed it couldn't happen where we came from – a festival taking its name from an oil company – but we also agreed the people were lovely, every one of them, and we'd feel dirty if we went home and crapped on them in interviews: 'Well, I said Yes thinking, Pan-Canadian, that's got to be one of their big festivals. Then I got there and it was PanCanadian *Petroleum*!'

We had a festival in Tasmania not so long ago which

had the timber industry as a minor sponsor. The organisers emailed months in advance to let us know, and to tell us there were protests being planned and the protesters would attempt to contact us and get us on side, and that they, the festival and its representatives, defended utterly our right to free speech, etcetera, etcetera. It was several hundred words of numbered points about how fine it was that we would have our own views, and that was enough for me. It reminded me that I'd prefer pristine forests *and* a way of keeping people in work and I wasn't sure how that would happen, so I lay low, put Emma between them and me and just did the job when the day came.

But Calgary wasn't like that. Dave Stone and I paid private lip service to the ozone layer, confessed to each other our motor vehicle ownership, and agreed that we were both probably as dependent on fossil fuels as the next person, even when the next person was someone in an executive position with PanCanadian Petroleum, as was likely to be the case in the room in which we'd found ourselves.

I helped myself to a third glass of wine, he took another orange juice and we agreed we were as conflicted as all right-thinking people must be from time to time, and that a lot of what we did might or might not be seen as hypocritical, depending on how you were disposed to look at it. Dave Stone, some caviar caught in his shaggy Viking beard, confessed he even bought Nike shoes, but only because he couldn't get others to fit. I told him to call me the moment he started to contemplate buying his young nieces and nephews gift packs of cigarettes for Christmas.

We went off separately and schmoozed. I told myself people who work in the fossil fuel industry are, of course, people too. I spent a good ten minutes being silently intensely political, wondering if I should be more committed to public transport at home – catch a bus once or twice, write a letter to the papers about it – and then I gorged myself on the Pan-Canadian Petroleum canapés. There are people less shallow than me who have already evaporated.

Quick, more prawns. There's no compromise in me, only surrender.

Perth – Tuesday

THE CANAPÉ DIET: you know you're famous when you never have to deal with food bigger than your own hand. Actual meals mystify famous people, and cutlery is something they're almost nostalgic for, from childhood.

In fact, that's probably not the case, even if it is part of my routine. It's probably more applicable to corporate lifestyles, the medium-to-high-level jobs involving endless networking, but somehow that's not as funny. It's funny if Brad Pitt forgets how you eat a meal, but unremarkable if a guy in a dark suit eats more wontons than he needs.

Now I'm tired, a new level of tired. It's long into the New Zealand night and I'm holding onto that one fact as if it's the explanation for everything.

I was well publicisted all the way to the lift, Felicity, as she should, leaving nothing to chance. In the room there's just the low hum of airconditioning, the voices of the late TV news, no pressure to talk, or make sense, or live up to any expectations.

My itinerary sits in a pile on the desk that includes my

per diem envelope and some Cabcharge vouchers. Everything else is dumped around the place – my suitcase, damp laundry, other bags, my boots with the jumbo paperclip holding the left tongue in position.

Nothing gets fixed.

That's the thought that occurs to me, sitting on my bed not concentrating on the news but noticing my boots and the jumbo paperclip. Nothing gets fixed. Not the tongue on my boot, not the blown lightbulbs at home, not the leaky taps.

I washed some clothes in Christchurch last night, in the bath in my room at the hotel next to the one once stayed in by Bill Clinton. At least they're sort of clean, if not dry. I rig my portable line up from the shower head to the towel rail, and in Perth they can take as long as they need. I'm here for five nights. Five nights on the twelfth floor of Rydges with a view to the south and east – city buildings, the wide dark body of the Swan River, suburbs glinting off in the distance.

After a while, we all end up with hotel jokes in our routines. Little observations that we accumulate like the ones we used to pick up at home, and that were the first things we found funny. Why is it that the main difference between four- and five-star hotels is that five-star hotels give you the mirror that lets you watch yourself on the toilet? Boom boom. You realise you've been touring too long when you get home and you can't go to bed unless there's a chocolate on the pillow. Boom boom.

But it's not all like that, not all about the distinction between four stars and five. You get used to city hotels that are set up for business – for calls, faxes, interviews – and the only new experiences come along when someone offers you a regional tour and you play Rockhampton or Bendigo or the Moranbah Workers' Club.

I searched far too long for the phone once in a room in Townsville, before finding the note pointing out the convenience of the gold phone under the stairs next to the office. I stood there reading it, a couple of sentences typed badly on a lined card years before, and warm summer monsoon rain lashed my balcony and I knew the stairs were some distance away. And I thought, is this what I've come to, creeping out at night dodging the Townsville rain with a handful of wet coins to phone home and talk about the fun I'm having? Is this it? And what happens when I really make the big time? Do I get to use the platinum phone under the stairs?

Emma didn't understand the system either, driving them crazy calling the office number after hours, when the phone was diverted to the caretaker's flat. And Murray too, calling from home. I don't think I had the mobile then.

But I *was* having fun on that tour. I ran down the stairs barefoot and phoned home wet, and I could hardly hear Murray's voice through the noise of the rain, but I cupped my hand around the phone and told him everything I could about my day, until the money ran out.

I take my bloody-drool shoulder stain to the sink, and I rinse it and squeeze it and rinse it and squeeze it until it seems to be gone. At least it's not a white shirt. I wring out whatever water I can and hang it over a chair, its crinkly damp shoulder facing up and ready for the airconditioning to go to work.

Felicity and I didn't quite synchronise tonight, but it's hard to invent rapport out of nothing in the dark in the back of a moving vehicle. She turned up with energy – worse, a nervous kind of anticipation – I turned up flat and in the wrong time zone and poorly slept. They're on their way home now in Adam's car, both of them saying 'I thought she'd be funnier'.

I had my thighs Glad Wrapped today, dammit, and how can anyone come out of that with enough self-esteem to scintillate?

Somewhere in my suitcase, I have the *Sunday Mail*'s 'Ten Best Butt Exercises' article from some time last year. I've been spreading my butt across plane seats most of the day, but the article manages to do no more than cross my mind. Anyway, there's no sense in working out only your butt. Tomorrow I'll swim, and that's far better. I only brought the article for times like this, days when I don't move and then find myself in a hotel room late in the evening, thinking I might as well do something to keep my body working. Something to use my muscles, tire them out, put myself to sleep.

I lie on my back on the bed. There's an ad break in the news. I can remember three of the Ten Best Butt Exercises, or four, but none that can be done while lying on a bed not moving.

I'm here, I'm checked in, my laundry's out, the 'Do Not Disturb' sign is on the door. If only someone with energy would come and clean my remaining teeth.

I expect I'll dream, though I'd rather not.

I picked up an apple from the silver bowl at the reception

desk, a hard green apple, and I take a bite of it and chew it with the left side of my mouth. I'm sure my mother used to tell me not to eat lying flat on my back in bed. 'You'll only choke doing that,' she'd say, as if it'd almost be my just deserts since she'd told me enough times before.

The gun in the dream has a wooden stock and a box magazine with the right sort of capacity, so I've assumed it's a Thompson submachine gun, even though the man holding it is right-handed every time and I don't get the clearest look at it. I used to think it was an Elvis Costello song, the one about the Thompson gunner, but it was Warren Zevon. I found a best-of CD at a friend's house that I stayed at not so long ago, and I played it when they were out. It's about a mercenary in Biafra in the sixties.

I don't have dreams often, not ones that I remember. But there are some that come back on and off, brought out by travel and time-zone changes, things like that. Dreams in which I'm falling, or my teeth are loose. Dreams in which my car brakes don't work, or something's gone very wrong at school, or someone's after me. When my head's buzzing with overtiredness, it seems to flip through them like an old deck of cards.

My neighbour broke two teeth once, his front teeth, on a marble floor when he fell from a chair he was spinning around in, one afternoon while we were watching TV after school. Maybe that's where the tooth dreams started, though I've heard they're common. And I've lived in an era when plenty of news stories are about a war somewhere, and all stories come with pictures. And I was born in a place and at a time when the accents and the streetscapes in most of those stories were close and familiar, even though I lived in a peaceful village on the coast. You can't ignore it when it's in your own land, even if it's not your village, even if you're small.

So that's the dream that comes on some nights of poor sleep. Our village, those times. Taken and worked on in the way dreams do.

Men with guns, following me, chasing me through cities, forests, the woods close to home. The lights of silent cars turning into the lane. Old black saloon cars with suspension like a porch swing, rocking and swaying, the lights rocking and swaying like lanterns behind the trees. No noise, no noise, and the heads inside of gunmen, dark and shrouded. Weapons on their laps, cleaned, loaded, the glint of the moon on gunmetal, then the smooth click of moving parts – a bolt being tested, a magazine clunking into place, thirty-two bullets. Hands like farm boys'.

In a shudder, the night goes. I'm on a road, face down, I can't move. It's all about noise then, recovering noise from the deafness in my head. Crowd noise and smoke, the clatter and clatter of gunfire and its echoes, that's where I am, right at the heart of it. Right at the feet of the Thompson gunner, becoming as small as I can, wishing myself away.

The apple is fresh and hard, dark green and almost sour, and that's the way I like them.

I won't sleep just yet.

Ballystewart — 1972

IN BALLYSTEWART when I was young there were two apple trees in the garden of our white house beside the sea, but all the apples were good for was cooking. Mostly they would fall to the ground and stay there until my mother or father collected them in a bag and tipped them onto the compost heap.

'Why would you plant trees when no one can eat the apples?' my mother said. 'What would make you choose a variety like that?'

But my grandmother never liked to see them going to waste so sometimes she and I would pick them, her up a ladder and me below with her sun hat to catch them in so they wouldn't hit the ground and be bruised. She'd make pies and apple sauce for pork, and she'd put the sauce in jars and cover each lid with a bright piece of material cut with pinking shears. I wanted to help her cook, and I wasn't allowed to cut or peel but I could stir the sauce when I was tall enough. I was seven then.

I spent afternoons with her sometimes. She was the first

person to teach me card games and she let me watch *Doctor Who* on TV, though I had to watch the Dalek scenes from behind the sofa. My mother said I wasn't ready for *Doctor Who* – she said I'd have nightmares – so it was a secret when I watched it at my grandmother's house. And my mother would turn up later to take me home and she'd ask what we'd been doing and my grandmother would say, 'Oh, this and that.' I can't remember any nightmares though.

The news would come on after *Doctor Who*, and we'd change the channel or turn the TV off. 'It's all miserable,' she'd say, as the first pictures came on screen. 'Too many bad people doing things we don't need to see.' And the picture – an armoured car on the wet streets of Belfast, a blown-out shopfront – would fizz into nothing, and she'd lead me back into the kitchen saying, 'Shall we make something else, my girl? What would your daddy like?'

My grandmother stuck recipes in exercise books, and she had half a shelf of them. If we made a cake I got to lick the bowl and sometimes to pipe the icing on, squeezing it from a bag out through a star-shaped nozzle.

Even in pies our apples weren't sweet, but people make apple pie too sweet most of the time.

Perth — Wednesday

I WAKE EARLY, when the light comes, next to a half-eaten apple gone brown. My tongue's more swollen, my cheek a bit shredded. I won't sleep again and I know it, so I find the Q&A email from Emma in the mess on the desk and I get to work. I can make notes now and it'll cut down on emailing time later.

Q: What's your worst addiction?
A: 'Where Are They Now' articles in magazines just like this one.

Q: What's your burning ambition?
A: To go through life without sitting through or doing a PowerPoint presentation (must be a better word than 'doing') and to tumble turn competently.

Q: What's your worst blind spot?
A: An irrational hatred of drive-in dry-cleaning customers. Irrational? Maybe not. Think about it. It's the

ultimate self-indulgence, and they add to that by expecting an immediate place in the traffic. They're so lazy they can't put one foot out of their cars to pick up their clothes. Did I says cars? I meant Mercs and Range Rovers, obviously. Range Rovers that never go anywhere more rural than pony club. Yep – it's a blind spot, very blind.

Q: What's your least successful attempt at self-improvement?
A: Could be that 'Ten Best Butt Exercises' article from the *Sunday Mail* that I've carried for thousands of kilometres over the past few weeks and done twice – excessively the second time (typical) on a day when I thought I really needed it. It took a very expensive ski-lodge-style butt massage in Banff to stop me walking like a chicken the next day, to be frank. I'm assuming exercise articles confer at least some benefit if you pack them in your bag and think about them most days?

Q: What's been the highlight of your career so far?
A: Seeing my name in a mirror ball above Boy George's on the back of a fundraising anthology (check exact name of book and charity).

Not bad. And I think I carried off the dry-cleaning one with some conviction, even though it's actually Murray's and I could hardly care less about drive-in dry-cleaning.

I miss it, that misspent passion directed against people with big cars and an inflated sense of entitlement. Q: What do you miss? What do you miss most right now? I'm glad they're not going there. Where would I begin? A catalogue of endearing idiosyncrasies that are also infuriating, the laugh lines around his pale blue eyes, his hair in the morning that stands up like a jester's hat, the games he and Elli invent together and that make sense only to the two of them, the simple measured rhythms of a normal life and every small detail of it.

Q: What's the first thing you see in the morning?
A: I look for the windows. I look for the light. I look for a sign that will tell me where the hell I am.

That's the real answer. I think I'll skip the question. I think I'll get back to the rest of them later. At home the light comes in from the sides, both sides, and Murray's up already, opening and shutting kitchen drawers, his tie slung loosely around his neck, his hair still wet and misbehaving. There's coffee waiting when I get out there, on the counter already sugared and stirred. Murray's standing watching TV by then, eating a bowl of cereal and expecting that I can talk sensibly before caffeine kicks in. It's just not how my brain works.

But today I'm awake at six-twenty a.m., I'm on the wrong side of a wide country that already has light everywhere and my head is full of wrong, unhelpful things. The gym in the building next door opens at six-thirty or so, and I can get a pass at reception.

The lap pool's only about thirteen freestyle strokes long,

ten if I work hard on my style, but the gym is good – nothing like a hotel gym. My hand is sore again, this time from doing weights. It's sore near an old scar, but the discomfort goes while I'm in the water.

I have a resistance training routine that I do sometimes, though not as often as I should. I'm more into cardio, and particularly kickboxing or swimming when the chance comes along. At least swimming doesn't change too much from place to place. No two bikes or two treadmills seem alike from one gym to the next, and there seems no point in learning how any machine works. I always end up standing there poking at buttons until round about the right number of red dots appears on the screen. Then I have a minute or two staggering along looking drunk, but soon it's working smoothly and I'm flipping through channels on the TV remote, the usual mixture of CNN, BBC World, soccer somewhere in South America or Europe, local programming.

The gym at the Christchurch hotel wasn't bad, and it didn't take me long to get into the 'rolling hills' routine on the bike. There's something cruel about names like that, and their pretence to clean outside air and a view. The gym there was a small room underground, and I pedalled away getting teary-eyed watching a Nadia Comaneci doco. I don't know what time it was, but it was the wrong time for my body, and for my state of mind, and I was teary about her triumph, about how young she looked, about the stories yet to come to do with life back in Romania, Ceausescu's son, all that. In 1976 she struck me as a snooty overachiever, but in the doco, in my late thirties, every score of ten gave me a lump in the throat. Even as her public story was all about glory, her life was probably unravelling. As lives can do, without people knowing.

I cranked the hills up a notch, pedalled harder, and the burn set in in my thighs, the sweat fell from my hair and the screen showed all red dots and hard work.

Swimming became a habit in Calgary, and I usually had the basement pool all to myself. It had a low ceiling and warm water and the air was thick with the smell of chlorine, a smell that stayed on my skin afterwards and sometimes caught me by surprise since it seemed so out of season.

The Perth lap pool is on the rooftop, and the office buildings towering around it mark out a piece of blue sky shaped like a chunky badly-drawn star.

My turns still aren't right.

'This was the summer I learned to tumble turn.' It's not fully summer yet but if I could, at the end of it and long after, remember this summer just for that, I should be happy. It's like an old diary entry, a line from a novel about one of those summers when the central character starts to find their way in the world, or learns that anything might be possible. But that can't be. I'm far too late for my rite-of-passage novel. I'm simply not the swimmer I'd like to be.

I'm standing rearranging my swimming cap when my phone beeps with an incoming text message. It's business hours in the east, and I expect that's where it's from.

Five more laps and I'm done, and hopping around at the side of the pool to jiggle some of the water out of my ears.

The message is from Emma: 'Note to Mega – ensure rowing machine included in workout. Celeb canoe race only days away . . .'

I eat at an outside table at the CBD cafe, and the continental buffet is wasted on me with my broken tooth. I fill a bowl with yoghurt and a bowl with fruit, and I tilt my head to eat on the left.

I'm not sure why the tumble turns aren't working. My friend Julie, a champion swimmer in her day, tried to teach me the technique in a pool at Noosa last summer. But each attempt I make still involves a motion more like a tumble dryer than a tumble turn, and every time I surface I'm surprised by which way I'm facing.

A voice calls out to me, a young male voice shouting my name.

I look up and some school students are standing on the corner, four sixteen-year-olds with striped ties and bags too big for them.

'It was him,' one of them says, and his friend says, 'Bullshit, it was you.'

They come a few steps closer and they ask me what I'm doing in Perth and when I'll be back on TV. This is the part of my audience demographic I could feasibly have given birth to, but it's not something they ever seem to work out.

I tell them I'm here partly for the festival, but mainly because I've heard they've got great dentists. I tell them about yesterday, the bookstore, the experience with the designer and his sheaf of fabric. It's only when I'm nearly finished that I wonder about the wisdom of shouting out some story about taking my bra off to an audience of sixteen-year-old boys on a city street. It works for them though.

One of them hangs back when the others go, and he says, 'Hey, it'd be really cool if you could sign something.' He pulls his modern history textbook out of his bag and hands it to me with a pen and says, 'Anywhere you like. Somewhere near the end. We're not up to that yet. And it's Matt, Matt with two Ts.'

I open it at a photo of the signing of the Yalta Pact. I draw a cartoon of myself, a line sketch I worked out a while back for the times when my brain has run out of witty personal remarks. I put myself behind Churchill and Roosevelt, with a cartoon grin and crazy hair, and in the margin I write, 'Matt, having a fine time in Yalta with the boys. Wish you were here. Meg.'

'That is so cool,' he says. 'So cool.'

And he slaps the book shut and runs off after the others, his shirt half hanging out at the back, just as it should be.

I call Emma, and it's good to hear her voice.

'I got your emails,' she says, 'but I want to hear all the rest of it as soon as you get the chance. It's been weeks and weeks since we've talked properly.'

Emma is sitting in an office in a converted Sydney terrace house, sunlight coming in through the French doors that open onto the small courtyard behind her. I've visited enough times to have a picture of it in my head. There's a round table with the papers on it, but no one will read them until lunchtime. She's barefoot, but her shoes are nearby in case anyone comes to the door. Clients will call all day, in varying states of need and disarray. Venues and promoters and occasionally the associate producers of TV shows will call to book the clients, or to make one of a series of small but annoying changes to arrangements that have already been agreed upon. We won't get the chance to talk now, either of us.

'What about Banff?' she says. 'That night in Banff. What time were you emailing people?'

'Late. Or early, depending on how you look at it. There happened to be a terminal outside my room, and you know I can't miss a quick email check when the opportunity presents itself.'

Another phone line rings and she says, 'Could I just get you to hold on a second?'

The phone clunks down onto her desk and she takes the call. It's about a contract clause and I can hear her, in a voice that now sounds flat and far away, saying that archival recordings and national broadcast are two very different things, and she'll get it sorted out. It feels almost as if I'm eavesdropping on the conversation physically rather than remotely, as if I'm in her phone, on a file or a pile of letters on her desk and looking up at her talking, looking across the room, past the bookshelves and the table and out at the sky beyond the courtyard. Sitting in her office on an incidental visit to Sydney, talking through the plans for this tour, or another. Working out what happens next.

'Hi, sorry.' She's back, loud and clear. 'Now, where were

we? Felicity's good, isn't she? We've had a few nice conversations. I think she's quite a fan of yours. Oh, how's the tooth? I'm sorry I couldn't make it to Parramatta yesterday.'

'It was a flying visit. I didn't expect you to.'

'They said you were a trouper.'

'As long as they pay for the tooth . . .'

'They'll pay. It was their food. We've had that talk. They are mortified, you know.'

I can see Felicity inside the CBD cafe, no jacket this morning. I wave, but she's looking the other way. Emma's other line rings again.

'Bugger,' she says.

'It's okay. I think we've both got things to do. Felicity is roaming the buffet right now trying to find me.'

'All right, I'll email. I've seen your schedule so that's probably the best way to do things. But I expect a call as soon as you're back in Brisbane. All the gory details.'

Felicity reaches the hot food and turns, and this time I catch her attention. She's pulling the new itinerary out of her bag as she gets to the door.

'All fixed,' she says, and she sits down. She moves the sugar, sets the itinerary on the table and rattles her hand around in her bag until she finds her sunglasses. 'You're going to the dentist this afternoon, so the interviews this morning are the same as before.' She turns two pages, then a third. 'I've moved the two o'clock and the three-thirty to tomorrow and Friday, but you'll still get a break tomorrow afternoon for coffee with your friend before the opening party tomorrow night.'

She sits back in the seat and, perhaps for the first time, breathes out. I can't see her eyes behind the dark lenses.

I tell her I'm obviously in good hands and she smiles and nods, but looks uneasy about taking it as a compliment. 'There's still one or two to confirm.'

'Sure, but you get that.'

I've forgotten everything she's said already, I realise. My mind stayed stuck in the unfinished conversation with Emma. Gory details. She wants all the gory details, and I've told her next to nothing for more than a month. I should call her back. I would, but the other line would ring too many times. She's busy, I'm busy, it's not the time to talk about life.

'Tomorrow night's booking well,' Felicity says. 'And your own shows are, too.'

Calgary — two weeks ago

THE PANCANADIAN COMEDY FESTIVAL started with a big opening event called the Uptown Showcase. Before I flew in I'd had some ideas about what the Uptown part of that might mean, but it turned out that our venue was the Uptown Screen – an elegant old cinema that could seat about four hundred. I couldn't have guessed that.

'I hear Uptown's a Canadian brand of cigarette,' Dave Stone had said when we compared our schedules at the opening reception, so I told him I was pretty sure his first event was sponsored by the people who make clubs for harp seals.

The Uptown Showcase featured several comedians – two Canadians well-known from the Toronto club circuit and now TV, someone from Scotland, and me – as well as tumblers from Cirque du Soleil and a singer/songwriter called Rob Castle, who happened to be in town at the right time.

'I know it's eclectic,' one of the festival people said, 'but that's the idea.'

The show was being taped for broadcast by the CBC, so

variety helped, as did the apparent star power of Rob Castle who, I was told, was quite like Ryan Adams but a few years older and big only in Canada so far. We were to sit in the front row, all the performers, and then take our turns being interviewed on stage before doing our bit. So one edge of the stage was to be laid out like a lounge room and the rest of it set up for performance, with the CBC host disappearing into darkness once each interview was over. And I've done years of events, but that format was totally new to me. Then, five minutes out from show time, I was told there would be opening remarks by the Lieutenant-Governor of Alberta.

I stood in the green room with the minders and the other comedians and the muscular tumblers of Cirque du Soleil, and everyone but me was bustling and had some sense of purpose about them, or they were clustering in small groups to talk. In the distance, beyond the doors, the noises of a sound check could be heard – instruments, a voice, talking sometimes and then singing a few words.

I felt a long way from home then. The green room was dark and messy, and looked like it had hosted some other event just minutes before we arrived. There were tables pushed back, and a whiteboard with red scrawled writing on it that I was sure wasn't to do with us.

That's when I met Rob Castle, as I was having my 'long way from home' moment and using canapés to deal with it, as is my practice, ambushing the sushi trays on their way out of the kitchen. It's all those laps of the pool. I'd swum that afternoon, and carbs are essential. Rice, salmon, seaweed – a perfect combo. Along with the statement: 'No, Meg, don't eat more than fifty, or you *will* puke.' So I took a beer. Big improvement. The bubbles in beer occupy stomach space, and have no metabolic implications.

I wasn't up for meeting anybody just then, not even ready for a word of conversation, and Rob Castle turned out to be standing next to me exactly as I was feeling overstuffed with food and foreign and jet-lagged and strange. And crushingly stabbingly unfunny. What was I doing in Calgary? There's so much needing to be done at home, so much that in that instant looked wrongly abandoned. There were conversations I needed to have. I missed people, Murray and Elli. I missed our life.

And Rob Castle said, 'Hey, that guy, that guy over there,' pointing to the slump-faced husband of the catering coordinator. 'Is he Sam I Am from *Green Eggs and Ham*, or what?'

Those were the first words he said to me. And he was right. And the two of us had a mean secret laugh at this poor Dr Seuss character of a man, and I snuck a couple more small pieces of sushi into my mouth, and Rob Castle loaded up a handful himself and jiggled them around like dice and said like a shy boy, 'Rob Castle, by the way.'

So we had to sit next to each other after that, like perfect new best friends.

We rearranged the seating down in the front row of the crowded theatre, and we sat next to each other and kept up the mean secret laughing, at almost anyone's expense – the host, other comedians, the chunky tumblers from Cirque du Soleil, even the kindly Lieutenant-Governor of Alberta, a woman who reminded me only of my long-gone grandmother, someone I loved dearly. But Rob Castle and I, in our sly muttering way, were out to take no prisoners. We became quite obviously rude but couldn't stop it, talking behind our hands at inopportune moments, even after he said, 'You have to understand that I'm not always this impolite, but I just turned twelve and I think I could be about to dive into a very messy adolescence.'

And I giggled, actually giggled.

And he said, 'You know, I might share my lunch with you some day. You're that kind of girl,' and I told him, 'Hey, no way, boy germs.' But I don't know if they have boy germs in Canada, since he either didn't hear me properly or didn't get it.

It didn't matter. I'd swept up from my slump, I wanted my turn, I'd become completely fearless and I put in one of the best gigs of my life. I starred, and they didn't know that's not always where I fit in the pecking order.

Then the host called Rob Castle to the stage.

I couldn't believe how good he was, my new friend. Good enough that my first instinct was to feel surprise, and my second was to cry at the instant solemn sadness in his songs. I caught it on the way out and stopped myself, and reminded myself I was still part of the show here, down in the front row. There were eyes on me now.

It was probably just the usual tricks of the singer-songwriter at work, but deftly done. Songs about love and loss, the classic and essential topics, effortlessly poetic but each line true. He made me wonder, for one dumb romantic moment, if they all have broken hearts. One dumb romantic jet-lagged moment. I don't lead the life I invent for performance, after all, and I can't expect that singer/songwriters have only their own lives to tell us about.

And when he finished his final song, the last note hung in the air as if suspended or rising on an updraft, and the applause fell on it as loud as four hundred people could make it. Rob Castle smiled a boyish smile, bowed and waved and bounded from the stage for the seat next to mine, his guitar, quite by accident, still in his hand.

The Lieutenant-Governor of Alberta hugged us both on the way out. 'Oh, you two,' she said, 'you were wonderful.'

And I blushed fiercely, since I'd been so rude about her during her opening remarks, and because of the way she squished the two of us together in her broad grandmother's hug.

Perth — Wednesday

IN THE CAB on the way to the second radio interview, Felicity says, 'I've been meaning to apologise about Adam last night. We haven't been going out that long, and he really wanted to come and . . .' It tails off there, and she stiffens up. 'It won't be happening again.'

'Why? You've had him shot? There wasn't a problem, not as far as I was concerned.'

'Really?'

'Really. I think I was the one who brought up the subject of the boning knife.'

'In the airport. Yes.' She takes a quick laugh at herself for that misguided swipe at Adam, and she gives her head a shake as though it makes less sense this morning. 'He's probably sulking today. I'm beginning to think he might be a bit of a sulker. I'm not sure how I feel about that.'

'Oh, a lot of them are. He's got to have that sensitive side to be a novelist, remember? And the difference between sensitive and sulking's only a matter of interpretation.'

She laughs again, at the great creative sulking of her

stocky novelist-to-be boyfriend, presently pulling a surly espresso or two nearby in Northbridge. I tell her she should bring him to one of my shows. We should put his name on the door.

'Well, I don't know if I can do that,' she says.

'Maybe you can't. But I can.'

'Good,' she says, in an ambivalent way that I hadn't expected. 'Well, he'd love to come. I know he would.' She opens her bag, gives it a shake and reaches into it for her phone. 'I told him he was kind of banned, so that's how I know. But I can unban him now, I guess.'

She glances out the window, then checks her messages, makes a couple of notes on the itinerary. She underlines something more than she needs to, then puts a box around it.

I can see her going, 'You are banned, Adam,' with a finger-pointing sternness that he'd have to laugh at, which might make things worse, or better.

We take a detour around some roadworks and come out with a park to our left and the river to our right. We're back on the edge of the city on the way to the ABC studios. I want to tell her that boys like Adam like that kind of thing, some decisive treatment, but only a certain amount of it and it's not always easy to measure it out right. But what do I know? For a start, I don't know Adam.

'Tell me about this person I'm talking to next.' That seems like a better thing to say instead, and it's what I go with. Back to business. 'What are they like? What's the story?'

Two interviews down and we're back at the hotel thinking about coffee, but settling for mineral water. I can't help drinking it with my head tilted to the left, and that provokes another apology from Felicity. She tells me she should have had a dental appointment made for me before I got in last night, an appointment for first thing this morning.

'You're banned from apologising,' I tell her. 'Okay? Banned.'

The festival calls her, for at least the third time, and she checks that I'll be okay if she goes in to the office when the next interviewer arrives. It's the last interview of the morning, and she's marked the dentist's address for me on a Perth city mini-map, along with two Internet cafes. Everything's covered, and nothing's more than two blocks away.

'I might have Richard Stubbs later in the week,' she says. 'What's he like?'

'He's fine. He's a good guy. Actually, I think he'd be good company in and out of cabs and all that.'

'I hadn't expected to be working with you,' she says. 'I put my name down for you, but I didn't think I'd get you. Technically this is work experience for me rather than fully professional. I hope that's okay. I've got my degree and everything, but it's hard breaking into the business. I've done some freelance stuff though. Mostly I work in the coffee shop that Adam works at.'

'Well, I wouldn't have picked it.'

'Really?'

'No. You don't have the temperament to make coffee.'

She stalls, a strawful of mineral water on its way to her mouth. 'I'm kidding.'

She swallows and says 'Oh, good, right' and treats it as the joke it was supposed to be. 'You had me worried for a second there. I thought arriving in Adam's car was a bit unprofessional, but I don't drive and he really wanted to do it.'

'That's okay. I don't think I'm really the limo type. Adam's car worked for me. In London I've had drivers with caps. It's all too weird. And I end up in far too many cabs already, and quite a few cab rides here take a bit of a turn when the cabbie starts going, "Hey, you're that comedian, aren't you?" So I sell X-ray equipment. That's the story I tell them, and there's not one cabbie yet who's found it interesting. But it's not the only job that works that way, I guess, in cabs or at parties or wherever. There are plenty of jobs that chase you around when you don't necessarily want them to.'

'My mother's a doctor,' Felicity says. 'People are always wanting to show her rashes and lumps and things.'

'If you're a comedian, every time you leave the house you've got to be ready for people hassling you to say something funny and make them laugh. And they won't laugh. It's a dare. It's a challenge, and you know they'll hold out on you. And then they'll go, "Hey, I'll tell you something *really* funny. You might want to use this . . ." Any time your face is on TV it doesn't help, obviously.'

'Can I ask about the TV people?' Felicity says, more tentatively than she needs to. 'The ones Emma was talking about. Are they bringing your show back?'

'You noticed my show? That's quite flattering. And, obviously, rare. No, this is different. More acting than that. A series, probably. That's the plan, anyway. A drama. Action. It's a big secret at the moment. It's all this gym and pool time that I'm putting in. I figure I might as well get more out of it than just the cliché of a long and healthy life. I thought I might make it tax deductible, maybe turn it into a paying job.'

Felicity, from the moment I said 'big secret', has had no capacity to treat what I'm saying in any way other than seriously. She's nodding, and I find myself saying 'No, really . . .', about to revisit the tax deductibility remark.

I tell her I want to create a dynamic female character who has the brains and also the physicality to do things. Make her powerful, but with a bunch of normal human imperfections. I want her to be real, but I also want to have fun with the role. I want the show to have some subtlety to it. And I guess I want her to be able to be a kind of role model, but not in an obvious way, or a preachy way. Maybe I want that, maybe I don't. Maybe I'd be happy if it's good TV.

These ambitions have been through a lot since they started, I realise that now. Your character starts with a degree in art history and training in forensics, soon enough there's much more to it, much more at stake, and she's being parachuted alone into a rogue state at night, clanking with weapons as she drifts down into the waiting darkness.

One of the staff comes and takes our glasses away. The condensation under Felicity's glass forms a letter C and her index finger connects the ends and makes a circle.

'This is a lot more interesting than the office,' she says. 'You should have fun with that. With a show like that. I'm not very physical, so I'd like to see someone take that kind of character and give her more than just physicality. I'd like to see you do that.'

'Well, we'll see what it becomes. Once the network and the international co-production partners and everyone else has had their say, I expect she'll be a large-breasted super-spy. And I don't think we can ever have too many of those. I've got a friend who's an actor who says that every script she gets has men described in three lines of detail and women described as "beautiful". That's why I wanted to focus on creating a character, a fleshed-out character. It's like the assumption that all female comedians can do is "chick stuff" – as someone delicately put it to me not so long ago. Anyway, we'll see what happens with the TV plans. I can already imagine the wardrobe meeting, and it's all cleavage enhancement and grenades and knives and things. Are you getting worried about the subtlety?'

She smiles. 'I am a bit. I'd still watch it, though.'

The journalist we've been waiting for arrives. She's Alice from a student newspaper, and she gives me a firm handshake and a smile that shows a mouthful of perfect teeth. Felicity checks again that I'll be okay without her, and tells me she'll have her mobile on all the time. She's going to be good at this job.

Alice speaks in a speech-and-drama type of voice, but when I turn down coffee she suggests a beer, if it's not too early in the day.

The first open bar we find is at the far end of the mall and below street level. The beer smell rises to meet us as we walk down the stairs and into a large room with off-white feature archways and old guys with oily hair settled grimly into boozing. Horse races, somewhere, are running high up on several TV screens.

'Welcome to Perth,' she says, without overplaying the irony or even turning her head.

The interview is conducted in just the right spirit. She's immediately likeable, an arts student who saw the last show I did here and will be paid fifty dollars for this story. I buy the beers, and have to explain why I'm drinking mine half sideways. I already know how her article will open.

She takes out a notepad with a list of questions, and then an oversized tape recorder she's borrowed from the magazine office. It looks like it was knocked off from a high-school language lab in the seventies.

'I know,' she says. 'State of the art.' She clears her throat a couple of times, then presses play and record. 'Interview with Meg Riddoch, in a hand-picked Barrack Street brunch venue where ambience is not the word. Meg Riddoch, do you see yourself as a role model?'

'Alice, it's late on a weekday morning, I said No to coffee and I'm making you drink beer in a Spanish-mission style cavern, otherwise inhabited by a group of men wagering on what might be the fourth at Werribee.'

'So, I'll take that as a Yes?'

'Of course.'

The interview becomes a conversation – in the way that only some of them do – with Alice going back to her question list when she remembers to, or when a natural conclusion forms itself. I find out about her brother, her uni subject changes, her father, who hardly understands her at all but tells all his friends she's setting out to do the longest arts degree in the world. She asks the usual questions and others too, student magazine questions such as 'Club sandwich – yes or no?' and 'Who are you most like on the crew of *The Love Boat*?' Cable, it seems, has brought back more of these shows than it should have.

We're onto the second side of the tape when she scans down her list and says, 'Favourite chocolate available in block or bar form?'

I tell her that I used to have a thing for Old Jamaica, since it's at least an answer I can work with. 'The promise of dark chocolate, fruit and tincture of rum seemed like a hell of a combo when I was a kid. You could gorge yourself stupid on chocolate and feign drunkenness at the same time. Plus, it came with a kind of "pirate chic", despite the fact that pirates were generally bastards. Actually, the whole experience was: gorge yourself stupid, feign drunkenness and talk in a vaguely Cornish accent about your parrot, and slicing people from one end to the other. Not just a chocolate bar, but fun for all the family.'

'Excellent,' she says, maintaining the smile she's had throughout. She checks her list again, and looks up. 'Are you happy?'

The question comes without an agenda. It's the next

on the page. I've worked hard with chocolate, but the best I can do with happiness is a rather late, slow 'Sure' with the emphasis on the unspoken 'un' part of the word, and on the pause before it.

She wasn't expecting that. I've played the games I should so far and dealt creatively with questions that have called for it. She's surprised, I can tell, even though she's trying to hide it. I try to force a smile, as if the pause was only me dreaming about my own list, the long list of things that make me happy.

'Is that any kind of question to ask a comedian?' It comes out of me in an almost on-stage voice, the sound of mock confrontation. 'Aren't we all tapping into some deep seam of sadness?'

'Very eloquent,' she says, acknowledging the performance, but with a smile as though the issue's disappearing, not an issue after all.

'Or, alternatively, a bit of a cliché.'

'But nicely put, nonetheless,' she says, tapping the end of her pen on her notepad, turning it end over end. 'Your work seems very much about the everyday – about things you've done or noticed – rather than some deep seam of sadness. Even though some of the stories now are about TV or international travel, they're also about regular insecurities and have an everyday feel to them, if you get what I mean.'

'Yeah, yeah, they're about normal embarrassment even if it's in uncommon places, little rituals gone wrong. Small things.' We're back on track, or back on some kind of track at least. 'And I don't really know why, to be honest. That's just what found its way in there and people started laughing.'

'Early on it was more bitter and twisted,' she says with a half smile. 'I get the impression you've refined it, in a way. You pick up on different things now, and some of that stuff's not as prominent.'

'I lead a different life now. Maybe that's it. Alice, I was just a fool who once had a drink too many and got up at an open mike since it seemed like an invitation to slag off the last half-dozen shitty men I'd bumped into. And I have to say it felt pretty good. Quite cathartic. Sadly, in my mind I would probably have categorised that as very much about the everyday back then.'

'Really? Give me an example. Some cruddy everyday guy story from back then. Something that really happened.'

'Something that really happened? That sounds quite unwise. But what the hell. It's a long time ago. I did honestly go out with one guy who had a birthday when we'd been together four weeks, and I wasn't too sure how it was going and I didn't know what to get him. I didn't want to send the wrong signal. So I asked him for suggestions and he said that things were a bit tight for him at the time and, if it was all the same to me, he'd prefer the cash. And how did fifty bucks sound? But he was a shocker and I should have known it all along. Denial had been the glue in that relationship for at least three-and-a-half of the four weeks. He pissed in the shower too. Some men think anything's a toilet. But there was always other stuff in the act as well, except for that first night maybe. Soon enough I had something reasonably coherent together, and off it went from there. And I'm lucky it did. The coffee-shop thing never worked for me, no matter how hard I tried. And I did try, with a lack of success that could verge on the spectacular on a bad day. I make shithouse lattes, and that was the least of my worries. I needed the comedy to work, for my own sanity.'

She's right though. Whatever I might say about having other material, I gave the bitter-and-twisted chick stuff a good run when I started, and Felicity was too polite to point it out to me, back at the hotel. I stood up at that first open mike and I mouthed off, and I'm sure I'd had more than one drink too many that night. The problem wasn't always with the shitty men, of course.

'You were born in Northern Ireland,' Alice says, the end of her pen now touching the bottom question on the page, 'but you came to Australia with your family when you were young. What made your family move to Australia? Do you remember anything from before you came here?'

'Yeah. I was eight when we left, nearly nine.' That's the statistic, a standard stat and I'm used to saying it. I expected we'd go somewhere with my 'shithouse lattes' remark but we didn't. I realise, too late, that the stat alone isn't much of an answer. 'I shouldn't be having this beer. It's giving me pauses.'

I've got an answer for your question, I want to tell her, and it runs about six lines. Usually it comes right out without thinking, but not today. And it's no more the whole truth than the rest of my answers, but it is the truth and it does the job, and lets us knock the topic off in one go, every time.

It'll be there tomorrow, automatic as ever. Why couldn't we be talking tomorrow?

I had latte anecdotes, bad coffee shop experiences to talk about, but she missed her cue.

Ballystewart — 1972

I WAS EIGHT when we left, nearly nine, and anyone who asks if I remember anything didn't change countries at that age. Eight years is a lot of seasons, a lot of school, real friendships left behind, TV, music, rain, snow, sometimes sunshine, blackberries, barley harvests, plenty. Wet dogs and the wind off the sea, the slippery bladders of dark weed on rocks, wheel ruts in lanes, foxes, plenty.

And airports – Belfast, Heathrow, Teheran, Karachi, Singapore, Darwin, Melbourne, Brisbane. Days of that, with two dawns at least, Teheran and Melbourne. One with the sun breaking over purple hills and fans on stands marking rickety time in the airport waiting area, the other cold and clear over flat country as we wandered around the terminal, smacked with jet lag, waiting for that final connecting flight.

In Brisbane we were met by a man from my father's company. He had his hair slicked back and a box of chocolates and fat cufflinks. The chocolates had no list of what was what, and I'd always had a clear preference for soft centres. It left me with the feeling that this country mightn't be as easy as I'd been promised.

But that's the end of the journey, the end of my time in the other country, not the start.

I laid my earliest memories down in my first summer when the laburnum tree in our garden was in bloom and I was in my pram under it. I was wrapped up well and looking up at the bright yellow flowers, then on my side, nose against a seam in the plastic, feeling the pattern in the plastic, rough on my cheek. And the wind whipped up as it often did and flowers fell down onto me, dropping from the tree and landing in my pram. And that was confusing, exciting, strange, another new thing in the world to come to grips with. Along with birds – gulls flying in from the sea – bees out pollinating, the sound of my father's car arriving at the front of the house, wheels turning on gravel.

This is all still real, every bit of it, somewhere back and deep in my head. Just as real as everything that followed it.

We had whitewashed walls, and I'd get in trouble for picking at them, for picking at the bubbles in the whitewash and their flaky broken edges.

We lived four doors down from the local shop, and the man who ran it was huge and bald and always told my mother it was lovely to see her, a real pleasure.

My mother made her own skirts and took time with her hair so that she'd get it just right, and she was the woman in the village who looked most like Jackie Onassis. That's what someone's mother said once, and I remembered it, and it was true. Admittedly none of the others looked anything like Jackie Onassis so she had a head start, but she also had magazines that came with the right patterns and a sewing machine with all the features you could hope for.

She was a teacher, but not at my school, and I'd seen no other teachers who dressed quite like her. I never knew if that was a good thing or not, but she stood out in a shop where half the people had come in from farms, still with their boots on. She'd be there in shoes with real heels, and big round sunglasses and a pastel knee-length skirt with matching jacket.

There's a photo of me in those sunglasses and a pair of her shoes, and I'm wearing the dress that became known as my 'party dress'. It was cream and covered with dozens of red cherries, most of them in pairs. My mother made it too, and it was my favourite thing in the world when I was six. I would have worn it every minute of the summer in 1970, if she had let me. By 1971 it didn't fit and I'd moved on. She made me clothes that year too, I think, but I don't remember them.

By then when I went to parties I was content to look like everyone else there, and not like the different one with the special dress. If there was a special dress that year it was worn by a girl called Christine, who I never much liked, and it was made of royal blue velvet and had long sleeves. She was, as my mother said, 'a girl who was far too fond of herself', and we lived in a place that didn't suit attitudes like that.

The village wasn't much more than one street, two rows of houses roughly paralleling the shoreline, a place where cars might slow down a little but not stop. There were farms almost all around, though at one end the last few houses backed onto the woods.

We walked in the woods when I was very young, before guns were banned. People could still shoot foxes then, and they sometimes did. I remember the taste of the plastic of empty shotgun cartridges, and what they were like to chew. How young was I then, if that's my first memory of them?

My father took long loping strides on those walks, and his stride seems shorter now. He wore an old tweed jacket, and it looked like a farmer's. He'd often be ahead of me, his hands clasped behind his back as he walked, and he'd call out if there were puddles I should watch for. He'd find flowers even if they were very small, and signs of animal life – badgers, foxes and pheasants – and he'd crouch down to show me and I'd smell the tobacco that had once been in his jacket. He'd smoked a pipe, apparently, when he was younger.

I can remember the freckles and the fine hairs on the backs of his hands as he'd turn a feather over, or show me where the tracks of an animal went under the hedge. I can remember the smell of mornings like that, how they felt on my cheeks, how the daytime moon looked when there was just a pale white sliver of it over the trees.

And there are faint squiggly lines that I can see if I look carefully at nothing or at a plain surface or a clear sky, and that come, I think, from looking right at an eclipse. I wasn't a habitual rule-breaker, but I broke the obvious ones. I told lies when it was in my interests – but never in a big way, or a way that caused harm to anyone – I talked in class, I climbed higher than I should or climbed things I shouldn't, I patted dogs I didn't really know, I looked right at an eclipse.

Why did we leave? A lot of reasons, hard to weigh and package and sell as an anecdote. Life is often less anecdotal, less convenient, than we'd all like to think.

Perth — Wednesday

It's a question that comes up often enough on tour though, particularly in print interviews when they're trying to plumb deeper depths.

Why did you leave? Can you remember it? It's a Chinese-water-torture question, one that falls like a drip onto your bare forehead day after day and becomes nothing more or less than a way to spoil a perfectly good conversation about Old Jamaica chocolate or Spanish mission beer caverns, or some other topic you haven't talked about a million times before.

Are you happy? That's one that doesn't come up a lot either, at least not reduced to its three most direct words.

The Spanish mission beer cavern is near the Internet cafes Felicity marked on my Perth mini-map, so I picked up some lunch nearby after the interview and came back here to the better of the two. There's the usual spam to weed out, a few I can deal with next week in Brisbane, a photo of an acquaintance's new baby – still creased by the struggle of birth – and two new emails from Emma:

subject: nw

Hey Mega,
Got a call from *NW*. I think they want to do/are doing a story on you. Sounds feature size, so it might mean talking to other people for background. Shall we leave till you're home and talk about it then? That's not so long now.
Em

subject: elliott k

Hey Mega,
The lovely Elliott will be in Perth with a director and others checking out locations for another show with a scout. He says he wants to 'check in'. He thought he'd round up a few people worth impressing and you could 'do something'. Sounds excellent, no? I hope the I/Vs are going well.
Em

There's nothing from home. No Murray, no Elli, even though I emailed her days ago.

The lovely Elliott. Emma lives with me through every shift in the quicksands of TV, and we share complicated views of Elliott King.

How many of my character's subtle human imperfections will I still be holding onto if and when the cameras roll? Soon they'll be hiring a wardrobe consultant for my kickboxing classes and sending along a photographer, and there's no subtlety by then. Who am I kidding? There's not a lot of subtlety now, outside the notes I make on planes about character nuances.

Here's what it's reduced to: Eric Bana did Chopper and became a big star, ipso facto, comedians taking on serious roles works. And the head of drama at the network has taken to referring to my character – with an enthusiasm verging on the feverish – as 'an Australian Lara Croft'.

'Don't you get it?' he said, actually thinking there was something down that way to get. 'We could have something pretty special here. Lara Croft is *big*. And sometimes Australia's big, too. I'd like to see us go with this, and if we get the timing right we could even get a US presale, and that just doesn't happen from here. I mean a network. How about that?'

'Or,' I said to him, 'we could dress me in khaki and bring in some *biiiig* reptiles and . . .' And that's where I stopped it, before the bit that went 'a female Crocodile Hunter', because we all know how badly wrong that might have gone. *Would* have gone. Crikey.

I think it was Elliott's doing. Elliott who lapped it all up when I put my concept to him, Elliott who said, 'I think she's a new kind of woman for TV, a new kind of character, and it's all in how we craft it.' Elliott who somehow trimmed that sentence to 'an Australian Lara Croft' when it came time to pitch it to the network.

So I got Emma to go back to him the first time they mentioned Lara Croft, and I got her to say 'Meg's thinking of something a bit more subtle than that' and she said that Elliott's response was something like 'Oh, sure, sure, yeah'.

And she told them no guns, and they came back talking martial arts, as if we were haggling over a contract clause. So then we *were* haggling over a contract clause, since I wanted 'no guns' stipulated and then they wanted 'martial arts' stipulated in case I might change my mind on that one.

'Martial arts is great,' they said in the meeting they flew me down for the next day. 'And it's not off the track. It's fine. It's a good idea, women having self-defence skills. We know you like martial arts.' And I told them only for fitness, and they said, 'Cool – it starts off being for fitness, but there's this buffed guy she works out with, he's kind of her assistant . . .'

It's so pretty when they think on their feet.

I wanted to go, 'Yes, but really it's all a trap, and the buffed guy-assistant's brain has been hollowed out by the Evil Doctor Zoron and replaced by a genetically engineered super-smart hamster that peeps out through his nose and controls his every move using a series of gears and pulleys . . .'

But, by the time I'd thought of that, hours had passed and I was pacing Emma's office blowing off steam and the TV people were nowhere to be seen.

And Emma said, 'Oh, Mega, the bigger they talk and the more knives you have strapped to your thigh, the richer you'll be. It's TV – full-on commercial TV – remember? It's not that you can't have subtlety, it's just that the subtlety can't be very subtle. And it'll give you a break from touring. It'll give you that home time you've been looking for, if the deal holds together and they make it at the Gold Coast and in Brisbane. This is ninety per cent what you want.'

'Every time I look up your nose I see a hamster,' I told her. 'Oh faithful assistant . . .'

'No really,' she said, and her head rocked back as she laughed. I leaned forward for a closer look, and she flung a hand up to cover her exposed nostrils and then said, still laughing, 'What am I doing? There's no hamster. Trust me, Mistress. I haven't seen Doctor Zoron since he stopped bulk-billing.' And she rocked forward again in her seat and laughed at her own joke for some time, ignored the phone when it rang and then said, 'I'll get back to them and say No to the knives if you want me to, but they say they just see them as an extension of martial arts and part of the look. You wouldn't have to go stabbing people.'

Not in the first draft anyway, but it wouldn't shock me if some stabbing snuck in there at some stage. Backed up by a dodgy set of statistics, if it needs to be, to show that our target demographic would like stabbing, or expect it.

Emma promised me she'd go in hard for a 'no super-hamsters' clause, and might even push for one about genetically modified rodents in general, but I told her not to worry. I'd bust Evil Doctor Zoron right in the monocle, rodents or no rodents.

'I want you to know that I'm fully committed to your vision,' Elliott said later when he took me out for a drink to make sure that everything was back on track. 'Fully committed to *our* vision. And committed to getting this thing made.'

Emma's email is still on the screen, telling me about the lovely Elliott and his plan for us to do something. I click on Reply, and then I don't know what to say.

Elliott, the lovely Elliott, the past month. It's the past month that I really need to deal with, but I don't know where to begin – or when, or how – and that gets in the way of me coming up with a remark that's glib enough to do justice to Elliott King. All the gory details – that's what Emma said she wanted. And usually there's no one happier to oblige than me.

I wanted emails from Murray and Elli. I had an idea that I'd log on and there they would be, full of non-gory detail. Murray on how he's now heard enough Avril Lavigne to last a lifetime, but if his major parenting issue is persuading his daughter to spell 'skater' without a number in it, things aren't too bad. Elli on Murray's Sunday morning French toast going badly wrong, and how he had to stand on a chair to put a plastic bag around the smoke alarm.

The person at the terminal next to me laughs at an email she's just opened. It's a big backpacker place, this Internet cafc, but definitely one of the better ones, neither as soulless as a Kinko's nor as much of a cyber sweatshop as plenty of others.

The one down the street was all war-gaming boys when I looked in – rank with late-teenage pheromones and overrun with the clamour of machines. You leave those places feeling like you've been sprayed with Essence of Boy's Armpit. The air's so thick with it your instinct is to keep your mouth shut in case it'll coat your teeth.

If cyber war is like this, what does real war smell like? You'd have to hope there was a breeze or the collateral damage from boy smell could be grim indeed.

I'm killing time, sitting here dreaming about emails I'm not going to get and the blur that Internet cafes become as the cities go by. I'm killing time and paying for it, at the rate of about a dollar for each quarter hour.

My hands are sweating on the plastic armrests.

The X-ray is ready within minutes, and the dentist shows me the image, holding it between two fingers in front of my face and pointing out the deep intact root system that will allow the job to be done in one go, and this afternoon. There's so much of the tooth below the surface and, by the looks of it, even in the jaw that the X-ray suggests I've done no worse than clip three corners off the top of it, though my tongue tells me almost all of it's gone.

'So, this is good,' he says. 'We knew too much of it was gone to simply fill in the space, but we'll make you a crown. It'll be porcelain. Porcelain looks good but the main thing is it gives an excellent long-term result. I don't imagine you'll feel much at all when we get to work, but we'll make sure you don't. You might get a bit bored, though. In which case, you might as well watch a movie.'

I assume he's kidding, but he pulls an overhead TV monitor around and his assistant holds a folder up in front of me.

'Recent releases are at the back,' she says. 'This'll take a couple of hours, so pick anything you like.'

The list runs to a dozen pages or more, sheets of names of movies and TV shows in plastic sleeves. I ask if there's anything they haven't watched, as if we're three housemates standing in front of the new-to-weeklies at Blockbuster before we order our pizza.

'I'll probably be concentrating on the tooth,' the dentist says. 'But I've seen Mister Bean enough times, if that's all right.'

I pick *EDtv*. I missed its cinema run, since I was on tour at the time. I've heard it's pretty good but, really, if it's a crap movie and Matthew McConaughey gets his shirt off a few times, all is not lost.

The assistant straightens my bib, and fits a pair of massive sunglasses of the kind worn over regular glasses by people who are past caring. The dentist applies topical anaesthetic, then injects the local, which stings once or twice but never badly. A firm grip on the armrests gets me through. He keeps testing and testing to see that it's all properly numb, but I don't give in lightly and I jump at the merest hint of sensation.

'We'll make a start,' he says matter-of-factly. 'You can let me know if there's a problem.'

He pushes a blue rubber dental dam into my mouth and clips it around the tooth. The drill whines and goes to work, and the sucker that's hooked over my lower front teeth pulls water and saliva out noisily.

He laughs at something in *EDtv*, right when I'm sure he's working the drill down deep into my tooth. It's not one of the more slapstick moments, not even a great line. I think he's laughing at the nuances of a Woody Harrelson facial expression that is surely happening somewhere beyond his right ear, so what the hell's he doing to my mouth?

I manage to say 'Uuh' which had more to it in my head

but comes out in the language only dentists know, and he explains that he's seen the first part of the movie a couple of times, and he particularly likes this scene.

'Don't you think it's what he's best at?' he says. 'Playing this kind of character? Woody Harrelson, I mean.'

He keeps working, I fall for the movie more than I expect to. Matthew McConaughey takes his shirt off. The dentist finishes drilling, and then we wait as the computer gets to work designing my crown.

We've got fifteen minutes, the assistant tells me, and she points me in the right direction for the bathroom. I'm dizzy and I lurch to the door with my bib swinging loosely on its chain, the enormous sunnies still in place and the blue rubber dental dam hanging out of my mouth. Which is still jammed open with the hardware that fixes the dam in place, so I'm slurping up saliva as I go. On the way past, the receptionist pushes tissues into my hand. I head off down the corridor, as instructed, turning right and then right again, saliva, I'm certain, flapping from the free edges of the dental dam.

When I get there, it's a relief to be alone in the cubicle, and to know that the worst of the procedure is behind me. The window is frosted glass but I can hear noise through the vent at the top, the sounds of human traffic in the nearby mall, people with the time and opportunity to shop in the mid-afternoon.

I'm sure I smell sweaty, and the right side of my face is numb from the cheek down. I wipe my forehead with the tissues. Time to go back.

I turn right into the corridor and keep going until I reach a door. It must have been open when I was on my way down here, though I don't remember it, open or closed. I go through it and it shuts behind me. Shuts behind me, with a disconcerting locking kind of sound.

There's another door ahead, and noise beyond it. I have come the wrong way. I have come through the fire door, and it has locked behind me.

I wipe some saliva from my dental dam onto my sleeve, as if that's a better place to put it. I'm by myself here, in what must be the ground floor of the fire stairs. I'm by myself, surrounded by unpainted concrete walls and with the door that I have come through carrying a prominent sign that reads 'This door to remain locked at all times'.

I try the handle anyway. It moves up and down five millimetres. It doesn't open the door. Somewhere, back in the building, a computer is about seven minutes away from finishing a porcelain crown. My team is waiting. *EDtv* is paused and waiting too.

The best I can do is take a cautious look out of the other door and into the mall. If I'm near the main entrance to the building, I can perhaps sneak back in that way. I open the door, just a crack. I recognise nothing. I stick my head around it, my hand holding back the big piece of wet blue rubber hanging out of my mouth. Still nothing.

I have no choice here. I need help.

I step outside, and I take off one shoe and use it to wedge the door so that it won't lock me out. I will quietly ask someone where I am, and if they know a way back in. For the first time, saliva runs down my neck.

'Hey, Meg Riddoch!' someone shouts out. 'It is you, isn't it?'

I am standing wearing one shoe, sunglasses with lenses the size of TV screens, a bib that I'm drooling on and a sheet of blue rubber that's hanging out of my mouth. Not even my own mother . . .

'It *is* you,' he says excitedly. 'Oh, hilarious. I'm John and this is Liz.' He waves in the direction of the woman next to him. 'And this is our friend Paul. What is this? What are you doing?'

'We saw one of your shows in Melbourne a few weeks ago, a month ago,' Liz says, rushing to get it out and grinning as if she's just stumbled upon Christmas out of season. 'We live in Melbourne, John and me. We're here visiting Paul.'

'Um,' Paul says, a welcome confusion on his face. 'Is this part of the comedy festival – because I wouldn't put it past them – or are you actually having dental work done?'

I nod vigorously and, for some reason, point to him, as if it's a game of charades and he's just guessed what I've been miming. I tell him I'm in the middle of a dental procedure, and it would be great if he could help me find my way back to the dentist. Except I forget to factor in that half my tongue is numb, half my face is numb and there's machinery in my mouth, so when I go to speak it comes out as 'Uh uh uh uh-uh uh uh uh-uh uh-uh-uh' and I don't even get to the part where I ask for help because John's saying 'Hilarious' again and laughing raucously. 'As if it'd be part of the comedy festival.'

'Well, it might have been,' Paul says. 'It's the kind of stuff they do at festivals. They had the Angel Project here a few years ago. They had people hidden all over the city in angel costumes.'

'So what would this be?' John says, all too ready to start workshopping. 'If it was performance art with all that rubber hanging out of Meg's mouth? The Gimp Project?'

I gag on my dental dam when my next breath sucks it into my mouth. I sound like a failing pool filter drawing in water and air at the same time. All three of them are laughing now. I point to the door I've come through, and tell them I've got to go. The words make no sense, but the meaning should be clear.

Liz pulls a camera from her bag. 'I said to John after we saw you in Melbourne that we should have taken the camera. This is just destiny, right? Imagine bumping into you here. We can't let you go without a photo.'

Before I can make a move, she and John are either side of me and Paul is lining up the shot. The only quick way out of this is to let it happen.

'This is superb,' John says with feeling. 'It's so good to meet you. Hey, you're drooling. Can we get one more with me dabbing your chin?'

So here I am, on the Murray Street Mall, no more privacy than a circus animal, partially anaesthetised, incoherent and drooling, having my chin dabbed for posterity. I point to the door again once Paul has captured the moment, and this time they let me go. The last thing I hear clearly as the door shuts behind me is Liz saying they'll send the photos to the website. I sometimes wish people wouldn't do that.

I put my shoe on and I stand there, back in the ground floor of the fire stairs, wondering what to do next. I can't go outside again, so the only plan I've got is to pound on the inner door until someone hears me.

Before I can make my move, the door opens, and my 'Uuh uuuuhhh' has enough urgency to it that the woman standing there stops.

I mime frantically and she says, 'Oh . . . oh, you're locked out of the dentist.'

She laughs, as though events had the potential to turn embarrassing but she's saved me from that, and she holds the door until I get there.

'It's left at the end of the corridor,' she says. 'Then left again.'

The dentist greets me as though nothing's happened. The crown is ready, I can't begin to explain my adventure, I don't even try. I lie, happily, back in the chair and pick up *EDtv* from where I left off.

Hours later in my room the feeling is returning to my face, first as a hazy tingling and then as something more focused and defined.

I came back to a flashing message light on my phone, Felicity checking to see that it had all gone as it should, and telling me to call if there's anything she can do for me, or if I want to do something for dinner, if I feel like dinner.

When I realised that my tongue could move normally, even though I couldn't feel it, I tried twice to call Emma. I've let my mobile battery run flat and it's recharging, so I used the room phone and dialled her number from memory. Both times I called Amcor, the packaging company, who had a message telling me business hours were over for the day.

Outside, it gets dark. The street lights come on, and the lights of houses in the suburbs start to as well.

I missed the end of *EDtv* and I didn't even notice until I was back in the room. I hardly get to finish a thing.

The tooth is spectacular though, the best in my mouth. The dentist fitted the crown, then drilled it down to size. It smelt like a building site while he worked on it, like a drill working on stone, not like a tooth. He showed me the map of its contours on screen, and then took a mirror and showed me the tooth itself.

And I went out to the receptionist, put $758 on my credit card, and bought yoghurt and fruit on the way back here. They told me my new porcelain tooth is ready to go to work immediately, but I think I'll trust it more in the morning, when I'm confidently reacquainted with that half of my mouth. The Cajun chicken filo still has me rather food-shy, maybe.

The other part of Felicity's message was confirmation that tomorrow starts with 'Battle of the Sexes' on breakfast radio, and that it's a phoner to the room at seven-forty.

I eat yoghurt from the tub and my face feels strange now as sensation comes back in an abnormal, disordered way. It was easier when there was less of it. It's as if the nerves started by re-marking the old outlines and now their control has wavered while they're filling in the whole picture. It all looks fine in the mirror though, or at least less deranged than it feels. It's only when I smile that there's any hint of asymmetry, and it's getting better.

The sky is perfect, cloudless, clean, and taking on darkness as indigo first before black. I've never been so tired, I'm sure of it. I've smashed my tooth and had it fixed and no one knows, practically no one.

In the offices in nearby buildings, I can see unfinished work on desks, toys stuck on the tops of computers, work spaces of varying configurations. That's what I'm looking at, the small places where people go each day, five days a week, and the ways they make them their own. I'm sure I know how the whole floor is laid out. There are corridors with flat blue–grey carpet, a reception with two potted palms and a curved desk, meeting rooms without windows, kitchens with fridges where people steal your lunch however you mark it. And the fridges have kids' pictures on them, or those word magnets which someone always arranges into something profane and anatomically improbable, and spoils it for everyone.

I've been that person, naturally.

I've been the annoying temp who doesn't care, the permanent staff member who doesn't stay long, the account manager who, despite her habitually foul mouth and worse line in humour, is not looking to have sleazy moves made on her at the Christmas party. Not that it didn't turn out to be a source of material.

Every time I go 'What is it with office Christmas parties? Mistletoe has a lot to answer for . . .' most of the room is with me. Most of them have been there. And some of them have probably been the drunk co-worker who, late in the evening, thinks you just might put out for nothing more than a piece of parsley left over from the nibblies, if they hold it over their heads in a way that gets the mistletoe message across.

By ten o'clock it's all about bad music and worse groping, and those men grow a third hand. They've got one hand for their eighth beer, another to hover an enticing piece of parsley above their damp rubbery lips and somehow, out of nowhere, there's a third – the Christmas party hand – that gets plonked right on your arse. Because who wouldn't come across after a good clumsy bout of arse squeezing? And it's only worse when they turn on the charm and tell you that, the way they look it, you're pretty much a dead ringer for Nicole Kidman, just a bit stronger in the legs.

That's the routine, all but the last bit which I've managed to keep to myself. I don't know why I drew the line at that.

I was no wallflower at those Christmas parties. I often overdid it at work functions, whatever the time of year, but Christmas parties came with the most free alcohol and the added pressure of squeezing in every possible seasonal cigarette before the inevitable January one resolution, and the equally inevitable recriminations by about the eighth for having weakened and failed again.

I resented those jobs and most things about them, except the company of a few of the people, and I was angry at the end of each year that I was still stuck there and that my luck hadn't changed.

But it wasn't just about Christmas, and taking stock. I drank too much at any opportunity, and I smoked when I drank in a way that I would have called 'social' but that usually involved finishing my own packet quickly and then working the room for spare cigarettes the rest of the night, taking them whenever possible from the people I liked least. On one occasion, I'm pretty sure I slept with someone I didn't know. I can't be too shocked that someone occasionally lurched my way with the old parsley mistletoe stunt in mind.

Murray, who has only heard about those years, refers to them as my Keith Richards phase. I don't honestly think it was as bad as it can be made to sound – as bad as I make it sound when I tell the stories. When I finally put my mind to it, it wasn't that hard to decide to drink a bit less, though the nicotine took some shaking. I chewed a lot of Nicorettes before I was through it.

Angst came out of me like steam back in my twenties, as if I was overheating with it. I'm sure it did. I'm sure I radiated trouble. And I'd get up and do my man-hating self-hating act, and get more abuse and more applause than most of the others. I loved it all – I loved the release of it, the laughter, the contest. I loved hecklers and I baited them. I'm sure I could hardly even spell subtle until I was in my thirties, so I don't know why I think I can complain when TV people can sometimes recognise it but put ratings first.

I started out doing stand-up at the Story Bridge Hotel on wet nights early in the week when no one would leave home to go to anything. That must have been twelve or thirteen years ago. It was eight years from then to Edinburgh, via a Raw Comedy win, Melbourne Comedy Festival, occasional TV, regular TV, touring. Increasing amounts of touring.

My first regular TV job was as a sidekick on a talk show, which failed – though I came out of it well. The show wasn't bad, but it's fair to say it was patchy and it never quite found its feet. One Sydney paper called me 'one of the few genuine bright lights in an hour of television that otherwise stumbles along at low wattage'. I couldn't believe my luck scoring that job. It meant flights to Sydney and an overnight stay once a week, and a thousand dollars a time. It was a new league for me, a new set of numbers. I had to try not to be too much more grateful than they'd expect.

The thousand dollars was broken up into all kinds of payments to make it a strict one-off deal, but it was a thousand dollars so they got no complaints from me. The breakdown was the same each time, always ending with $2.42 for 'subsequent use on New Zealand cable, satellite or other'. Other? What on earth was left to be other?

They paid all my expenses and served meals in the green room, with two choices of hot food and two salads, and they kept a well-stocked bar. I learned not to drink before the show, though the offer was always there. On air the established regulars always looked like they drank too much – backstage they were sober and calm, even attentive. They'd done their time on the road, and gone through all the bad behaviour that comes with that. On the first night I was there, the host had one glass of wine once we'd finished taping, and he told me how attached he was to home now, and that he'd started writing a novel and it wouldn't be what people would expect. He said he was reading Carver again, and he hadn't since his arts degree.

I had, of course, been expecting loosely structured debauchery, spilt cocaine crunching underfoot in the toilets, worse behaviour off-screen than on. I had underestimated the element of performance, and the attention to detail. It was a better show than people gave it credit for, though international guests didn't always know what to make of it.

But I'd started to learn some of those lessons earlier, before I was a regular.

The first time I did TV it was 'Good News Week' and I was a last-minute replacement for a politician. Emma got the call on the Thursday afternoon for a Friday evening taping and Sunday broadcast. I'd watched the show regularly, so I knew how it worked – two teams going head-to-head over a series of embarrassing games based on knowledge of the week's events – but I had no idea of what had happened in the world that week. I'd done a night at the Story Bridge, I'd gone to a band on Tuesday, I'd temped every day in a real-estate agent's office. I bought the paper on the way home after Emma called me, but it hardly helped in the end.

I smoked, I drank, I worked myself up into a state, I told no one I'd be appearing on the show. I called in sick the next day and flew to Sydney in the afternoon.

The producer said, 'Don't be too concerned if you do something dumb or fluff a line and crash and burn. We edit, and we do a few takes if we need to, so you don't have to worry about it going to air. Unless you *really* crash and burn, of course . . .'

And I did. We were given props for one segment, props that told a story, and we had to work out what the story was.

My team had an instant camera, a coat hanger and something I can't remember. The props were rushed on in a break, and I ended up with the camera and hardly heard the instructions. I didn't know if I needed to. I didn't know what I was supposed to do with it.

I made such an idiot of myself on the first two takes that not only did all three make the final edit for the show, but they were part of the ad for it that was on air by midday Saturday.

Each time, the host would work his way along the team and get to me third and announce, 'And Meg Riddoch has...a camera', and I would try to open it with a single smooth proficient move, and each time blast a photo of the underside of my chin and jump in my seat.

A week before, I had arranged to have dinner with my parents on the Sunday after the taping, and they made me sit there watching the whole show. 'You were very funny with that camera,' my father said. 'Did you have to practise?'

It worked for me though, and there was no turning back. It's where the problems began, things like that that were also golden opportunities. They came with a real income, but they also came with travel and an increase in profile, and you're committed to the damage before you know it's being done.

'Your fucking, fucking job,' was how Murray put it one indelicate day, years later, after hiding his feelings for months and months since he didn't want to stop my fun.

'Fun?' I wanted to say to him. 'Fun? I do this to bring my share of the money in. I want to spend more time at home, but this'll pay off for us, just wait.'

But I said nothing because parts of the job certainly were fun and his work isn't like that. And anyway, he said it on a day when it was getting to both of us. I'd dragged us into something neither of us understood, and it was taking its toll.

'This is part of you,' he said. 'And I don't ever want to take it away.'

He looked sad and his hair looked a mess and I loved him for saying it when we were in the middle of fighting. And I tried not to cry because it was a truce, though not a solution, and some days you settle for a truce because there's not one good solution in sight.

In the nearest building, about two floors up from mine, an office light goes out. Someone else goes home, probably later than they should.

I settle in for a night of TV. A banana, a cup of chamomile tea and a night of TV. I expect other people will have arrived for the festival by now and they'll be down in the bar getting reacquainted till all hours. Tonight, my tooth gets me out of that.

My face is feeling better. I can feel my new tooth with my tongue, and it's smooth and sure.

I think it's Wednesday, but I've lost track of TV so I spend too long ineptly channel surfing. Something goes wrong with TV when you tour, even if you're touring in your own country. Entire seasons of your favourite shows seem to vanish, to happen only in a faraway and maybe better world in the lounge room you've left behind.

Even when you think you've got everything right and you're propped up in bed on four pillows and the wide screen is right in front of you at the perfect angle, the shows you want to watch aren't there. You have dozens of channels and, when you find the one you're looking for, it's not showing the show you want to watch – the show now screening in lounge rooms across the country, including yours, including lounge rooms in the same city as your hotel.

Instead you get a cavalcade of obscure sports and stock exchanges in which you have no interest. Darts, hurling, curling and the CAC-40. The Cac Quarante. Tubby English lads guzzle big beers and shoot for a hundred and eighty, you sit there mesmerised, quietly saying to yourself *Cac Quarante . . . Cac Quarante*. French is such a cool language even the name of their stock index sounds alluring. *Cac Quarante . . .*

Imagine a Frenchman in a suit saying '*Cac Quarante*', an Australian in a suit saying 'All Ords'. The latter is made even more ordinary by the comparison, the former, if whispered in your ear in the right circumstances, sounds like it could change the course of an evening. Today's share price of forty big companies turned into a thing of desire. It's a fascinating world in which, it's easy to suspect, a lot of Frenchmen get a lot more sex than they really should. Or maybe that's a myth, too.

Enough. Sleep now. Sleep and don't dream. Or dream of the Frenchman saying '*Cac Quarante*', though he's almost certainly trouble of the worst kind.

Calgary — two weeks ago

WE PILED INTO Jen's car after the Uptown Showcase — Rob Castle, me, and a couple of others. One was a visiting comedian, one a local guy I can't picture at all now and hardly spoke to. I think he was a student.

I'd seen Jen at the festival office in the hotel when I'd dropped in the day before. The volunteers were in baggy matching T-shirts, and she was standing with them but looking more corporate and acting decisively while they held back in a clump. It turned out she was one of them, but she'd worn a leather skirt that wouldn't have worked at all with the official T-shirt, and people who didn't know better assumed she was actually on staff and kept asking her to make decisions. Which, she explained to me in the car, she was happy to do. Someone had to, and no one else seemed to be stepping forward.

Jen was a student too, but she'd been away until the weekend so she'd had no chance to volunteer formally. She'd missed all the briefings and turned up yesterday just in case an extra pair of hands was needed. Which, in her view, it wouldn't have been if the volunteers rostered to the meet-and-greet desk hadn't been introverts who felt better rearranging the plates at the other end of the room and sneaking the occasional Danish.

I sat in the front passenger seat, the three boys squished in the back. As we'd walked towards Jen's small car, Rob Castle and I had stayed on opposite sides of the group, but even while Jen talked it was him I was listening to as he sat directly behind me and dealt with the experience of being thigh to thigh with the student, a major fan who had all his albums at home.

Sometimes you meet people, I told myself. You meet new people and you click. And gender doesn't come into play and, when you're old enough to know that, it's all good. It stays uncomplicated, you stay in contact, you've got yourself a new friend.

We stepped out into the freezing air, and it seemed several degrees colder than just minutes before when I'd left the Uptown Showcase on a post-performance high.

From the outside of the Ship and Anchor there was no sense of what you'd find inside. It was low and quiet and sealed against the cold. How do you ever know these places are there, if you don't know already? It's not like home, where all year round the crowds spill out of the Regatta and the RE, and the beer garden noise travels across the neighbourhood.

The air was thick and warm inside. The others had their coats off as soon as we were in the door, but I kept wearing mine. I haven't hung a coat since I was eight and my mother wasn't there to remember this one.

But Jen saw me stuck there with it still on and said 'I will remember your coat' in an ideally maternal way that placed emphasis on each word, so I went with it then and trusted her. 'I will remember your coat and, believe me, so will you if you get two steps out the door without it.'

I wasn't thinking that way, since it's never that cold at home. I lose umbrellas all the time. The second rain stops, they're out of my head. With a cheap umbrella that's no calamity, but the jacket I was wearing was borrowed from a friend and made from an expensive synthetic thermal fibre. She hikes in New Zealand with it, above the snowline.

Jen's coat was the real thing – ankle-length and elegant – and I looked like a tourist who didn't know much. She held my jacket at arm's length and looked at it and said 'You are so Australian' and in that context it was clear that 'Australian' was a kind Canadian euphemism for clueless. 'I bet you throw the first snowball when we get to Banff.'

The Ship and Anchor had wood trim everywhere and smelled like old beer and warm damp wool. It was full of people and noise – alcohol-driven conversations shouted over the music. It was obviously the place to be on a Friday night in Calgary, if it was in fact Friday. I'd been less certain of the days ever since I'd crossed the dateline. I always make a habit on tour of knowing what's coming next, what my itinerary has for me tomorrow, since that's what I have to deal with, but it does mean your understanding of everyone else's calendar can start to drift.

The name of the day counts for less when you move on twice a week. No matter how much you like people, you can't make regular plans with them when you're on tour. Neither one of you gets to say 'How about next Tuesday?' since you won't be there. There's just tomorrow and maybe the day after, then email and the small chance that future itineraries will collide, or that you'll be back some day.

We sat at bench seats on either side of a long wooden table that someone called Gary had been holding for us against all odds. He was a volunteer too, a college student trying to grow his first beard, and we all squeezed in – we'd picked up a couple more people by then – and the others started talking about friends and writers and bands I didn't know.

Gary sat opposite me, picking up the conversation about writing and making a point about authenticity, saying that authentic writing from Calgary would have people not walking on the streets at times like this. They'd use the fifteen-plus walkways that go over the streets, whereas a foreigner mightn't know that, and might send their characters outside and write the story as though it was happening in a half-populated city. Which wasn't what Calgary was at all, and they'd just be exposing their lack of any real connection with the place.

'I think a lot of what creates place gets down to detail,' he said. 'The small details. That's where the truth is. Like, how do people get around? Which beer do they drink?'

I was a foreigner there, and nothing made it plainer than the fifteen-plus walkways. They hadn't become part of my Calgary story, and they never did. I don't understand walking fifteen feet above everything, and I find streets hard enough to navigate at the best of times. I wouldn't last one winter in Calgary.

We drank Big Rock Traditional Ale, and Jen taught me to call it Traditional so I'd get it right when it was my turn to go to the bar.

With the movement of people around our table, I ended up opposite Rob Castle when I got back, and he said, in a lull in the music, 'Hi, stranger. Imagine seeing you in these parts.'

After another beer or two, we all sang along to 'Blister in the Sun', though I wouldn't normally sing a note when sitting across the table from anyone musical. I was the last to join in, but Rob Castle said, 'C'mon, Meg, it's the Violent Femmes. It's not about singing. And it's perfect with beer.' And he nudged my leg under the table with his foot, as if he were daring me. I felt like a schoolgirl whose ponytail had just been pulled by the cute boy in the playground.

I joined in at the next chorus, as loud as the rest of them, and Jen reached over and clinked her glass against mine. I avoided Rob Castle's eyes, and told my cheeks not to go red. I took another mouthful of beer, Traditional, before the verse, and I remembered Elli at seven sitting on the floor at home with a jigsaw puzzle in front of her singing 'Why can't I get just one fuck', and thinking that's the last of that Violent Femmes album for about ten years.

Next up, with people in the mood for singing along, there was a song that's either called 'The Saskatchewan Pirate Song', or at least referred to that way. It's as funny and rollicking as it should be, and all the others could sing along with it as well. Jen leaned forward during the second verse and explained something about the improbability of sea-going piracy in Saskatchewan. I didn't catch it all, but I picked up the sense of it and already knew from the map that oceans weren't an option there.

In the bathroom shortly after that I sat in a cubicle, drunker with the brightness of the light in there, thinking more about Elli and the Violent Femmes. I felt a nausea that I put down to jet lag, but a deep head-swirling nausea that made me cry into my hands even though I didn't feel particularly sick. I didn't want this, I didn't want to think about it, I didn't want to be reminded. Outside the cubicle door, girls were talking, planning their lives in the coming days and weeks, and discussing the boys they were with, all of whom it seemed had had too much to drink and were creating a very poor impression.

I washed my face, and drank no more.

In the street perhaps an hour afterwards, we walked and talked and the group reshaped itself in a way that put me next to Rob Castle. The temperature was close to freezing then. It must have been. I had my hands in my pockets, since I don't have gloves, and only my face was exposed and it felt like it was stiffening up.

We walked along streets I hadn't been on before, past closed cafes and offices and a cowboy-themed bar where the doors would swing open for a second or two and whooping and hollering and crowd noise would surge, and then be clipped off as they closed again. A hum still passed through, but as an indistinct mixture of music and people, and easily drowned out by the occasional passing car and even the wind when it gusted.

We stopped to look in through the high windows and I could see girls dancing on tables in cowboy hats, but I got no clear sense of whether they were staff or patrons.

We turned away and started walking again, and I said something I forget now and Rob Castle said 'You crazy thing' and he messed up my hair with his hand.

I was feeling very tired, physically still not myself in this new place, and I felt tears well up, out of nowhere. Maybe it was just the cold dry air on my eyes, but his gesture seemed way out of line, and great, and perfectly friendly, and almost unbearably intimate. His hand settled on my shoulder for a second, then moved away. The others were two steps ahead of us down the street by then, beyond the windows of this crazy place, breathing vapour, smacking their gloved hands together, heading for the traffic lights.

And I said, because it seemed the moment for it, 'Your music, it's so sad, some of it.'

And he said, 'Well, I guess it is. I don't know that I mean it to be, always, but I pick up my guitar and ideas come along and I guess they become what they become. And I'm not very metaphorical. I want to get to the heart of it. So they're simple songs. I'm surprised how sad some of them become.' We walked a bit further and he looked down the street and into the far distance and he said, 'Maybe that's just in us, that capacity.'

And the guy on the door at the cowboy place called out

'Hey, aren't you Rob Castle?' even though we were five steps past him by then, and onto something else.

I called him in his room, but at a time that turned out to be three-fifteen a.m. I thought my head had just hit the pillow, but that my eyes had snapped open because I suddenly had one more thing to say. He answered with a sleepy edgy voice, like someone expecting bad news, or a fire. And that's when I woke up enough to look at the clock, so the first thing I said was 'Oh my god, it's three-fifteen, three-fifteen a.m. in Calgary'.

And Rob Castle said, the edge gone from his voice and an amused kind of warmth in its place, 'Meg, I was missing you. Meg the talking clock . . .'

I told him I was sorry, terribly sorry, even saying the word 'terribly' though I never would usually.

'Oh, no, it's not very rock of me,' he said, still with the warmth and one of those fuzzy not-quite-woken voices. 'I was just three hours into this deep deep sleep, and I was hoping you'd call and update me on the party situation.'

Here he was, my new best friend with his Dr Seuss references, his capacity for sad sad songs and his shy-boy charm, and I was calling him at three-fifteen a.m. and there was no fire, no news of any kind, no party I knew of where people more rock than either of us weren't giving up on this night just yet. I was stuck between things to say. I wanted to talk, I realised, but I didn't know how to put that. Suddenly, I was less sorry, less tired, and wanting to talk to Rob Castle. Wanting him to be a little more rock, and to wake up.

And that's when he said, 'Could we have breakfast maybe? We could meet in the lobby, say eight-thirty? There's a cafe in the mall, the Good Earth, I've been there a couple of times. I don't know what your schedule's like . . .'

I told him my schedule was good, nothing till ten or so, and I lay awake until four or later, wondering why I'd called him.

He was in the lobby at eight-thirty, as planned.

We walked outside on the way to the Good Earth, since he said he preferred the fresh air unless it was seriously cold, and he didn't really know how to navigate fifteen feet above Calgary anyway. I looked like crap that morning, I'm sure I did. Washed out, with bags under my eyes that my concealer stick was struggling to hide. The wind blew right at us on the way to the mall, and the cold came through the legs of my jeans. He didn't seem to feel it. His jacket was wide open, his hands in his pockets in a jaunty sort of way, pointing forwards and gesturing as he talked.

'I'd recommend the spinach and feta scones,' he said, once we'd sat ourselves at the window table at the Good Earth.

He was right. They were just as they should be, crusty on the outside, soft in the middle. The coffee was good, too.

We each had a scone, and he broke his into pieces with a fork and then looked at the plateful of crumbs and shrugged, as if it hadn't quite worked.

We talked, mainly about inconsequential things. We

talked about touring. He told me he always kept his house keys in his pocket so that he had some connection with home. He ordered a second coffee. He signed an autograph on a paper serviette for a customer who was on her way out, and he did so very obligingly.

We sat and looked out at the mall. I looked at the people traffic in this place that I hadn't seen before, the hundred-year-old buildings, the shops that were closed or being refurbished. The lack of people traffic, actually.

'My father was a travelling salesman,' he said, and I think it linked to our conversation about touring. 'He was away a lot when I was young. More than I would've liked, anyway. I was the last kid in my class to learn to ride a bike because no one got around to teaching me. But it was an era of travelling salesmen, and there must have been kids like me all over North America.' He laughed at himself then and said, 'Where am I getting this melancholy vibe? Do I really think you've got any interest in my bike riding?'

We talked about when we were young, and he guessed correctly that I'd been a big *Anne of Green Gables* fan. He also guessed that I would have picked Shaun Cassidy over David back then, which wasn't right, though I had friends who would've gone that way. He told me his first crush was Carly Simon, without a doubt, and his second was a girl in his sixth-grade class who never noticed him.

'I wrote a song about that once,' he said. 'Well, kind of.'

He yawned and stretched his arms above his head and out to the sides, and I apologised for my late night call, about five times, and about five times he said it was no problem.

He said he'd slept either side of it, hours each side, and he'd slept pretty well.

He told me he'd been expecting more 'chick stuff' when I got up on stage, so I told him that, after a while, the general hopelessness of men starts to look a little obvious.

He laughed and said, 'I never get sick of seeing that kind of act. Men can do with reminding, you know. Some of them are appalling – full of tedious stories about absent fathers, and what it's like to be a twelve-year-old with trainer wheels.'

Outside the window, a busker stood with his back to us, tuned his guitar without any real hurry and started playing Bonnie Tyler's 'It's A Heartache'. But his only audience was a magician on the other side of the mall, the Great Cosmo, who stood at a boarded-up shopfront, his name surrounded by spangly gold moons and stars on the small sign hanging from the tray table jutting out from his waist. He wore tails and a top hat, but his face let him down by being not even a little mysterious. He dealt cards out onto the table, executed a trick for practice or simply to keep his hands doing something in the cold. The busker played on.

'He's quite terrible, isn't he?' Rob Castle said to me behind his hand. 'And yet I can't look away.'

The busker finished and bowed from the waist to the empty mall, and the Great Cosmo called out, 'That was special, Hal. You're making it your own, I'm thinking.' And the two of them laughed in a way that was about sharing the absurdity of it all, and getting through it.

'It's a goddamn Larson cartoon,' Rob Castle said and, as was fast becoming usual, I thought it was brilliant.

On our way out, I threw the busker a dollar and I noticed his case was mainly full of one-cent coins.

'I hear they met years ago,' Rob Castle said when we were well beyond earshot, 'on the festival circuit, and that's what becomes of such things.'

'A chance collision somewhere and, years later, you're facing each other down in an empty mall and playing for pennies.' That's how I put it, but it sounded wrong so I said, 'Something happened there. That was way sadder than it was meant to be.'

And that's when I told him about Murray, breaking up with Murray two weeks and three days and several hours before, for the time that Murray insisted was the last time. And that it probably really was the last time, because we'd worked through it and fixed essentially nothing, and that had taken a lot of energy and some months as well, and he hadn't returned my calls in the last seventeen days. Not that there had been many, because you get the message soon enough.

And I told him I knew that was too much information and a stupid thing to talk about, but he said it wasn't, and for a buck he'd do some Bonnie Tyler for me, if it'd help. His arm was around me then, which was good.

Perth – Thursday

'BATTLE OF THE SEXES' – who starts the day this way by choice? Across the country, commercial radio stations wake people up and welcome them to the morning with this girl-versus-guy tussle over inanities.

I should get Emma to add it to my list of tour requirements. Needs access to a gym, ideally with lap pool. Needs a regular supply of fruit and water. Will not do stupid dawn or red-eye flights. Will not participate in 'Battle of the Sexes' under any circumstances.

The last time I did, I gave the guy a pounding, simply because I was so irritated with myself for forgetting to tell Emma I'd never do it again. Of course, the guy's always a sitting target. He's nervous about being on radio and annoying me merely by phoning in, endorsing the 'Battle of the Sexes' concept and keeping it on air. Plus, he's up for a prize and I'm not. But I can't let that have too much of a bearing on my performance when I'm fighting the battle for women everywhere. I can't look weak, caring, nurturing. It's in the interests of challenging stereotypes that

I have to set out to pound him. And he should understand that.

He's Tyson today. He's standing at the breakfast bar in the kitchen at home, wearing a cap, just old enough to shave semi-regularly and wondering if the fuzz on his chin might amount to something if given the chance. He's on his parents' phone, he's taken completely off-guard by seven-forty a.m, just fast enough and just slow enough to be the sixth caller, not a chance when it comes to best-of-three-questions any time before ten o'clock.

That's the Tyson I'm seeing anyway and, when one of the hosts asks if I'm ready to go, I'm psyched enough to say, 'I'm going to crush you like a bug, Tyson. Like a little bug.'

The hosts both go 'Oooooh' and one of them says, 'Sounds like fighting talk, Tyson.'

Tyson comes back with 'Um, yep, righto . . .' and then, when they start reading question one, he talks over them with a better comeback and the question has to start again.

I'm up two–nil inside a minute, feeling a sudden flicker of the urge to nurture, and three–nil looks harsh. They ask a sport question. I give him a few seconds but all he gives back is silence.

'You're looking down the barrel of a whitewash, Tyson,' the male host says. 'The blokes are relying on you. Come on, it's a sport question. Come on, Tyson, you've got to know more about this one than Meg.'

That gets to me more than it usually would, and I hit him with a 'Yeah, Tyson, who's the girl now?'

In the studio, the breakfast hosts – both male and

female – cheer, and I want this all to be over. Tyson is stuck in his parents' kitchen staring blankly at the birds in the back garden, his mouth gone dry, the phone cord coiled in his fingers.

So I give the answer, it's three–nil to the ladies, and Tyson, the pressure all gone, thanks me as if he means it and says it was cool, the way I laid it on him.

At the gym, I start with weights. I bench press more than usual, pumping away my stupid 'who's the girl now?' line. In my brain there was irony all over it, in life I suspect there was none. I should know better.

My hand hurts again, in the same place as on the plane, on the back in a muscle near the base of my thumb. My gym instructor in Brisbane often tells me not to overdo it. I suspect that's what he'd tell me now if he were here.

So I pick up my towel and I go up the stairs to the pool.

I get about eight laps done before Murray, Elli and life sweep back into my head and won't easily be put away.

I stop for breath and tip water out of my goggles. I push off again and concentrate on technique, on long freestyle strokes and making all of them count. My hands look pale when they hit the water, crashing through the mirror of the surface and pulling bubbles down with them.

Where did we go wrong, Murray and me? We paid good money for the answer to that question. We bought ourselves quite a few answers in the end, but it was the end by then and you need answers earlier than that, while you're still prepared to work.

I think I was still prepared to work. And that could be, might be, *am* still prepared to work, but it's no good thinking that way.

We spent too much time apart due to our jobs, mine more than his. In hindsight, it's a factor that's important and uncomplicated, and on it went from there. Too much time apart, Murray not understanding why I couldn't say No more often, Murray telling me he couldn't say No since he's not in charge of his life the way I'm in charge of mine. He works for a big company. He always has. He doesn't understand anything else, he doesn't understand jobs you invent as you go along, and put together the best way you can. Not that he didn't listen, not that he didn't try.

We both tried, fruitlessly, and it tore us apart. But quietly, like a seam coming undone or something unravelling. There was nothing ugly about it. It stopped working. We stopped having something to work with. It stopped, from Murray's point of view, being worth the grief. From my point of view it still was. Is.

He's in Asia now with work. Shanghai, I think. Elli's with her mother, where she usually is. Making the usual amount of trouble, I hope.

I'm used to him emailing me every day when he's away with work, emailing or calling. That was part of our plan. Every day in some way we would be in touch, and that's how we would beat geography. But we haven't, and it's clear to me every time I check my email or arrive at a new hotel and there are no messages waiting.

We were together seven years, and I don't know what

I'm going back to in Brisbane if I'm not going back to that.

Months ago, I talked Elliott King into bringing the other TV people to Brisbane for a look around. It was an earlier stage of the show's development then, and I took them to potential locations, specific and generic, and we visited the studios at the Gold Coast. I worked as hard as anyone could to get myself a steady job close to home. But I still have no power to decide where the show will be made, if it will be made, and there are still no guarantees. Sometimes I work for a big company too, and I don't sign the cheques. And my plan – that part of it – is holding together so far, but it's taken too long.

Tumble turns work better when you think about them less. When you leave it for your leading arm to show you the way, just like Julie said. And the arm goes, and you go after it and you push away from the wall with your feet. The next lap begins, a rhythm develops.

Rob Castle had messy hair and a denim jacket and an acoustic guitar. He looked a little like John Corbett from *Northern Exposure* and *Sex and the City*, and those guys are always sensitive, right? And he seemed a little like Woody Guthrie to me, and those guys are always out pursuing noble sentiments. The image I have of Woody Guthrie, right or wrong, comes from one photo – the photo of him on a street somewhere, his back to the camera, I think, a guitar over his shoulder and the words 'This Machine Kills Fascists' written on it.

So in Calgary I spilled the beans, and had my first conversation outside our counselling sessions about my break-up with Murray, there with a sensitive singer/songwriter on a windswept mall thousands of miles from home, east of the Rockies in the Houston of the north.

That's enough now, enough laps.

My muscles feel good, having worked. I'm sure I have raccoon eyes from the goggles, but I don't think I have a photo shoot till this afternoon. It's very quiet up here around the pool when there's no one else, as close to silent as you could want. The air is warming up, and I wonder if it's a lump that I can feel in the cool shrivelled skin of the back of my right hand, or if I'm imagining it. It's sore when I press it. I think it's a lump.

I get as dry as I need to and go down the stairs, past the muscle shots on the wall and the 'Twelve Things You Should Know About Step' poster.

Back in my room at the hotel there's a message from Felicity, telling me how great I was on 'Battle of the Sexes', and that she'll see me in the foyer at nine-twenty.

I shower and go to work with my eye cream and a lot of moisturiser, and my skin feels better right away. My hand's okay now, too.

I'm listening to CNN with the bathroom door open. There's a story to do with Northern Ireland, but I don't catch the details. An American, who is clearly pro-republican, is accusing the other side of sabotaging the peace process. It's never pointed out to him that he's referring to the other side of a complicated conflict an ocean away from where he's sitting. He says, 'I'm Irish and proud of it, and that's why I'm saying these things.' And he says it in a Boston accent and, when pushed about the money his group has raised, he insists that it gives comfort to families, and that anyone who says otherwise – anyone who says that one cent of it has been spent on guns – is an enemy of the peace process. 'That's just more sabotage,' he says forcefully, 'like I said.'

What chance do people have of a balanced view when this is put forward as a piece of the story, and the story is put together by media in countries that can't know? What chance do they have when there's no balanced view anywhere? The whole situation is driven by a lack of balance, its instability maintained by agendas that go back generations. And simple lines can be drawn an ocean away, and funds raised and spent for a mixture of purposes, and people can be left feeling good about a contribution they're making to something that, on the ground, is never that simple. Never as decent as they'd like to think, whichever side they're on.

You can't back a side in these conflicts. You can't know what it's like from a distance. You can't know who's right, if anyone's right, but that stops being the issue early on anyway. Whatever you stand for, wherever you are, you shouldn't get to be called a freedom fighter if you're breaking into people's houses at night and shooting them because they don't agree with you.

From an early age, my parents always told me that you can do better than pick sides. They didn't pick sides. They got on with life, made that kind of contribution, and it now seems like a noble one to me. They believed that things would improve if there were more people like them, people whose way of dealing with the world was governed by an even-handed decency.

They said everyone was entitled to their own views, and to speak them, but that most differences between people were inconsequential, or at least not enough to justify intolerance and violence.

They're retired now, and my mother runs a group in their area that links refugees with health care and the services they need. It's not political, she says. There's a need, and she's responding to it.

'Do you know what *halal* actually means in practice?' she said to me when we last spoke. 'It's a lot more complicated than you'd expect.'

'What made your family move from Northern Ireland?' the journalist from the *West Australian* says, glancing at his notes. He's in his late fifties, with no-nonsense steely-grey hair and pages of background info printed from websites.

Felicity has us sitting down the back of a King Street cafe that's wood from top to bottom and has signs of an earlier, possibly industrial, life. It's stylish and busy, and the coffee is very good. I've told her we should only do coffee-shop interviews in places that can actually make coffee. She's outside at the moment. She's taken a call and is pacing in the street with the phone to her right ear and a finger in her left.

'There were a few reasons, really,' I tell the journalist, having allowed a pause so as not to make the answer seem automatic. 'My father got a job at the Port of Brisbane – a better version of the job he'd been doing – my mother was a teacher, so that was pretty transferable, and 1972 seemed like a good time to take your eight-year-old and leave Northern Ireland for somewhere like Brisbane. So it was a combination of factors, probably. And a good decision, a good decision they made.'

That's the answer. Almost every time it's the whole answer. It's a small question in these interviews, it gets taken no further and the answer usually doesn't appear in the article. The article, if it mentions where I was born, usually says nothing more than 'moved from Northern Ireland to Brisbane at the age of eight', though sometimes it says nine. I've read other ages, too.

'Just a couple more details,' he says, in a business-like way. 'You and your partner – are you married or de facto? If you don't mind me asking.'

'No, no, it's fine. We live together.'

'And for about how long now?' Just the facts, that's all he's looking for.

'Seven years.'

'And it was Murray, wasn't it?' he says, already not really listening, on the brink of packing up. All I have to do is nod. He turns the tape recorder off. 'We've got some good stuff there. Plenty for eleven hundred words. It'll be a good profile piece.'

He looks at his watch and tells me he's got six hours. The Saturday magazine section has a five p.m. Thursday deadline. 'Easy,' he says, and he stops to confirm with Felicity on the way out that the photo shoot is still in the itinerary for three o'clock.

We walk down King Street back towards Rydges, and

he leaves in the other direction. Felicity has her phone in one hand and a bag over the other shoulder, a canvas courier bag today, more like something a student would carry than the one she's had with her so far. She power-dressed to meet me the night before last, I realise, and I'm glad the pressure to do that seems to have passed.

'Good interview, great latte,' I tell her when she asks me how it went. 'My exacting standards are being well met. Good gym, very good dentist . . .'

In the cab on the way to the next interview, I admit that there was more to the dentist than I've mentioned so far, more than good service, a movie and a spectacular new tooth.

'I had this incident . . .' That's how I begin it. 'One of those collisions between life and art, that's how I'm seeing it now.'

She laughs when I tell her what happened. She starts laughing early, when all I've done in the story is take a wrong turn and end up stuck in the stairwell. By the time I'm outside trying to explain myself in my dental-dam voice, she's laughing through her hands, her eyes wide, seeing the funny side and the survivable horror.

'But don't think I'll make a habit of it,' I tell her. 'For the rest of the week you'll see nothing from me but impeccable self-control. I'm only telling you now because you never know where people's photos might end up. I don't want you thinking I'm out drumming up my own publicity by running round the mall with a blue rubber dental dam shoved in my mouth.'

'Oh, I wouldn't have thought that,' she says. 'You told me you're more about subtlety now, and that wouldn't be very subtle, would it?'

At the ABC I'm on after the two o'clock news.

'We've met before,' Prue, the presenter, says as she reaches out to shake my hand. She's good. I remember her. 'You've been busy since you were in last time. Plenty to talk about,' she says, going back to her side of the desk and picking up her headphones. 'They must be missing you at home. It looks like you've been away for a while on this trip.' She clicks two buttons, pushes something I can't see. 'There's just under two minutes of news left before we're on. I noticed there's quite a few Irish comedians on the program. Can we talk about that, since you're from there originally? Along the lines of whether or not there's something about Ireland that inspires this kind of view of life? Comedy? Storytelling? That kind of thing?'

Ballystewart — 1972

IT SOUNDS LIKE an Irish story.

I was born and lived in the village of Ballystewart in the last of a short row of two-storey terrace houses. Like all the others, it was whitewashed. It had a green door, bottle green and glossy and I can only remember it freshly painted, though I should assume it wasn't always. I was there almost nine years, and can remember most of them.

We were within spitting distance of the Irish Sea, my mother would tell people later and, from my bedroom window with the right wind, it's possible that we actually were. Within spitting distance of the Irish Sea, a stone's throw from Millisle and Donaghadee, on the same stretch of coastline as Ballywalter and Ballyhalbert. All of these are names that aren't much known to the outside world, at least not the parts of it where I've been.

From my window I looked out to the grey sea in the distance, and to our garden with its wide flowering laburnum, its two apple trees, some rose bushes that never did well, a trellis of sweet peas and a back lane that curved behind the hedge, then curved again and led to the Donaghadee road. There were two hives in which someone had once kept bees, but they weren't used in our time.

We'd go to Donaghadee to do the banking. I remember my mother queueing at the tellers but I was never high enough to see over the counter, so my strongest memory is of the lifeboat over near the far wall. It was a model, but a huge one, and there was a collection box which always had money in it. My mother often added some.

When I could read enough I read the signs that went with it, about a lifeboat that went down in a storm with lives lost. My mother helped me with the harder words. I read each sign aloud to the end, my mother sounding out the longer words with me and explaining any I didn't know. When we'd finished I knew the whole story, and the model boat couldn't be the same again. Before then, it was like a great toy gone astray in the bank and, if you put money in, maybe they'd get more of them.

All of a sudden it was about people gone down in a lifeboat, and I'd thought lifeboats couldn't sink. If lifeboats could sink, what could save you? So every sea shanty about drowning might be true, and the sea was right there. The harbour was just across the road, with the lifeboats, not as safe as I'd thought. I wondered why that had never been explained to me, and I read every sign I could from then on.

My mother wouldn't remember it that way, I'm sure she wouldn't. That would apply to a lot of things.

I know it's the case because of what's been said since, and because it's how memory goes, how it must go as time passes.

We'd remember it differently because we saw it with different eyes, but also because all things remembered are to some degree imagined. Recollection has an irresistible urge to tell a story and is more likely to fill gaps than to leave them, if you work at it.

But I can't be persuaded that I didn't see the things I saw, and that I didn't do the things I did. And no one would call me on the bubbles in the whitewash or how the sky looked from my window, though they'd say I was wrong in some areas. They'd say I was eight and I wouldn't know, not really.

The politics, for instance. My parents would say my memories were wrong, but they aren't. They're right, they're sharp. My story is not their story, but it's not less real just because I was eight.

At eight you can be just old enough to know quite a lot and to keep it in your head. You have your own life then, or at least you're starting to. You have some sense of yourself, some sense of your own of the world you're in, and you learn that your parents' protection is not absolute. You learn that there are limits to what they know, and what they can control. Despite them, people are killing and being killed. There are bad people out there, going out with bombs and guns and killing on their minds, and they can be very hard to stop. You learn that because it happens and it makes the news.

They can come to your door in the night, and sometimes they don't even knock.

My mother and I read the lifeboat signs, and then we

went for ice-cream. It was a clear day in early summer with a flat sea. She held my hand when we walked near the harbour, but we didn't talk about what the lifeboat signs had said. My father worked at a harbour, though not that one. I was quite afraid, but I didn't let my mother know it. Every night, the lighthouse beam swung over our house, hoping to keep boats from the rocks.

My parents had a context for what happened in Northern Ireland when I was young. They were in their thirties when I was born, and both of them over forty by 1972. They had lived both young and adult lives already, and every new development could be tested against what they already knew.

I had only the context I was putting together at the time. That was my entire frame of reference. On one day in early 1972, I walked in the woods with my father, I read Enid Blyton, I stood still while my mother held the pinned-together pieces of a dress against me and said I'd grow into it, and I watched Bloody Sunday on the evening news. If that's life no one can change it, and no one can tell you that it's not how life is. At eight, if you've got all those things in your day, then that's how it is.

I'm hazy on the Bloody Sunday details though, and more certain of the things we found in the woods. Perhaps my parents steered me away from some of the TV coverage.

I've stayed away. I couldn't see the movie, though people told me it was good once you adjusted to the accents. I still don't know how many people got shot by soldiers, or why.

Looking back on it now, I had a *Famous Five* childhood

in many respects, but it developed an edge to it. I did all the things they did, but I did more. They never seemed to watch the news. They never had their car searched by the army.

My life was mostly like theirs, though, and close to perfect in those respects. My parents were very much in favour of blowing the cobwebs away on any clear day, so I spent a lot of time outside with my friends, at each other's houses or in the woods.

At harvest time, we'd build forts in the fields out of hay bales and no one ever stopped us. In the woods we'd see ghosts and terrify each other and run like hell. And we'd clamber over the lorries in the McKendrys' field, coming to grief repeatedly in there. There was plenty to fall from and to fall onto, but again no one told us not to climb the way we did, though they did tell us to be careful.

We'd find ways to get around in there that we were sure no one knew, and we'd give them coded names. If anyone came after us, that was where we'd escape them. We'd lose them in the McKendrys' field. We knew the quick ways through, and the dead ends, and where to hide. I don't know how many lorries there were but there must have been at least dozens, and tractors and other broken-down equipment. I don't know why. Nothing ever seemed to leave. No adult seemed to go in there, and everything in the field seemed long past salvaging.

So there it was, an entire field of rusting vehicles at one edge of a farm, and I never thought to ask what they were there for.

I went to school with Sammy McKendry, one of the

sons of Sam McKendry the farmer. He and I and a couple of others spent a lot of afternoons in the field, and there was endless scope for an eight-year-old's imagination there.

We once found a pile of smashed windscreen glass that we called diamonds, and we kept it in an old leather glove that Sammy had noticed under the seat of one of the lorries. It was a big man's glove, with quite a capacity for diamonds. We shook them down into the fingers and filled the palm and called ourselves a country, or a band of pirates, depending on how we were feeling. We had the wealth of a country, surely, but we were pirates at least as often, and we'd found the diamonds at the bottom of the ocean or taken them from worse brigands than ourselves.

We hid them in a glove box in a particular broken-down Bedford – whatever the story, that was constant – and we swore each other to secrecy. Even if they came at night and got us, we had to keep the secret. Deny the diamonds, deny we'd ever seen them.

One day, we'd buy an island with them, or fast cars. Later it was guns, maybe a tank or a helicopter, green with a gun either side.

Perth – Thursday

I KNOW SOME of the tricks for photo shoots.

Put one foot forward and rotate just slightly at the hips if you don't want to look wide. Lean forward, not back – back has chins in numbers. Push the middle part of the tongue against the roof of the mouth to draw up the skin under the jaw. Open the mouth slightly, but don't gape. Deal with the camera affectionately, and as though you're letting it in on a secret. Let your whole face slump between bursts of shots, then toss it all freshly into place as required. Work it, baby. Beautiful.

And no Glad Wrap necessary today. A good amount of technique and a suspension of the natural human fear of photography, and all is well. Or as well as it can be. If you tell yourself you'll look like a bag, a bag is what you'll look like, and that's the first thing to know.

I'm so good at this I could teach it. How can I criticise a TV producer for being reductionist about character outlines?

The photographer from the *West Australian* comes

without too many big ideas, but he's shooting colour for the magazine so he gets the guy behind the bar to mix me a big red cocktail. We're in the club I'll be working at tomorrow and Saturday. There's a small stage at the end opposite the bar, and French doors all along the side letting in more light than the room can handle. The wooden floorboards look grey, as though they've never been treated. There might have been carpet in here once. We're upstairs in a pub, in the kind of room that hides its flaws with mood lighting at the right time and gives up every ugly secret in daylight.

The photographer closes in for a tighter shot – me, my red drink, my red lips, my red dress. He's making a theme out of red, and it's starting to feel as if he's pushing it too far.

I changed at the hotel after the ABC interview and tried to sort out my hair. There was no time for a shower, no time for much, but time enough to fake it, and that's when my red Tim Lindgren dress is always the choice. It's travelled everywhere with me since I modelled it at a Melbourne Cup charity fashion event last year. It was my fourth dress on a hot humid day and the others had all looked very wrong, but as soon as I put it on I felt great and I knew that I'd regret it if I didn't buy it.

We do some shots with the drink and some without. Some with me on a bar stool and some standing. When I follow his instruction to lean casually against the bar he tells me I look like a shearer about to order a beer, and then he takes about ten shots of my response, and says, 'Excellent. I don't think I've seen anyone who looks less like a shearer, but you've had far too much practice having your photo taken.'

He finishes the roll of film, and says he's done. Felicity gets me moving towards the stairs while he's still crouching down disconnecting his flash.

'We'll be a few minutes late at the hospital,' she says. 'I might call them and tell them.' She waves down a cab as soon as we're outside. 'Now, what else do you need to know? I found out that the canoe race is raising money for a cell separator. That's the specific project. It's some kind of cancer research machine, I think. I don't think I have anything on the person we're visiting, though – only that she really wants to meet you.' She tells the cabbie the address, and starts pulling sheets of paper out of her bag, printed emails, hand-written notes. 'The PR people found her, the hospital PR people. Just to give a kind of human interest angle to the race, you know, connecting it to where the money goes.' She stops, and reads through an email. 'We've got a ward number, so I guess she's actually in hospital. They really only need one picture of the two of you. You'll probably even be early for coffee with your friend.'

So, we're getting there. Felicity has both weekend papers covered, I'm knocking off another day in my itinerary. A few more photos, then something as normal as coffee with Claire, then a couple of hours all to myself. A couple of hours in which I can shut up completely, run, walk, swim, watch TV, take a long, long bath. Then off to the opening night party, where I'll do my twenty minutes, then probably drink like a shearer. Some nights you can't hide in your room.

The main building of the hospital is large and brown and brick, and the carpet inside the entrance is a vibrant blue with geometric shapes in other colours, the kind of carpet that keeps people awake at airports. The hospital PR person is waiting at the reception desk.

Her name's Desley, but as we walk through the hospital to the ward people call her Dee. She wears glasses of a style and size that haven't been in for ten years, and power shoulders, and she accessorises with a bright scarf. She says it's great of me to come in for this, and to line up for the canoe race on Sunday. She says she's been at the hospital fifteen years and supposes she'll stay till they carry her out in a box. The journey to the ward involves four corridors and two lifts, and I start to wonder if we'll come out in the Pan-Canadian building in Calgary.

The photographer from the Sunday paper is in the ward when we get there. One of the nurses has brought her own camera, and Felicity says she'll take a photo of the two of us together.

We stand in front of a filing cabinet and the nurse starts to blush and says, 'Come on everyone. It should be all of us.'

She waves her friends over into the shot. One of them has roses she's about to put in a vase, and we take one each and clench them between our teeth. Felicity laughs and takes the photo, then we rearrange the group, strike a new pose and take another.

I sign their noticeboard with a red Nikko, adding the much-practised cartoon of myself, and they say they'll never wipe it off. I tell them about yesterday's trip to the dentist, and the dental-dam voice gets better each time I try it.

'I don't think we've ever laughed so much in this ward,'

the nurse in charge says, as she gathers us up and steers us into the corridor. 'We should do ward rounds like this all the time.'

She sweeps us along – me, Felicity, a nurse, the photographer, Desley – and she stops us halfway down to knock on an open door.

'You have a visitor,' she says brightly, and I'm propelled forward and into the room.

In the bed lies a girl whose smile is huge but about the last thing I see. She's emaciated and on a drip, pale and losing her hair, and then I realise that her right leg ends above the knee.

'Oh my god,' she says, with a young glee that's for a moment oblivious to whatever it is that's destroying her. 'Oh my god, you came.'

The nurse's hand is on my back, steering me forward, and I hear her say, 'Well you did tell us you'd like to meet Meg. Meg, this is Courtney.'

Courtney sticks her hand out, ready to shake, and her IV line rattles against the metal bedhead. Even her bones feel small when I take her hand and shake it as gently as I can. Courtney must be about to die. I tell her it's good to meet her. I try to look as though I'm not still reeling from the shock of seeing her without any preparation, but she's full of excitement and bordering on awestruck so she notices none of it.

I have a sudden urge to cry or be sick, but I simply have to push through it so I ask if she'd mind if I sat on the edge of the bed.

I put myself closer to her, and I try to think about what

she might want from this. That feels more important than the photos. They should have told me, dammit, they really should have told me. I've done two hospital photo shoots before, each time with someone who was getting better. That gives you expectations. Expectations that you're about to sit in on another good news story.

Courtney's lying on a sheepskin and, now that I'm near, I can hear the rasp in her breathing and see that she has ulcers in her mouth. I pick her hand up again and hold it and preposterously say, 'So, how have you been?'

And she says 'Good' in a chirpy way. 'What are you doing in Perth?'

'Oh, you know, a couple of shows, a bit of canoeing, that kind of thing.'

I have no idea what I should say. She might be fourteen or fifteen years old, but she's shrunk back to twelve and her time is surely very short. Elli keeps coming into my mind. She's years younger then Courtney but tall for her age. I don't want to think about her now.

I can't help but feel that there must be something much more useful I could be saying to Courtney, or doing. I could have been great here, with some warning. I could at least have entertained her, and been the version of me that she'd want me to be.

It's Courtney who reminds us all that we're here to take some pictures. 'So, are we going to do this, or what?' she says, urging the photographer to get to work.

I swivel around in the bed so that I'm sitting next to her instead of facing her, and the photographer moves to the windows. Desley and Felicity look uneasy, stuck in the doorway. Felicity looks as if this is all new to her. It was supposed to be another clever way of putting my picture in the paper, just another item in the itinerary we could put a line through in the cab straight after, and forget.

Courtney grins like a maniac in every photo. I keep holding her hand. Her skin has almost no colour at all, and I can see veins on her cheek and temple.

I ask her if she's okay with all this and she says, 'Sure. It's for the papers. You and me in the papers,' and the okayness of it is a truth she holds to be self-evident. We have burst in on her in what must be her last days, but she's asked for it and she wants it now it's here.

The photographer doesn't take long. He doesn't even change film. When he's done he pulls a small notepad out of his pocket and checks the spelling of Courtney's name. He says he'll need a few quick details, if that's all right – Courtney's age, why she wanted to meet me, a bit about her health problem, if that's okay.

She's fourteen, she's as quotable as can be on the issue of wanting to meet me, and then we get stuck.

'What I've got,' she says matter-of-factly, 'is osteoblastic osteosarcoma. It's in my lungs now, but it started in my leg.'

The photographer's pen hovers over the page. He looks at me and then towards the doorway, but the nurses have gone. Desley looks back at him helplessly. The room is silent. None of us can spell Courtney's cancer.

'Oh, shit, how embarrassing,' she says when she works it

out. 'It's *my* disease.' She closes her eyes. 'Okay, osteo . . . O, S . . . I'm pretty sure it's only one S . . .'

Desley stops her, and says it's easy to check the file. She says it's a big name and she's sure a lot of doctors can't spell it, if you can read their writing at all.

Courtney looks defeated. 'Well, you could just put "bone cancer" I suppose,' she says, and the photographer nods and writes it in slow capitals.

I offer to stay for a while after the others go, and Courtney says, 'Really? Would you do that?'

We talk for about twenty minutes, until her dinner comes. The meal trolley rumbles along the corridor, stopping to serve each room, and I help Courtney to get set up in bed. I help her move, and she's all bones. The meal comes on a tray, and a hot steamy institutional food smell comes out when I lift the steel lid off the plate.

'Usually I spew,' she says, 'but I'm getting this new drug in the drip that means you don't spew and it even makes you hungry. Even for this.'

She already has the fork in her hand.

'That hospital PR person should have done much better,' Claire says, sounding affronted on my behalf. 'The festival publicist should probably have asked her for more information, but it's really down to the hospital PR person. You want to be ready if someone's seriously ill. It means something to them. It's not just a picture, then.'

We're at the Blue Duck cafe above Cottesloe Beach,

drinking coffee and eating cake. Claire interviewed me once a few years ago, and it was only a phoner – she was in Perth, I was in Brisbane – but neither of us had any time pressures that day and we talked for half an hour or more after she had all she needed. This is our second meeting since then, and we email sometimes.

Claire is a freelancer who does a lot of celebrity pieces, as well as some food and travel. She has dark eyes and dark straight hair and rings on most of her fingers, some obviously from generations ago, some much newer. She's the kind of person who probably has a story to go with each of them. She thinks intently about things. She'll sit, holding her coffee cup in both hands and weighing the arguments up in her mind, and she'll come out with a firm view about what she thinks is right or wrong. And we've agreed every time in two-and-a-half conversations to date, so coffee with her is one of the better parts of a visit to Perth, one of the parts that most resembles life.

I don't blame Felicity for what happened at the hospital. Felicity is already good at this job on her first attempt, and she can't cover everything. I got the chance to say that before she left the ward. I followed her into the corridor on the pretext of checking the details of the evening event, and I spelled it out to her that it was not her fault and I did not want her dragging herself over the coals about it, while expecting me to watch. I took a Cabcharge voucher from her and had it in my hand when I went back in to Courtney. It made it look as though some business had been done.

It also gave Courtney something new to be amazed

about. We talked about the Cabcharge voucher and how life on tour works, and about the people you can end up doing events with. I told her some tour stories and made out that they were the type of insider stories you never get to read in magazines. That's what she wanted, something that was hers alone.

Claire and I are sitting at a table on the deck, above the beach and with the afternoon sun dazzling over the sea. We compare notes on several people we've each met once or twice. In most cases we have the same sense of them, but sometimes they've shown us something different – perhaps urbane conversation with me over a drink at a function, evasiveness in interviews with her.

'He was quite charming,' she says of one author, in a way that suggests she wasn't entirely charmed. 'But all he gave me was quotes. He was very good at quoting other people, which doesn't surprise me – he's a great stylist and you get the impression he's very well read – but he didn't give me much about himself.'

Claire does not expect me to be a comedian in front of her. I don't have to pick up the flowers on the table and clench them between my teeth, I don't have to drag up the old stories. I can take in the view, I can listen most of the time instead of talking, and we can discuss things. Actually discuss them. Discussion, on tour, can be painfully rare at times.

She did a phoner this morning with the actor Simon Baker in Los Angeles. It was the second time she's spoken to him and she says he seems like a genuinely nice guy. He lives with his family at Malibu and seems unaffected.

'It's interesting that he and Russell Crowe and Guy Pearce were all in *LA Confidential*,' she says, 'and they've taken such different paths since then. Simon's role in that was quite small, of course. Have you ever met Guy Pearce? He seems very genuine too, but the only time I've spoken to him it was a phoner and I suppose it's their job to seem genuine. Some of them could try a bit harder, though.'

The best I can manage is a third-hand story about Guy Pearce, Russell Crowe and Guy's thirtieth birthday party in LA. It's gossip, and only low-level gossip at that, but I can't stop myself telling it.

Claire laughs and says, 'Well, that sounds like typical Russell Crowe, if you believe what you read. Still, it'd be hard to stay normal with all the sucking-up those people get. And all the time away from home.' She takes a bite at the biscotti that's come with her coffee. 'Speaking of which, I took a look at your website. It's quite a tour that you're on.'

'It's nearly done,' I tell her. 'And it's had its moments.'

'It can't be easy for you, being away for these long stretches,' she says. 'And it can't be easy for your partner, either. I suppose you find ways of making it work. Does he ever come along? Does his job let him do that?'

My coffee cup is in my hand, and I can't remember whether it was on the way up or down so I set it back on the saucer. I still had my Guy Pearce story in my head, trying to work out the hands it passed through to reach me, and I don't know where to start the story that would answer her question.

'I could do with some time at home, to be honest.' That's

all I can say, and she knows there's more. She's too good at getting information out of people for her not to know. It isn't in me to tell this story. Not here, not today, not yet. This afternoon at the Blue Duck is too good, too clear, too unspoilt so far.

She asks if I'd like another coffee. She says she might have one, maybe decaf this time.

My whole face feels congested, and I try to focus on her question but I start crying anyway. I grab a serviette and blow my nose.

'It's that poor girl,' I tell her, and the tears keep coming. 'Courtney. It was pretty upsetting.'

And she says, 'Yes, quite a shock. They should have told you.'

'She made me think of Elli – Murray's daughter who lives with us some of the time.' People are starting to look over our way. I take another serviette and wipe my face, and try to look calm about it, try to take control of my breathing. 'She's with her mother at the moment. Murray's away with work, too.'

Claire pulls a squashed box of tissues out of her bag and passes it to me. 'Aloe vera,' she says. 'Much less scratchy than serviettes.'

Calgary — two weeks ago

I WOKE TO A BED that was empty but for a note on the visitor's pillow. It read:

Meg,
Last night was special but I have a wife and three children in Thunder Bay, Ontario, two girls and a boy (the youngest) and one of the things most important to me is being a good father to them. I don't know that that came up last night. Which was a special night, sincerely, and a special memory, and I don't think either of us wants it spoiled by a single unhappy word.
I will be thinking of you.
Rob

Two small pieces of Fremont Palliser Hotel Calgary paper, there on the visitor's pillow. He'd tried to cram the message onto one but perhaps, with three children, it hadn't been easy.

I was stunned at first, angry with him by lunchtime, and in the afternoon I went back to my room alone and cried half a bucketful, though I told myself it wasn't to do with Rob Castle at all. And then I realised he disappointed me most by writing such great songs and yet such a mediocre note, and I was stuck with the simple clear thought that the night had deserved better.

I had needed his company desperately after breakfast the day before, as the wind skidded in from the Rockies or across the prairie and froze my cheeks and we walked from the mall back to the hotel. I had needed an arm around me, and preferably his, and from there one thing had led to another.

Late in the evening we had ended up at the door to my room, me with my key card jittering in my hand, Rob Castle with his jacket folded over one arm. We had stood there with the door open, my foot against it, several ways for saying goodnight in my mind. I can remember the moment when the last of them went unsaid, and I pushed the door fully open and he followed me in. His folded jacket fell to the floor, its arms splayed out on the carpet in the last of the hallway light as the door closed.

Over the next few hours I had times – seconds only – when I let myself think that this was a kind of proof. Proof that I could move beyond recent weeks and the past seven years, proof that I could and would fall again for someone for reasons of great sentiment. And I could smell the sweat lifting from his warm bare shoulders and his hair as I held him. It was his own smell, new to me. And his hair fell unevenly onto my face, brushed my closed eyes, and I told myself it was physical, all this. That's how I should see it.

I'm left with those ideas – too many of them – and the sharp recollection of my hands on his shoulders and on his back, of the noise of bodies between thick starched sheets.

I fell asleep first. I remember him stroking my hair, saying something.

Jen picked me up for the show on the evening of the day of the note, and I did the show and I bought her a drink afterwards, several drinks. On her fourth, when she'd decided to leave the car for the night and take a cab home, I said 'Guess what I did last night?' and she said 'What?' and I said 'I fucked Rob Castle'. Because that's how it looked by then, no better.

She took another mouthful of beer and made a frown and said, in a tone that fitted perfectly with my 'guess what' way of putting it, 'You know, I'd wondered about that. Not in a judgemental way of course.'

So I said, 'Did you know he was married with three children in Thunder Bay, Ontario? I now have a note to that effect.'

And she said, 'No, I didn't know that. Was I supposed to? It sounds like essential background information. A note about the family? How considerate. Was this note in lieu of a conversation, or as well as one?'

It had immediately become a kind of joke between us – which was such a good way to play it. It was as if her chaperoning wasn't up to scratch and that's where my trouble had started – I was 'the talent' and might take it upon myself to sleep with anyone or anything in the absence of contrary advice.

She told me that she thought the festival should have given me a better briefing, and that she wished she'd come on board earlier, or at least given herself a lot more time to read trashy magazines. Because this was Rob Castle, after all, and his home life couldn't possibly be a secret.

She blamed the whole business on the demands of her studies, and on the number of festival volunteers who were only in it for the T-shirt and an occasional surplus Danish.

I gave her the note and she read it and said, 'I thought he was a better man.'

All I could add was, 'Or at the very least a better writer.'

I explained myself a bit further when I could, which might have been another beer later or simply when enough time had passed after telling her, and I'd got my next lot of thoughts together.

'I was the loneliest person in the world when he and I went out for breakfast,' I told her. 'That's how it felt. Life hasn't been good lately. And the mall was such a sad place. I feel horribly guilty now, of course, don't think I don't.'

But he got all my back story, I got none of his. I knew nothing of his life beyond the Uptown Screen, the mall and the elegant Fremont Palliser Hotel.

Jen stayed on my side, and I needed that. I finished the night glad about Big Rock Traditional Ale and her company and sometimes even the sex with Rob Castle which, I had to admit, had been very agreeable and perhaps necessary at the time. But I also stayed worried about the other members of a family in Thunder Bay, Ontario, and what might one day become of them.

I didn't know – couldn't know – if the heartbreak in his songs was real or just clever invention, as it should be and as I'd thought it was. Maybe he's not creating it for the songs, and his heart breaks all the time. Maybe it broke once, long ago, and that was enough to harden him, leave him open to misadventure, and damn the consequences. Not that there would be any, this time.

Perth — Thursday

THE RUNNING SHEET for tonight is waiting for me back at the hotel, in an envelope tucked under my door. There's a list of minibus times with it, and another copy of the program, which describes the venue, the Watershed, as 'a hub disguised as an installation — part club, part performance space, part pool, aquarium and sink, but above all, it is the hottest place to be cool in Perth this summer.'

I couldn't tell Claire about Murray. I've only met her twice, and every time the break-up surges back into my head it feels like it'll burst. I didn't want to crack up in front of her, and the crowd in the cafe. I didn't want to get into any of the details, and hear good well-meaning things in return. We had a conversation going, our usual conversation, about the worries of the world and about people we almost have in common, and that's what I wanted this afternoon, something normal.

Somehow that didn't apply on that cold morning in Calgary with Rob Castle, or it stopped applying because Calgary was so unlike home. I wasn't quite myself there, from the moment I met him.

He should have told me that he had a life back in Ontario. What kind of expectations did he think I had? A future together? Him and his lovelorn songs, me and my domestic observations, out on the wide open road playing every town on the CNBC weather map from Whitehorse to St John's? Me, working on my chick stuff, amusing him and reminding him that there are shitty, dishonest men about, travelling with all the charm and tenderness they need to wreak quiet havoc and then move on?

I want to see him again just to scream at him 'I got what I wanted' and then to say, in less than a scream, 'And you're welcome to Thunder Bay, Ontario, but you had plenty of chances to talk about that and you took none of them because you knew we wouldn't have slept together if you had.'

And that's the simple truth of it. The complex part, the connectedness I felt, I can't be sure of any more.

I fell for a guy – nose-dived for him, plummeted for him – because of how brilliantly he referenced popular culture, from the things he noticed and the way he noticed them, to his hair, to the well-made look of longing in his eyes. And, like a lot of men in popular culture, he was ultimately disappointing.

I struck him when I was in a moment of great need, but he wasn't what I needed, even if the story had stayed simple and we'd woken up beside each other and our tours had quietly disentangled themselves the next day when he moved on to Edmonton.

I'd like to say that I was in control, rational, and that it wasn't so much about him. I chose sex over cigarettes, and because I couldn't find a kickboxing class. But there were hours when we were together and I wasn't sad. I don't think I was sad at all.

His writing in the note was at different angles. The paper had moved. He'd paused, and looked at me asleep there, and known what he was doing. He'd given it thought, and still it was such a lazy crappy effort.

After a shower I can convince myself my eyes are less puffy. I can't make a decision about what to wear though, and my suitcase is half-empty before I settle on my 'Alby Mangels – Ladies Man '88' T-shirt and my favourite black Dogstar pants, which always make my thighs look great (athletic, yes, but not Tour de France). The seven-twenty minibus is about to leave when I get down to the foyer.

I sit across the aisle from the two other passengers, and the nearer one says 'I'm Niall' in an Irish accent, but from the south. 'And this is Ken.'

The driver slams the door shut and the minibus goes dark.

'I'm Meg,' I tell them, and Niall reaches out to shake my hand and then Ken does too. 'Are you both on the program tonight?'

'Niall is,' Ken says. He's facing me, but the bright foyer lights silhouette him and all I can see is the shaggy outline of his hair. 'I don't start till tomorrow, but they tell me there'll be free beer backstage, and that's enough for me. Besides, we've only got two nights in Perth before we move on to Sydney, so we've got to fit in as much hospitality as we can.'

His accent is different, less of a lilt, harder on the vowels.

The minibus jerks away from the kerb and into the traffic. We cross King Street and pass the bright lights outside the theatre.

'And where are you from, Meg?' he says. 'Somewhere in Australia other than Perth I'd be guessing, if you're staying in the hotel.'

'Yeah, Brisbane. And you're from Belfast? Or somewhere near Belfast?'

'I am. How did you know that?'

'I spent the first eight or nine years of my life on the Ards Peninsula. We left in 1972.'

'And why wouldn't you if you had the chance?' he says. 'We'd be about the same age, you know. Funny that we'd meet in Perth. 1972? Yeah, I was eight then as well. We should have a beer or two tonight, when you're done.' The minibus turns a corner and he grabs the window frame for balance. 'I've got a big brother who got caught up in a lot of stuff that year. He was an angry bastard then. I used to run some of his messages.' He stops himself, and smiles. 'But I was from Ardoyne. I guess you and I would be as likely to meet in Perth as anywhere.'

We're stopped at some traffic lights, waiting to turn, and the headlights of the oncoming cars come in through the windscreen and I see Ken properly for the first time. He shrugs and smiles. His hair is greying at the temples in an attractive sort of way, his teeth are uneven. He's holding a packet of cigarettes and pulling one of them in and out.

It's a knowing kind of smile that he's giving me, and

I nod and say 'I guess' and I can feel myself smiling too, in the same way he did.

'Well I'm from Cork,' Niall says, 'so don't mind me.'

Ken laughs, puts the cigarette in his mouth and takes it out again. 'Am I right in thinking they don't want us to smoke in the bus? It's not made easy for smokers in this country.'

I tell him we'll be there soon, a couple of minutes.

He's from Ardoyne. He ran messages for the IRA. He knows where I'm from too. We wouldn't have met.

We take a right turn and, as the minibus goes dark, my eyes are on his hands which are fidgeting with his cigarette. He's still got the smile. He says he could kill for a beer.

We turn left past the train station, then left again. We're at the Watershed already. A volunteer meets us and takes us in through the back entrance. Ken lights up, and offers his cigarettes around.

'You did well coming here,' he says to me as he puts the packet back in his pocket. 'The heat's something, though. Is Brisbane like this?'

The green room is crowded with T-shirted volunteers, comedians and several people I can't account for. There's food on a long table and beer in plastic tubs.

'Ah, we're in business,' Niall says. 'What are your thoughts, Kenneth? Domestic or imported?'

They set off to plunder, and in seconds they're elbow-deep in ice and talking through their options. I pick up a paper plate and put a couple of strawberries on it. Felicity comes in the other door, her mobile phone clenched in her hand. She sees me, and mimes a big sigh of relief.

Her first words to me are 'I'm so tense' and they come out as though they're under pressure. But she's excited too, excited at the prospect of the festival finally starting and the sell-out crowd we'll have tonight.

Once they see us talking, a couple of volunteers come over and ask about TV, and how I got started. They want to talk about how it works, and about stand-up, and about how it isn't easy to get a break in Perth. They get me to sign their T-shirts. A cluster of people forms around us, and it's like doing the show early – six, seven faces turned my way and waiting for the next funny line, demanding the next funny line. 'You're hilarious,' one of them says, though I'm frankly closer to heartbroken, my head full of more wreckage than the McKendrys' field. Murray, Rob Castle, that poor dying girl this afternoon, Ken and his IRA messages. I'm pushing it away, all of it, just to get the job done.

Felicity interrupts and says, 'There's a sound check to do. I've got to take Meg to do a sound check before we let the audience in.'

'Oh, I was supposed to do that,' one of the volunteers says, still trying to make out the scrawl that I've put on her T-shirt. 'I didn't know that was now.'

I get my first real sense of the venue when Felicity takes me outside. Its walls are temporary and it has no roof. It's built over a pond at the entrance to the art gallery. There's water and light and scaffolding, and it's a clear starry night. Beyond the screens, I can hear people talking, a crowd forming. Sound feels different here when I test the mike, but I know it's going to work. It's going to be fine.

We don't rush back inside.

Felicity says, 'Do you ever get sick of that? All the same questions, all the questions about TV?'

Her phone rings. She looks at the number and says it's only Adam. I leave her to take the call, pointing out that it'd be preferable not to refer to him as Only Adam when she answers. She gives a laugh, puts her finger in her left ear – where it now seems to spend half its time – and as she turns her back I hear her saying 'Hello again'.

The first two acts have ten minutes each, then I have twenty. I could be out there in not much more than half an hour. I sneak out the back way, around the side of the building, as the gates open. This is exactly the time when, years ago, I would have been setting off for a walk with my packet of cigarettes in one hand and my beer in the other, collecting my thoughts, wandering around murmuring my routine to myself, getting the feel of it back, putting the punchlines in place.

It was the morning cigarettes and the ugly binges that made me give it away. I still liked the pre-show solo cigarettes all the way to the end. They came with a sense of anticipation. They marked the last minutes of calm when I had nothing to do but blow blue smoke up at a dark sky before stepping into the light in front of hundreds of people.

For a while after giving up, I'd still head out patting my pockets, my hands looking for the packet and at best finding sugarless gum instead. Now a work night involves none of the cigarettes and half the beers. I'm older and wiser and that affects most things, though probably not enough.

The first act starts. I can hear an announcement over on the other side of the building, and applause. It's a big crowd all right, a big noisy crowd, and the thought occurs to me that I wouldn't give this up for anything. That's one of those things people say in an offhand way, but it looks like I've gone and done it. I've put it to the test and here's where I am, about to go on stage again.

Thank you. Start with thank you. And it's great to be back in Perth. And great to be here at the Watershed helping kick this comedy festival off. Actually, the first time I did a big event in Perth it was a debate a few years ago and it was broadcast on ABC TV ... thought I should go a bit glam ... turned up with a dress that needed a strapless bra. And had I thought that through? No, of course I hadn't. And at the ABC they don't have much money, but they're great at improvising. So the make-up person found a roll of ABC tape – white with blue logos – and taped me into the best cleavage I've ever had. I felt like a fighter pilot being buckled into her seat, but trust me it cleaved like nothing you've ever seen. And, since I hadn't thought through the dress, I really wanted to think through the tape. She told me no way would it come unstuck under the studio lights when it warmed up, no way would the lights make it visible through the dress. She was full of guarantees ... then on to the after party, dancing in a club, UV light, the tape fluoresces through the dress, with ABC logos showing prominently around my breasts. And, of course, no one tells me for ages.

... and on we go from there. And nice work too, making all those bold assertions to Felicity about female comedians doing more than 'chick stuff', and then opening with a story about a frock and my breasts. But it's there as a Perth story, and after that I think I can get through without relying on gender-specific body parts, or garments, and without a single brand name being dropped.

The second act's started. I'm ready.

Later, hours later, while the band was playing and the comedians were cleaning up the food – but particularly the beer – Felicity put her phone away and drank too much and I did too. Not a stupid amount too much, but more than I'd meant to. And I caught a cab back to the hotel, leaving the others to finish the green-room stocks before roaming the town for the next drink.

I'm sitting on my bed with the lights off, CNN on low volume. I'm on my third glass of water. It's not that late.

With the doors shut it wasn't difficult in the green room to talk over the band, but it was cooler outside so we spilled out onto a balcony where the music was louder. But it didn't matter. Bands are there to make noise, and they weren't bad at all. A breeze came in from the west and I looked up to see some clouds blowing in across the stars.

I told Felicity about the last time I'd played in Perth, at a festival a couple of years ago, when one of the acts was the famous throat singers from Kazakhstan. She said she'd seen a show of mine that time but missed theirs, so I did my best to demonstrate and beer churned up from my stomach and fizzed into my nasal passages. Just at the wrong moment for Felicity, who had taken a mouthful of beer herself and reversed it out her nose too.

So we leaned over the railing, both of us dealing with the great discomfort of beer travelling backwards.

'The famous stomach singers from Australia,' I said to her. 'You've heard of them?'

And I noticed how much she seemed to have changed from the person who met me at the airport, though perhaps I was seeing only a change in circumstances. Here she was, beer in her hands and dripping off the end of her nose as she leaned out over the garden bed, laughing and spluttering. I asked her about the jacket she'd worn the night I arrived and she told me it was her mother's. They'd talked, though Felicity hadn't wanted to, and her mother had insisted that I would expect a jacket.

'Speak in your accent,' she said then. 'The one you had when you were eight.' So I did, and she said, 'That is so cool.' She found a tissue in her pocket, or a serviette from the buffet, and she wiped her nose. 'You get asked the Irish question a lot,' she said. 'The one about Irish people being writers and storytellers and comedians. You don't seem to like it much sometimes.'

I told her I was supposed to hide that. It wasn't a question that should surprise me, and I'm supposed to have an answer ready to go.

'The problem is that people get all kinds of views in their heads,' I said, knowing she'd just asked the Irish question no one else had. 'And I'm too in-between to deal with them. I'm from there and I'm from here as well, so I don't know.

I don't know what influences what really, and it's not my job to bother too much about that. I'm just sick of people who have these simplistic views about the place when they've hardly got any connection to it. They've hardly spent any time there. Which'd be me, obviously. But I'm clearly talking about the other people.'

I felt like a tired drunk digging a clumsy hole through their own argument at that point, but it didn't stop me pushing on. I told her I'd had enough of the romanticising that goes on around the tale of the downtrodden Celt. And all that crap about craic and the funny instruments and, really, why the fuck can't they move their arms when they dance? And all those stories about being dirt poor in Limerick where it was rainy every day and, to be sure, we had to lick the moss off the very stones for sustenance, and then we went on to worthy achievement in the New World, now a major motion picture.

She asked me if I'd actually read *Angela's Ashes*, and I asked her if she'd let me be a hypocrite in peace. I hadn't read it, as such, but I had seen the trailer for the movie. And she couldn't deny there was an awful lot of rain in that trailer.

I tried to rise above the wreckage of my case – or tried to do something but I'm not really sure what – by saying, 'Anyway, the whole notion of the "the Irish" or "the Celts" isn't as straightforward as people think. There's centuries of migration.'

And Felicity said, 'Yeah, I heard Colm Toibin talk about that. You know, the Irish novelist? He was here for the

Writers' Festival once. His name's French, I think. Maybe Huguenot.'

She thought we were arguing the same point, but I didn't know any more. I'd finished my part of the show and coasted along for a while on the post-show high since it had all gone well, but by that part of the conversation I'd had a few beers and I was losing my staying power. I was about to talk about time zones and bed and stopping drinking, she was about to produce a Cabcharge voucher. That's where I saw the night heading.

Then the door behind her swung wide open in the breeze and clattered against the wall, and I saw Ken and Niall inside, at the far side of the room, charming the volunteers with their affable Irishness. And I told Felicity that we had a Huguenot castle in the woods not far from where I'd lived, and that I used to walk there with my father on Sundays. At least, it's in my mind as a castle, though I can't recall the building too well, only the woods, and the lane that took us there.

She said she wondered how it would have been if I'd stayed, and grown up there, if I would have been dragged into the politics and all that.

And I explained that it didn't really work that way. You don't get to grow up first, and it's not so much about dragging if it's all around you. I wanted to stop then, but my mind was a blur and I was already telling her that there's no one more passionate about their politics than an eight-year-old being brought up in the wrong place. If you don't know much about the world, you can be far too sure of whatever it is you do know. We don't get that here. We don't understand it. There are armies of ten-year-olds with Kalashnikovs in Sierra Leone.

I said it all, right up to the Kalashnikovs and Sierra Leone. And I thought about Elli then, who is also ten, and war is a million miles from her world, as it should be. She's growing up fast, but there's a lot I hope she never gets to know.

Felicity, at the end of a long pause, breathed a deep contented sigh, took a fresh mouthful of beer and said, 'It's been such a great night. I'm such a big fan of yours, you know. I'd be your biggest fan in Perth, maybe the whole of Australia.'

And that's when I knew we should go home, both of us, Felicity back to her parents' house and me to my room at Rydges.

CNN is running a breaking news story about another suicide bomber in the Middle East. I eat a banana in bed, and I change channels.

Elli will be okay. She hasn't learned to hate anyone. She hasn't learned the way of hating blindly, making it part of your being, making true sworn enemies of people you'll never know.

What is that quote? It's something to do with the Jesuits. 'Give me the child until he is seven and I will show you the man.'

If you were a fanatic anywhere and conscience didn't enter into it, you'd train children. They will take on your views, they don't get afraid in the adult way, they present a small target. Everything's wrong about it, except it makes too much sense.

Now more than ever, I want to call Brisbane. I want to check that everyone's okay, that's all. But it's two hours further into the night on the east coast, and there's not a reason I could give. Elli's safe in her bed there, and Murray's in Shanghai, in the same time zone as Perth and in a hotel room that, I imagine, is much like this one. He's looking out across the lights of a half-familiar city that will never be home, spreading himself out across the king-size bed and, like me, watching the breaking news on CNN.

We were together long enough not just to know each other's habits, but to see some of them converge. Bed TV is the unheralded luxury of the hotel stay, and it didn't take me long to turn him. We ironed out a lot of differences over time, I'm sure we did, but most of them may just have been habits.

I went after Murray when my career was on the way up and not much to speak of. I made the moves, but he held back for a couple of weeks and later admitted it was partly because I wore a man's watch.

I'd stopped smoking by then. I hit thirty smoking and wheezing, losing it at high speed. I went for Nicorettes and a lot of exercise to kill the tension and it worked, but maybe I was lucky and not as addicted as some people. I wandered around the floor at work at the times that would have been my cigarette breaks – I was with a health insurance company then – I drank water from the water cooler in little paper cups, I banned myself from going to smoky places where I'd drink too much and where one wrong nostalgic song might magic a cigarette back into my hands. I made it a mission, and I'm good with missions.

My body changed. It toned, it firmed. And there might be thigh cellulite that I'll take to my grave, but that wasn't the point. Parts of me that had done nothing since school netball got going again, and I was determined not to let them down.

I ran in the morning, I got myself my man's watch since it was better for timing. And this is where I'm bad with missions. I started to get competitive, way beyond my means. I snuck onto the running track at the uni campus after hours, and ran a lap or two. I put my name down for a fun run with ten thousand other people and got so keyed up about it that a friend had to take me aside the day before and say, 'You realise you aren't going to win? They aren't even going to let you start at the front.' I'd stopped realising any of that, even though the big names in the field were Olympians.

I linked up with Murray some time during this process that now looks like a metamorphosis. I had been depressed in my twenties, sometimes. My thirties were better.

He told me later that he couldn't read me at first. The man's watch, the tough-girl hair that I might have had then, the career I was pursuing. I met him the first time through mutual friends when they had eight people to dinner and sat us two seats apart. Two weeks later, I made them bring him along to something I was doing at a comedy club. I was on early and joined their table afterwards. I tried to keep him at arm's length and charm him at the same time. I tried to play it cool but I didn't. I made him agree to have a drink with me, just the two of us.

We had the drink the following week and it was pretty awful as we each pretended that it wasn't happening, and that it happened all the time, no big deal. He talked about the finality of his recent divorce, I cringed inside because most of the routine he'd heard me do was about men being crap in relationships.

'Well, that was great,' I said at the end of my second drink, subtly invoking the past tense, and with a meaningful look at my man's watch. 'I'm glad we did that.'

And Murray said 'Yeah' and it rang equally hollow. Then he took a look at the small stage where, on a better night, a band might play and he turned almost back to me and said, 'You know, I eat too many meals that are dip and a packet of biscuits, and I quite like to cook.'

And with that we were on our way to our second date, by which time we had something to talk about since the first date had been so grim.

Comedy was starting to work for me then, and the more it worked the harder other jobs became to bear. I developed a need for it, a need to be doing it, working in front of audiences, getting a response, working hard to get better at it. Lucky breaks came when I least expected them.

I didn't stop taking them, I didn't stop pushing for more. You get into the habit of pushing, so you don't stop when things start to move the way you want them to. And I went on with the simple belief that, in the end, it must be workable – there must be a way to combine life and the job you most want to do. The steps forward did sometimes seem to come at a cost, but I kept going as if they didn't or at least shouldn't. I kept going in the expectation that it could all be made to work. Because any other outcome would be really unfair.

I left Murray stranded back there, somewhere. That was the word he brought up once with the counsellor: stranded. 'I'm sorry, but that's how I feel,' he said. 'Sometimes.'

Elli was three when we met, and Murray not single by much. We both had issues to deal with, him more than me, and we decided we'd make it out the other side together. Maybe that's an assumption you shouldn't make. I was shaking off some listless years and getting more determined, but neither of us knew what that might mean.

It would be good to know that Elli's happy, and to hear about what she likes at the moment, what movies she's seen, school.

Concert rehearsals should have started by now, and she's in the choir. Before I left, the teacher told me they'd be doing Louis Armstrong's 'What a Wonderful World'.

Ballystewart — 1972

We sang songs in the schoolyard when we were playing games. Popular songs of the time, but often with new words and I don't know who made them up. It was none of us, I'm sure of that.

In the rest of the world, the song line 'I'd like to teach the world to sing' became 'I'd like to buy the world a Coke', but we had a different version. We'd sing it when we were skipping or playing hopscotch or running around throwing a ball at each other, a game that was called brandy when I got to Australia but I think we had a different name for it in Ballystewart.

And the version of the song that we would sing began 'I'd like to crucify the Pope' and then went on to say what we'd do with his blood. I think the final word of that line in the original ended with 'love'. The only other part I can remember was the line that I think was our last: 'with Bernadette and Gerry Fitt to keep him company'. Bernadette was Bernadette Devlin. I asked my mother who Gerry Fitt was. I don't know what she said, but I can remember asking. I think I have the name right, though I might not, and I think he was a Catholic politician.

These people are now largely forgotten by the wider world, and I don't honestly know what they meant to it at the time. There was no CNN in those days, and not the hunger we now have for twenty-four hours of story.

My mother asked me why I wanted to know who Gerry Fitt was and I said, 'I heard his name.' And sang about his crucifixion in the playground at school, but I wasn't going to tell her that part.

I tried to work the song out, but I couldn't completely. The only crucifixion I knew of was Jesus with a thief on either side, and that was a bad business all right but necessary for there to be a resurrection. If we were to do to the Pope what they did to Jesus, wouldn't that say he was a hero?

Our song didn't work that way. When we sang about crucifying the Pope it was about killing him, and showing people. It was about turning religion on him for a last laugh, killing him that way. It made me scared, a little, even to sing it with the others, it was just so horrible. But I did. I sang it anyway because it's what we sang. But I knew it wasn't a song for singing at home. At home we played Nana Mouskouri and Cliff Richard.

I remember seeing Bernadette Devlin on the news, and another woman whose name, I think, was Corrigan. And sure they were the enemy – the word was passed on at school, and we sang about it – but seeing them might have been the thing that put in my head the idea that I had as much right as any boy, as much responsibility as any boy, to pay attention, to take on views and believe in them. And I heard stories about Catholics at school, and not one of them favourable.

At home it was different. There wasn't the same sense in my parents of duty, or purpose, of a historical rightness going back centuries, of the need to refight old battles, the necessity of not giving an inch. At home, the only thing that was ever said back then about Catholics was that they thought Mary was really important, but we believed she was just Jesus's mother. I knew we were right, of course, I knew there was nothing too special about her, but I also knew the issue wasn't as simple as a debate about religious technicalities. The TV news never had people arguing about the importance of Jesus's mother, even if that's where it all started.

But you always lead different lives at school and at home and in the various different aspects of your life. And each part is what circumstances make it, and the whole of it is the life you define as normal and then measure others by. That's what happens.

And I watched afternoon TV and I read books, I learned to make pancakes, I made pictures by gluing seeds on paper. I had the best doll's house of anyone, made by my grandfather to be quite like our own house, with curtains cut from the scraps of our curtains. I had a doll who looked like Jeannie from 'I Dream of Jeannie', and I decided I'd be just like her when I was older, when a full-sized house exactly like ours would be mine. She was my best doll, my favourite. Her limbs were very flexible and her hair would let you style it in different ways.

Her house was furnished in whatever way I could manage it, much of it with pieces acquired from elderly relatives – candlesticks, a chair and a table for the kitchen, toy furniture made for children very long ago and which my best doll would never really have chosen since she was so very modern and perhaps even a flight attendant.

Even the toy soldiers they gave me were old. They were the remaining pieces from an Afghan camel troop, six soldiers in a wooden box that had once been used for pencils. I thought they could live with my Jeannie doll, but my parents said they were real lead from a hundred years before, and lead can make you sick so it would be better to put them on a shelf and not play with them too often. They were too small anyway, and some of them were made permanently bow-legged for riding, though I don't remember being given any camels.

I liked them – I liked their hats and their orange jackets and their bent lead rifles – but they were wrong for the house, little heavy men with no moving parts, standing rigidly in the sitting room as if it was always up to one of the newer dolls to make conversation.

I remember visiting my parents' old aunts and uncles, going round to dark houses that had tall clocks and lace, and where every long-gone death was talked through again each year. 'Keening', I think my mother called it – that hopeless, sad kind of remembering. 'Sure, we're missing our Eddie. It would have been his birthday yesterday.' That's the kind of thing they'd say, wringing a lace-edged handkerchief in their hands. And I'd ask my mother later who our Eddie was, and she'd tell me he had been a cousin of theirs, maybe a second cousin, who died of a fever in 1912.

'Honestly,' my grandmother said once after a bout of this, 'those sisters of mine – they go to funerals of people they don't even know. They're forever looking them up in the paper. Could they not do something useful for the world instead of getting up to their nonsense?'

My mother laughed. The car wasn't even out of their street by then. I twisted around and looked through the back window, but they'd gone and the gate was shut. My grandmother kept talking as though her sisters had irritated her since about 1912, my mother kept laughing.

There were toys in the attics in those old houses, and people's best dresses from the 1920s kept on mannequins or in boxes, everything saved in case another generation might have a use for it. But there were relics in every room – old board games, a collection of spoons, a cabinet of trinkets and treasure from the world wars. It was the great-aunt who missed our Eddie who collected those, and she gave me my two favourite pieces before we left for Australia – a matchbox holder made from a shell casing at Ypres and a booklet of pictures from Hitler's glorious tour of the Rhineland at the end of the thirties. And she'd tell me how to pronounce Ypres and that soldiers called it 'wipers' as a joke, and she'd thumb through the Hitler booklet and shake her head and tell me about the neighbour's boy, who they'd lost in the D-Day landings.

Mostly though I'd sit still and eat cake, and adult conversations would be had. There were sometimes threads of stories that I could pick up afterwards – times past that were only alluded to, so I knew I should hold my questions until we were in the car and on the way home. There was, for example, my grandmother's cousin who married a doctor who went off the rails and had another family in another town and also took some of his own strong medicine. Which is where I thought the expression about giving someone a taste of their own medicine began, but his case seemed particular. They'd put him away for that, but he was also long dead by 1972, a figure on old peripheries and not much talked about, only talked about at all to explain the surname that my grandmother's cousin had.

All these houses are huge when I recall them, and they weren't. But I know that's a universal experience when remembering childhood places. All their staircases go up and up, and they didn't. But that's what it's like to go in there at six or seven or eight and fix that picture in your mind. If those memories are all set at eight, grandfather clocks are all twelve feet tall.

Perth – Friday

I'M WOKEN IN THE DARK by a male voice singing. It sounds like a nursery rhyme, but I can't make out the words. I can hear it through the wall, interrupted by the buzzing of an appliance. There's a female voice in the background, sounding completely bored. Maybe it's people, maybe it's a TV in the next room.

They're gone when I go to the gym in the morning, even though it's early. There's a dishevelled breakfast tray outside their door, toast with a few big bites out of it, a napkin in the cereal bowl. Maybe it was the sound of shaving during the night. Why were they leaving so early? Are they going somewhere? Another city? Back to their respective houses, slipping in quietly while it's still dark? I won't ever know. I get too many fragments of stories in this job.

I let it occupy my mind for my first few laps, in case any of what I saw and heard might be clues, but it successfully keeps its mystery. Did the voice actually wake me, or did I wake first and then hear it? I don't even known that.

I'm learning more about tumble turns, learning that

if you work the last stroke and pull into the wall with the turn, rather than stopping, your legs tense like a spring. The power in the turn comes because you don't stop. I can lap in nine strokes when it works well.

Months after we met at the dinner party, Murray and I worked out that both of us had been made a clear promise by the couple hosting it that there would be no set-ups, so we figured then that it must have been one after all. We had each said that we didn't want to meet their single friends and that, if we were to meet someone, it would happen in its own good time and of its own accord. I was tired the night of the dinner party, quieter than usual and perhaps a better observer because of that. I liked his hands and the way he gave people time to tell their stories, even when he was desperate to interrupt. I recall that I liked his pert butt when he went to the bathroom too, and I had to turn around to see it so I'd obviously noticed a few things by then already. I'm all class, all class. I could cry into my goggles if I'm not careful.

I roll into my final turn, swim to the other end and get out. My phone is under my towel, and there's a new text message when I check it: 'It's paintball tomorrow – Em.'

I call her and she says 'You know, paintball, skirmish, little guns that fire globs of paint' as though that clarification is all it will take.

'Would you sound half as relaxed if it was you doing it?' There's water still blocking my left ear, and I'm not yet loving the prospect of running around in battle fatigues with Elliott King.

'Of course not,' she says brightly. 'Come on, Mega. Your chance to shoot some TV people. That doesn't come along every day. And it's just little globs of paint. They're really keen. I'll can it if you want me to, but I think they see it as a bonding exercise, a chance to get out and have a bit of fun before working more together.'

'What about that thing you do with an empty milk carton where you all stand in a circle and try to keep hitting it up into the air? That's a bonding exercise.'

But the deal is done, and I know it. And there is a certain appeal to the idea of splattering TV boys with high-velocity paint.

I wonder how it'll be this time if it comes off, trying TV without so much pressure to be funny, or immediate. A writer on a comedy show once told me that the host monologues she put together had to have a laugh every two-and-a-half lines, and she meant teleprompt lines and there's not a lot of words to one of those.

When my own show went to air, it lasted five weeks and three timeslots. The media campaign ran for longer than the show. There was a two-line mention in everyone's January article on what was coming that year, along with one listing as a 'Hot New Show', one more as a 'Watch out for . . .' but not much else. The network had hoped for better.

The optimism – the mistaken optimism – only kicked in in the weeks before we went to air. There was wide newspaper coverage then and a lot of radio, since comedians work well on radio. There were network parties and plenty of other manufactured opportunities for me to have my photo taken. I held a lot of champagne that month, and kissed a lot of air.

The first proper whiff of doom blew in around nine-forty a.m. on the morning after the first show was screened. I was rating a full twenty per cent below expectations. I never clawed it back and, without me knowing it that day, we were already only two weeks out from going through the motions.

When the show was axed, one of the network execs said, 'You should have come from Sydney or Melbourne. We think that might have made it easier.' So that was what it was down to – my dumb parents, migrating to the wrong city in 1972.

The show is often not specifically remembered now, but it's there in the air when people talk to me, as some vague sense that I'm closer to genuinely famous than I once was. Sometimes I see them struggling with the vagueness of it, and I want to put them out of their misery and go, 'TV. Remember? I was on TV in a semi-regular brief capacity. That's why I'm one small step ahead of the pack.'

At least one magazine listed my show as a 'heroic failure' in its TV picks for that year.

A few months ago, I was trying on clothes in one of those annoying stores that doesn't have a mirror in each cubicle, and a woman started talking to me. I must have walked past her three times by then to take a look at different outfits. What she said was innocuous enough, and I've forgotten it now, but I noticed her daughter getting that agitated embarrassed look that parental behaviour can provoke in teenagers, and when I went back into the cubicle I heard her say, 'Mum, stop it. You're hassling someone who's borderline famous.' That's where I am. Borderline famous.

And why would any sane person wish for more? The most vacuous ambition in the world is 'I just wanna be famous'. Be famous to sell your product, be famous to do something useful, but don't go wanting it for its own sake. Get a life. A life can be good, and is much underrated.

What's it all about, anyway – the pursuit of fame? Money? Neediness? I'd settle for a good-sized Lotto win and regular positive feedback from the right half-dozen people. That'd be enough, surely.

Not that I buy that talk from the genuinely famous about yearning for the simple life. If they did, they'd walk. Maybe they yearn for simplicity on a press junket between the day's fifteenth and sixteenth interviews, but not most of the time.

Sure, I'd take the simple life, and I can see it now – the rainforest setting, a creek out the back, a garden of mixed legumes. But I'd take it on top of the Lotto win and the positive feedback, and I'd have a guy to work it for me. And his name would be Julio, and he'd be muscular, yet lithe, and always shining with the first sweat of a morning's work. And I'd watch him hoe. Hoe, baby, hoe. Tend my vines. Already it's vines now ...

I complicated the life I had, back home. No Julio will bring that back.

Some time ago, I set off down the track I'm on because I wanted to do the work. I want to do good work. That's another one of those Hollywood things, like yearning for the simple life. They all 'want to do good work'. This is so wrong. I seem to come with the full set of Hollywood pretensions, but a fraction of the fame and none of the money.

One person who remembered me after my five weeks of heroic failure was Elliott King. I had his card – Elliott King, King Pin Pictures – from meeting him at an awards ceremony while my show was in production and soon to go to air.

'You were the best thing in it,' he said, about one of my ventures that was already gone and hadn't been nominated that night. 'If you've got any ideas for anything in future, I'd always be interested to hear them. And it doesn't have to be comedy, either. I'm sure you can do more than that.'

Seven or eight months later I called him, with Christmas coming, a new year to plan and my show axed long before, and I told him I had an idea. I'd found his card in my bag, where it had stayed since the awards night. I'd left it there and given it no thought at the time, since I'd planned for my show to run its scheduled thirteen weeks with a likelihood of renewal.

He flew to Brisbane and he took me to lunch. He heard my idea out, and he got it. He asked the right questions, made the right observations and at the end he said, 'We can do this.' And I walked back to the station to catch the train home, realising I had confidence for the first time in months. Confidence that it wasn't just my own mad notion that I could stretch myself, try something new and make it work.

That's what I owe him for, that one clear moment on Ann Street. More than anything else, maybe. And it's not his fault that two years passed before the money came through to let us start work.

Felicity is later than I was expecting, so I've eaten too much bircher muesli by the time she arrives. I've replaced the appetite centre of my brain with a publicist, and that can't be healthy.

It's Friday, the itinerary tells me: celebrity canoe race practice, two interviews and an afternoon off while Felicity runs around town with Richard Stubbs.

'It's all okay,' she says. 'It's the pick-up time in the itinerary, not the time we have to be there to meet them. We're on schedule.'

'And it is just practice, isn't it?' I'm overloaded with food and not feeling competent. 'Just technique rather than anything too vigorous?'

'And a photo shoot, maybe. You and your partner.' She leads me out through the foyer to the taxi rank, stopping on the way to pull her sunglasses out of her bag. 'That's okay, isn't it?'

'Sure, but why me? I mean I'm fine with it, but there'd be bigger names in the race. How I do I get the practice shot as well as the hospital shot?'

She's around the far side of the cab now, and she stops with the door half-open to give me a look, as though what I've just said is a poor attempt at false modesty. 'I don't know the whole line-up, but maybe some of the other big interstate names are still interstate.'

'And my partner?'

'I don't know. There's no butterfly swimmers, so I tried to get you a footballer. But I'm not confident.'

We drive off down Hay Street, and I'm starting to realise I haven't paddled a canoe since school. I've used a rowing machine, certainly, but not a canoe, not anything in water. And I'm going to get screwed when it comes to partner selection. The comedian always gets screwed because it's allegedly funny.

The Barrack Street Jetty is only a few minutes away, hardly a cab ride at all.

As we go in search of the people we're meeting, I can't stop myself telling Felicity that my arms are a bit tired from swimming. I was lapping less than an hour ago, after all. It's my first pre-emptive move on an excuse, and she sees it for what it is and laughs and says, 'Yeah, right.'

At the far end of the jetty there's a canoe being lowered into the water. I'd settle for a pole vaulter – they've got good shoulders – or a gymnast with the strength to do the rings. Either of those would be quite acceptable. But it's not to be.

'Gawd, look at those divine arms. I think you'll be the engine, Darl, so you'd better take the seat up the back.' Those are the first words of my partner, a fey boy interior designer from a TV lifestyle show, just as I'd predicted. Worse maybe. This one would overbalance if his hair had to carry one gram more of whatever it is that's holding it vertical against gravity.

Felicity puts so much effort into not laughing that her cheeks flush.

The newspaper photographer never turns up, but my partner's network has a news crew there and they shoot bits of everything. The safety briefing, with him clowning around and playing dumb. The life-jacket fitting, with him clowning around and playing dumb. It's all very attractive.

His name's Anthony, and he says, 'Just don't ever call me Tony and we'll get along famously.' He has slender pale arms, and their pallor and slimness are only emphasised when he's engulfed by the bulky bright yellow life-jacket.

'Apparently they don't come in blue,' he says to the camera indignantly, and then shrugs his shoulders, which pushes the life-jacket into his ears.

The artistic highpoint comes when he tells the crew, 'Just get some footage of us paddling along and we can run it sped up – that always looks funny. You know, with music.'

They take it all impassively, we flail about on the water for a minute or two, he does nothing but splash me. And then he declares that his arm muscles are getting shaky and he'll have to stop.

'Maybe everyone's got someone like that as a partner,' Felicity says afterwards, as we walk along the edge of Langley Park towards the ABC studios. 'It mightn't be as bad as you think. Maybe some canoes have two of them.' She laughs at the prospect of it, a race of floundering canoes crewed by the famous and talentless. Frantic splashing, nothing much moving forward, not a hair out of place. 'Or maybe every other canoe has two footballers. Or canoeists.' That's a prospect that amuses her more.

There's a ride-on mower cruising up and down the park,

and the air is full of the smell of cut grass. I was expecting to sweat at canoe practice, and now I'm going to the ABC studios in gym pants.

I'll be home in three days, Monday morning. It feels a lot closer now. It's hard not to wonder what I might find when I get there, when I get home and open the front door. When I think of our flat, I can only see it with a mixture of Murray's things and mine and ours. I don't want that to have changed yet. But that's really just the first part of not wanting it to change at all.

Felicity walks me to the door of the ABC building and makes sure that I'm expected. The receptionist takes a look at the list on her clipboard and then calls the Master Controller to let him know that I've arrived.

'No worries,' she says, when she puts the phone down. 'He'll be here for you in a second.'

I sign in and stick my visitor's name tag on my chest, and Felicity checks that I'm okay to do the two interviews without her. I tell her to make sure she wears the jacket when she picks Richard Stubbs up from the airport, because he's done a lot of TV and he's got his own radio show and it's made him very fussy.

'Very funny,' she says. 'What's he like, really?'

I let her know that she needn't worry. He's a nice guy. He'll be nothing but pleasant company, cruising Perth with her in a cab this afternoon. As long as the banana situation's sorted out, the eight bananas a day he requires to be delivered to his room.

'He's convinced he's got some problem with his potassium,'

I tell her, as though he's a madman but must be indulged. 'And bananas are the only potassium source he's happy with, apparently. He always lets people know and they forget it all the time, and he can really turn then.'

Felicity is on the phone to the festival office in a second, before I can stop her and tell her it's a joke. The Master Controller is swiping his tag on the other side of the glass security door, and then telling me to come on through.

Felicity's waving to me, waving me to go ahead, while saying, clearly and firmly, into her phone, 'Where you've got "no special requirements", does that mean he actually told you – like, definitely told you – that he's got no special requirements, or does it mean that you don't have a list of his special requirements?'

I take two steps towards the studios and she turns away, still talking. The security door shuts behind me and, as Felicity leaves the building still deep in damage-control mode, I'm being led down the corridor to the green room, the Master Controller talking through what we're about to do and telling me he'll be back in five minutes, plenty of time for me to have a glass of water and a sit down.

He leaves me there, with the local radio station turned up loud. There's a faint smell of incense, and the walls are covered with black-and-white portrait shots of local presenters and certificates from cancer charities thanking the ABC for their support. There's no water in the water cooler, though someone has left a half-full cup on the coffee table, with a fat lipstick mark along the rim.

There's an interview about healing under way, someone

talking about a healing expo with teepees and Hopi ear candles. That's the incense smell, and the lipstick. The room's last occupant is now on air.

The Master Controller appears in the doorway again and says, 'Bunbury'll be ready for you in a couple of minutes. You might as well come in and get settled.'

He pushes his steel-framed glasses back up his nose, though I don't think they'd slipped, and he leads the way to the booth. He opens the door for me, and tells me we shouldn't have any problems, but he'll be in the next room monitoring everything just in case. The booth is about the size of a walk-in wardrobe, with a cork board on one wall crammed with the business cards of previous inhabitants. I sit in the only chair, facing a window with closed blinds on the other side. As I put the headphones on, I notice the sign he's written that says 'Please switch off all mobile phones and pagers.'

I have Felicity's number keyed in, and I take the headphones off my right ear and call her. She's in a cab on the way to the airport. There's engine noise and static and she sounds like she's in a tunnel.

'Okay, I don't know what to believe now,' she says, when I tell her I invented the Richard Stubbs story. 'I think I'm going to get one bunch of bananas just in case. I'll get him four. That's half a day. Then I can ask him if he wants more.'

A voice comes through the headphones into my left ear. Bunbury is ready to start talking.

It's the email from Elli that I open first when I see what's waiting for me at the Internet cafe. And it says:

> hello annoying one,
> well i AM sad.
> this is cr@p and i am angry with both of you :-(((((
> will you still always be my friend like you said?
> simple question
> e

It's an email that leaves me forgetting to breathe, stuck between breaths and dizzy. It sits there on the screen, with all the starkness of typed text. I wish she were here. I could type all day and not manage a whole reply. Two things I shouldn't do: send her five thousand words, and collapse in a heap.

I should keep it short, or write as much as I like then cut it back to the message at its most straightforward, deal with her simple question. Next week, I hope, we'll talk face-to-face.

Years ago, when I was working on some new material, I had a bit pencilled in in which I talked about adjusting to being Elli's father's new partner and being 'in loco parentis' to Elli every second weekend and some weeknights. The joke centred on the apparent literal translation being 'in madness, a parent', but I never used it. There was no madness about it. It's been great. And if I'd run that material once and she'd heard about it, it would have been very unfair. It's been a privilege to watch her being every age from three to ten.

Friendship perhaps describes our relationship best. 'Will you still always be my friend?' It's no throwaway line. By the time Elli was six we both knew that I couldn't simply explain her away as my partner's daughter, so the answer to the question 'Is she your daughter?' had naturally become 'No, she's my friend'. And if more was needed – if there was a new teacher involved, for example – I could add 'We've known each other for years. I live with her father, so that means Elli and I get to live together some of the time too.'

I've been in close proximity to two-thirds of her life – there when she broke her arm, there while she's learned a lot, there through that proud stage of newly being able to read aloud, a stage that came with its own regular highlights.

We were in adjacent toilet cubicles once at an airport, and I heard her small voice drifting over the partition as she said to herself, 'No matter where you are going and where you are from, always use a condom. Whatever you're into.' There was a long, long pause when I wondered if we might be about to cross into a new phase of knowledge, and then she said, 'Going to Sydney, from Brisbane, into McDonald's, chocolate and sometimes glitter. And I'd like a horse.'

I don't want to write this email. I want to have a conversation with her instead.

Suddenly, today, I feel as though I'm on the margins. She'll live with her mother Laura some of the time and with Murray the rest, just as she has been doing, but I won't be with Murray.

I hope I can still see her. I don't know what happens in these situations. She reads a lot, and I've always liked reading her books with her. 'We can share this one,' she'll say, 'if you want to. It can stay here and we can share it.' It's a gesture of friendship, and not required by anything else. We would be two friends who shared the books they read together and talked about.

I never wanted children. I never thought I could work out how to parent. There were years when I would have been dreadful at it. I was too selfish, too erratic, and no one would even have me back as a babysitter a second time. Toddlers would scream and scream, six-year-olds would refuse to go to bed and we'd still be in the lounge room dancing to Abba when the parents came home at midnight. I didn't have a clue, and I didn't want one.

Elli brought some child-bonding need to the surface, and met it at the same time. Murray wanted another, he wanted her to have a sister or brother. He said he'd like it if it happened, but the idea seemed to go quiet eventually. I travelled more, he got promoted and travelled more, and we settled into an arrangement that seemed to work for everyone involved.

We share a lot now, Elli and me. I can't imagine life another way. I'm nose-diving towards the 'collapse in a heap' option. Don't go there.

My dear E,
Simple answer: always. Always your friend, and that's the deal.

And I'm sad too, but we get what we get sometimes.
And sucked in that you're using the school library computer
and need to w@tch your l@ngu@ge.
Back very soon. Missing you lots in the meantime.
Love
M

Ballystewart – 1972

Mark Macleish lived on a farm that had a two-storey whitewashed house with a big barn opposite it, and high walls on the other sides making a kind of courtyard. He bought Commando war comics for 5p a time. A few of the others at school did too, but Mark never missed one. I read his, because I didn't usually have the 5p and it would have taken too much talking if I'd brought one home.

That's how my parents were, and it was one of the many ways in which they weren't like everyone else's. They weren't local, for a start. My father was from Carrickfergus, but he worked for years in Scottish shipyards and then ports in the south of England. My mother had travelled too and lived in London for a while, but they'd met in Scotland. They'd agreed to live not too far from Belfast, but on the water. Ballystewart was where they'd ended up, and my grandmother – my mother's mother – had moved nearby, to a small house in Donaghadee, around the time I was born.

My parents weren't like other people in the village, I could tell that. They were seen as all right, but separate, and therefore not to be told certain things. And it doesn't matter if you're seven or eight, you still know what those things are. We didn't talk about the Commando comics. I thought they wouldn't like them, but it was more than that.

I liked them though. Commando comics were set in World War Two, and no one read them with the eye for detail that Mark Macleish and I did. Mark was skinny and he got asthma sometimes, and he had big round glasses and a bowl haircut. He was no good at football, but he was smart and his eye for detail got him respect. His father was a big man and his brother Paul was broad-shouldered and strong, so no one knew how Mark fitted into that family.

Mark wanted to be an astronaut, even though not a lot of astronauts came from round our way and his mother said it'd mean going to school practically forever. She also said he'd have to take a much more responsible approach to his asthma if he wanted to be an astronaut, and I think he did after that. Paul wanted to run the farm, but he was taking ages to learn how you keep the books, and he didn't much like that side of it. He said he'd just do what his father did – marry someone good with numbers and bills and all of that.

It was Commando comics that taught Mark and me about the Thompson and the Sten, and no Tommy gun in a Commando ever came with one of those gangster rotary magazines. They came with a thirty-round box mag, and the Sten with thirty-two rounds but a magazine sticking out to the left. The details were in the stories, but also on the inside front and back covers, along with pictures of football players. We followed Manchester United, but if you did that you called them Man United. We all followed them, round our way. Or most of us. My father followed a team in Scotland but they played in a different competition, and not one that we heard much about.

There were guns on the news too, of course, and soldiers. Guns were banned, fireworks were banned, every day we saw footage of soldiers in the streets. Commando comics read like another part of the news to us.

Then Mark Macleish got some new school shoes and they came in a camouflage box with a booklet of commando hand signals. We started learning them that same afternoon. It also had information about military ranks and survival skills and battlefield techniques.

It's only now that I realise how poorly I must have fitted in when we moved to Australia. I must have seemed like a weird kid sometimes. I felt like a weird kid, but only because of my accent. That's what the others at school focused on, and they'd keep coming up and telling me to talk so they could hear it. I didn't like being the outsider. In my family, I'd been the one insider where we'd lived before. I knew it was a privilege, and I resented losing it. But I got rid of the accent and the problem went away. It made it seem as if it must have been the only different thing about me.

Once, not long after we arrived here, nits or lice or some other hair infestation ripped through our class and a lot of us got short hair. Mine stayed that way. I kept telling my mother it was what school told us to do. I got shorter and shorter hair. Don't-mess-with-me hair.

I did well at school though, much like before, and that

seemed to be the main thing. Good marks were the best measure of a healthy adjustment. Good marks and having a good time, which I did even though I felt a bit adrift. It wasn't a feeling I could put into words. It wasn't just about missing what I'd had before, and all my friends. I could talk about that, and I did. I felt uneasy, and I kept that feeling in my head and it took years to let it go.

But I made new friends, and I adjusted. I could be funny, and that always helped. I hung out with boys. I learned to kick a ball that wasn't round. I remember thinking they were weak, soft, unworldly. I didn't know the word 'unworldly' then, but it best describes what I thought of them, that side of them. They were good friends, though.

I think I first made friends with boys in Australia because that's what I was used to. In Ballystewart none of the girls in my class lived anywhere near us, but some of the boys did.

So, I took these four Brisbane boys, I taught them the hand signals, and I taught them how they should crawl if they ever carried a gun. One of their parents saw us doing it, so they took us to an adventure playground one weekend and we did the obstacle course so many times and drank so much cordial that Andrew Hailey vomited bright red.

And my don't-mess-with-me hair was soldier's hair. It reminded me of where I'd come from. And no one knew.

In 1972, we had Cubs and Brownies once a month in the Scouts' and Guides' hall in Ballystewart. We never went camping because it wouldn't have been safe and, for the same reason, there were some badge activities we knew we'd never do. I did the art badge. I got it for gluing seeds on paper to make a picture. We didn't mind really that we couldn't do badges. We played a lot of games and we had a good time.

The first time I saw a real gun was there, when Mark Macleish brought it along in a bag. He said he'd found a few of them at home, but the bolts were kept separate so this wasn't the whole thing, and the ammo and magazines were kept separate, too. We didn't mind. It was a big moment anyway. The gun was treasure in that bag, the best secret I'd ever been in on.

I wondered if it had killed anyone yet, or been in a war somewhere and come home. I put my hand in scared, but the barrel was safe and hard, cold and precise.

We were supposed to be doing something with flowers that night, but I'd already finished. Dried flowers and twigs, that's what we had to work with, and instructions to make something decorative for hanging on a wall, a gift we were to give someone. I sprayed mine all gold and left it to dry and went down the back where there were drinks, and where Mark was waiting.

When I got home on those nights, my mother would say, 'Did you have a good time at Brownies? Did you learn anything?' And often we didn't, but we did our best to that week. We cross-referenced the gun with the diagrams in the Commandoes and we tried to teach ourselves to strip it and put it back together. It might have been a Sten, that gun, and it was heavy but not so hard to take apart into its bigger bits. Not that we got much of a look at it, since we had to keep it in Mark's bag as much as possible, but we could take it to bits all right, and he went home with his bag clanking as though it was full of tools.

That sounds unlikely now, but it feels like a memory. It feels like it shouldn't have happened that way, or at all. My parents have always said that most of the province was peaceful, and made it clear that their views are more informed than mine. So it was easier to learn to believe a little less in what might have been my own life. It would have been harder to talk, and I'd always said I wouldn't.

Toy guns had been banned early that year, I think. Soldiers shot a kid in Belfast when he came around a corner with a plastic Tommy gun. They banned caps for cap guns, they banned fireworks. We had a box of sparklers from before all that, and my parents would still let me light one inside sometimes. We'd shut the curtains and turn out the lights, and the sparks would prickle on the back of my hand and the air would smell stronger than an old gun for a while after.

I was always a bit scared though when we did it, because fireworks and toy guns had been banned at the same time as each other, and the boy with the plastic Tommy gun had been shot dead. We talked about it once at dinner at the Macleishes', and Mark had asked why the soldiers couldn't have just wounded him instead, but his father said they had no choice.

'You can't get too fancy about shooting someone,' he said. 'You just aim for the middle. The minute you try lining up a foot or a leg you'll get shot yourself. Anyway, it was Ardoyne.

He would have been out in the streets in a year or two with a real gun.'

I knew about the first roadblock to go up outside the village. I knew days before that it would be on the weekend, even if I didn't know which day and exactly where. It was Sunday morning, and we drove through without being stopped. No one said what they were looking for, but I figured it was something to do with Catholics, and probably the IRA. We'd talked about it at school, and that's where we sang the songs about the Pope and Bernadette Devlin, after all.

My father slowed the car down but they waved us through and he said, 'See, it's nothing to worry about, really. I know they might look scary, but it's all okay. If we just look straight ahead and don't make a fuss, we'll be on our way home in no time.'

We drove between the two tractors they'd parked in the road, and there were people on them with sticks and knives, and handkerchiefs on their faces – some of them even handkerchiefs I'd seen at school. They had a point to make, and it wasn't about disguise. Sammy McKendry lifted his hand in a small wave to me as we passed through, and one of the bigger McKendry boys – the one with the gun – nudged him to stop it. But the gun was just an old shotgun, probably the one I'd first heard in the woods when I was three or four.

Later, on a walk with my father, I'd seen the fox it had shot, the little dead fox, and I'd been terribly sad. And the shotgun cartridges tasted mainly plasticky but also something else, and I could leave marks in them with my teeth. Then my father saw me biting them and took them away because they were dirty and because you don't eat anything you pick up off the ground. I can't have been more than three, maybe younger. But I wasn't afraid of the shotgun, even though it had killed something. It was more like a tool, and that was its job. The fox had been killing chickens, probably, or killing something that it shouldn't, at least.

I practised morse code in my room with a torch, sending messages to the far wall, but I was never very quick at it. I'd sit at the window if I couldn't sleep, watching the back lane as far as its bend, watching how black the night became if there was no moon. And I'd signal morse code into the night sky, usually just 'Hello' one time after another. Light was amazing. We'd learned about it at school. The beam would travel forever, and sometimes I scared myself by wondering who I might be saying hello to. They might come to earth, come to my house, come for me.

I knew aliens wouldn't speak English, not as their first language, but morse code was harder than English, so if they could crack that the meaning of 'Hello' shouldn't be too difficult.

And I'd shine the torch into the lane sometimes, but the beam was too weak when it got there so I couldn't see a thing. If the bed had been higher, I would have slept under it. That would have been better.

Perth – Friday

VISITING HOURS START at two p.m., so I decide to go and see Courtney at the hospital.

When I recall my father at the roadblock – when I think about the scene now, years later – I can see that his aim was to get us through it and on our way. He wanted to get me through it without me becoming too fearful of what was going on. That was his focus, and behind all his calm talk. What I didn't see at the time was that his sense of calm was forced. He seemed genuinely calm, and I was too, so the roadblock never seemed out of the ordinary.

We drove on and talked about my grandparents – my father's parents, who would be coming from Carrickfergus to visit us for lunch – and we talked about the kind of spring we looked like having, or at least my parents did, and around then they must have begun making plans for us all to leave. We needed to leave. I was learning to hate people I'd never seen, and hate is wasted energy on its best days, and sometimes far more destructive.

I want to get something for Courtney, maybe a book.

I don't expect I'll see her again after this. She's in a hospital bed being consumed by that cancer with the long name, and I can't believe that she handles every minute of it matter-of-factly. I want to tell her that I've noticed her there, that she wasn't just a photo op, that she's still in my head.

I find a large bookstore in the Murray Street Mall and the staff direct me to the young adult section on the basement level. Courtney is four years older than Elli, and that's near enough to a generation at their ages. The hospital says it is – ten-year-olds are treated as children and fourteen-year-olds aren't. I know Elli's books. I can't guess what would be right for Courtney.

The manager of the section seems to have read everything, and she makes the choice for me when I tell her it's for someone who is fourteen and very sick.

'How about something funny?' she says. 'Something that's funny but also a good book.'

With my Perth mini-map, I find my way back to the hospital. I will tell Courtney about canoeing practice, and that she shouldn't be putting any money on me. I will tell her I'm lined up for paintball tomorrow, and honestly not looking forward to it but sometimes you end up doing stupid things of other people's choosing, allegedly in the name of fun. I will tell her, yes, this is my life, the weekend ahead is no aberration. It's how it is. And part of what I like about the job – though just a part of it – is that it regularly throws me things I'm not expecting, and not good at, and invites me to try them out in a ridiculously public way. It fascinates me – it still does – that that can be part of any job.

There's not the same sense of excitement when I get to the ward today. A young doctor is by himself in the office area, writing in a file, and he doesn't look up. He sniffs and clears his throat and keeps writing. I never see anything of him but the top of his head.

A nurse appears from a nearby room, pushing a blood pressure machine on a stand, and she stops abruptly and says, 'Oh, it's you. I didn't think we were expecting to see you today.' She takes the stethoscope from around her neck and folds it up in her hand. 'But you're very welcome, though. Courtney's been talking about you ever since your visit.'

'I didn't get to talk to her much yesterday, and I've got a gap in my itinerary this afternoon, so . . .'

'I know she'll be glad to see you. She's just in her room. Reading the new *NW*.'

Courtney's door is the fourth or fifth on the left, and it's open when I get there. I'm reaching up to knock on it when she sees me. She looks surprised, but it's not the same look as yesterday. She's watching a soap, with the voices distorted by poor reception on the small TV. She's holding a magazine, the new *NW*, with the obligatory Nicole Kidman cover. And 'Meg's shock break-up' as one of the stories flagged.

'Meg's shock break-up' next to a face that doesn't look like Meg Ryan, but looks a lot like I might in an off-guard moment.

It hit us both hard, Courtney and me. And she had less hair than yesterday, I'm sure of it. There was a brush next to the bed, set down beside her with her hair caught in it. My visit was useless. I gave her the book on the way out. She was distraught on my behalf. She hoped the article was wrong, all of it, but one look at my face when I saw the magazine told her it wasn't.

I had to explain how these things happen, even to people who care about each other very much. It took a handful of her tissues for me to get through it. I found myself saying things I'd said to Elli weeks ago, and again today in my head in the Internet cafe, about the bad luck at the heart of this. I pulled up short of only some of the detail, but what the hell, she'd read the magazine and it turned out details weren't being spared. I told her she shouldn't be put off by it, that sometimes relationships work and keep working and then I realised she would die soon, almost certainly, and I wondered what the hell I was doing.

Meg's shock break-up. There I am, in a photo from Canada: 'Meg Riddoch partying hard in Calgary with Canadian alt-country star Rob Castle and a friend at the PanCanadian Comedy Festival.' I look drunk in the photo, but I'm not. It was early in the evening, after the Uptown Showcase but before anything else, and I've got my arms around Jen and Rob Castle, and a Big Rock Traditional Ale in one hand. The photo was taken in the Ship and Anchor, before we'd even sat down. It was Gary who took it, I think, the guy who talked about writing and the fifteen-plus walkways.

Soon I'm on the couch at Claire's place with a copy of the *NW* that I picked up on the way. And she's out of herbal tea, and I'm staring at the article when she hurries back in from the kitchen with two peppermint Cornettos.

'There you go,' she says, and we start eating them. I'm well into mine before it registers. 'I know,' she says. 'I looked in the fridge and it was the closest to comfort food. I thought we could do with one. Should you stop looking at the article now? Just for a bit?'

She takes the magazine from me and sits in a nearby chair with it in her lap. For a minute or two she talks with her hand over the story, as if it would be wrong to look, and then she picks up her glasses from the table, and she's reading it, and responding, and I'm moving her on from the 'Oh my god, how could they . . .' phase, and finding myself working through useless distinctions. I'd just met Rob Castle when the photo was taken, for instance. I'm confident that it was my first beer, and jet lag never comes up well.

But she's reading on, charging into battle for me again. 'Are they implying . . . yes, yes, I think they are . . .'

And that's when I realise I've spent all my energy keeping this at arm's length – out of my head, away from Emma and anyone else – and I have no energy left to lie. I could do it. I could get away with it – these stories are all about speculation – but I don't want to. Claire's support is too necessary but, more than that, it's too honest. She's right in front of me, slapping the magazine down on the table, outraged on my behalf.

The picture's face up – three people with hardly a thing to care about, which was a lie even then, for me anyway.

So that's when I have to admit that I slept with Rob

Castle. I have to admit it in Australia for the first time. Admitting it to Jen in Calgary was one thing, when the incident had happened hours before and was almost part of a dream, but it feels worse owning up to it in Perth. I was a long way from home, I explain to Claire, and alone, very alone, and the weather was wild and cold and something happened that night at the Uptown Screen that I couldn't rationally account for. And the next night too, back in my room.

I was single then, I tell her, but she's already leapt deftly to stick by my side.

'These things can happen,' she's saying.

'It had ended with Murray, weeks before.' The fact of it comes out of me as if it's not something I can control, or pause to word a better way. 'Weeks ago, or a month now if I add it up, and I was very sad one day in Calgary and I couldn't tell you yesterday. I should have but I couldn't.'

And she says, strongly, 'Of course' with a look at me over her glasses as if it's mad to even think it. 'Of course you couldn't. This is all far too painful. And we were just having a nice cup of coffee and some cake at the Blue Duck.'

The afternoon passes in a stupid haze.

Emma leaves a message on my voicemail saying, in a fake-calm voice, 'Hi, don't know if you've seen it yet, but I just picked up a copy of *NW*. Give me a call.'

I can't talk to Emma. She likes Murray and I love him, and I can't bear the details. I can't bear to have to put it into words. Next week I can do that, next week when the tour is over.

I tell Claire about Rob Castle, though this isn't ultimately about Rob Castle. I tell her about his wife and three children in Thunder Bay, Ontario, and about the note, which I realise I've almost committed to memory word for word, despite making myself tear it into pieces in Calgary as a first step towards getting it entirely out of my life.

'I don't even know what alt-country is,' I tell her needlessly. 'Not that I can say it would have had a huge bearing on my actions. He sounded kind of folkie to me. How did they get that photo? I don't even know that. I never wanted to see his face again. How do they get photos like this?'

And I tell her about Murray, but I want to talk about why I was with him, not why it ended, though it'll make me sad either way. I tell her about Murray and holidays, because we've got one booked for a month's time and I'd forgotten until now. We made the booking almost a year ago and I don't know what's happening with it. It's two weeks at the start of the school holidays.

Murray loses the plot on holidays, in the nicest of ways. He'll obsess about one CD and play it to death, day after day. Somehow the record industry seems to know there are men like this, so they always bring out something like *The Best of Tom Petty and the Heartbreakers* at the start of summer. He'll drink litres of orange juice as if he's just discovered it. He'll buy a juicer, and oranges by the bagful, carrying them up the stairs to the apartment on his shoulder, talking to Elli in a voice he is suddenly calling his 'peasant voice', and then handing around glasses of Freshly Squeezed Orange Juice (and don't dare leave any of that out and just call it orange juice, since that doesn't give the peasant his due).

He'll eat bagfuls of pistachios too, and there'll be fragments everywhere and handfuls of shells in any empty glass left sitting around. He'll try three days in a row to make a packet cake. At home, none of this is ever mentioned. No orange juice, no pistachio nuts or nuts of any kind, and he's a pretty good cook but only savoury.

On holidays he'll hold out on shaving and relent no more than twice, each time shaving in stages. He takes a week of beard and sculpts it back to nothing, via the look he calls his George Michael look, then the Satan beard, then his porn star mo, which is far too Saddam Hussein when it really gets down to it, and a few minutes of Hitler at the end before he's clean-shaven. Each stage comes with its own enthusiastic caricature, with me interpreting it all for Elli in the best way I can.

For Elli, that's life, that's Dad. It's hilarious, but it's also unremarkable. It's more than that for me, and this year I won't have it.

The article says it was mutual, according to a source close to us, but I guess that depends on your definition of mutual. It calls it 'a communication breakdown' but it was really more of a dead end. We never stopped talking, not until it was over. Another fine and irrelevant distinction. The article is as on the money as it needs to be, I turned myself public years ago, this is part of the deal.

'Yes, but . . .' Claire says, and I'm not sure that there is a but.

Murray anecdotes are in my show. Murray, poor bastard, got pulled into the public domain. I took our lives on the road, I put our lives on TV, this is the consequence. But I never thought I'd be this interesting. I thought we were safe because I'm well-known but not famous. I thought there was a line there, and that I knew where it was drawn. And that I had some control over where it was drawn. I didn't think I'd be worth a two-page feature or any sort of close scrutiny. I thought I still had privacy of a kind. I thought that was the deal I'd bought into, not this.

'He had to take my photo down at the office,' I tell her, remembering the day he came home with it in his briefcase. 'And it was one he'd always liked. He had it on his desk. And then he started saying I was just an ugly rumour.'

'Rumour alone would have sufficed, I would have thought,' Claire says.

'Well, yes, that's what I told him. Thank you.' She smiles, and I wipe my face with the back of my hand. 'But he said it was more convincing that way. And I know why he had to say something. People wouldn't leave him alone. Or at least that's how he felt. And he still kept hearing things about me anyway – the kind of things that go around about people with public jobs, people who do jobs that put them on TV or in the papers.'

'That can be horrible,' she says, and the look of concern is back on her face.

'Or in my case stupid, a lot of the time. He went to one meeting where two separate people were convinced I bred dogs as a hobby. No one in the room knew that he had any connection to me. I just came up in conversation. One of his complaints was that the rumours weren't salacious enough and that he'd have to start something better. It could be pretty amusing. But it got in the way as well, and I think it boxed him in. We hadn't expected it. We didn't know it might be part of the deal. We thought that, if my career worked out, the good things we had going for us might get even better, not that they'd end up . . .' I'm trying to find the right word '. . . neglected.'

That's it. That's what happened. The good things in our life were done no harm – not directly – but our attention was turned away from them, long enough that they faded, or somehow stopped being what they once had.

I get melted Cornetto chocolate all over my hands, Claire brings a cloth from the kitchen. There's a small chocolate patch on the sofa too, but she tells me to forget about it. And on my pants. Did any of the bloody chocolate end up in my mouth?

'It's a hot day,' she says. 'Very melty.'

I explain that it all got complicated with Murray and now he's in Shanghai, where he would have been anyway. He said I was shutting him out, ultimately, that I was getting his full story and 'What is it with you? Some days I don't know you'. Most days he did though, and where was the credit for that? We all have moods. So what? He knew me. He knows me as well as anybody does.

Through counselling we reached 'a conclusion'. That's where we found ourselves, with an agreement that it was over, and that we would be in contact only when we were both back in Brisbane, and then only to finalise details. I broke the rules by calling him several times. He screened me to his voicemail and I didn't hear from him again. I knew I couldn't keep doing that.

And Claire says, 'You're rubbing your hand. Is it okay?'

I can feel a lump, a small hard lump, and I tell her it might be glass, a fragment of glass from a long time ago, an accident once. Or it might be scar tissue. There are scars there from the incident with the glass – a small scar at the base of my right thumb in the shape of an Arabian dagger, another at my wrist like a star, a third in between and fading. In time maybe they'll all fade, line themselves up with creases and wrinkles and disappear, and my hand will just be old and not injured. That's what I've been thinking. It's been years since we last found glass.

I'm falling apart, one bit of me after another – this and the tooth and the knee I whacked on the ice above Lake Louise last week or the week before. I'm sick of running repairs. I want to be home, I want these things fixed.

Claire has two friends coming over for dinner and she lets me cook. My show's on late this evening, I can do that. I tell her there's a recipe I do, Argentine chicken, that I took from a TV cook but I like to think I improved on it, so if they're okay with chicken that'd be a good one.

We go out for ingredients, and I buy a forty-dollar bottle of wine and tell Claire this is what per diems are for and there should be no argument. And the same applies to the replacement box of peppermint Cornettos.

I stand in the kitchen, searching my brain for the recipe, for the grinning face of Ainsley Harriott out on the pampas. I cut the shallots with the whole bunch in my hand, and the blade of the sharp knife slips right through and sends little wheels of shallot across the board. I add garlic, because I always do.

The guests arrive. I think I hear ground rules being discussed at the door, but I'm busy frying the shallots with garlic and cumin and paprika, and thinking it might be time for the tomato paste. Ainsley doesn't do the garlic. That's one of our differences, but the big one is that he uses chicken mince and I grill minced chicken patties and chop them into cubes. People comment on the texture as a plus, every time.

The guests meet me with the caution due a crazy person with a knife, and that works for all of us at the moment. Something goes slightly wrong, the cooking takes longer than it should. I send Felicity a text message saying 'with friends – won't make the minibus – see you at the venue'. She calls back and calls back and I don't answer. On her fourth call she leaves a message, saying okay.

I can't talk to her yet. I don't know the Felicity version of this. She's off with Richard Stubbs, sorting out his banana rider, and the *NW* article is too fresh for me to work out how to talk to her, how to explain the many things I've said over the past few days that, when it all comes down to it, amount to lies.

Claire says she'd come for moral support tonight but she's got a phoner to London and I tell her I've had the moral support for the past few hours and that's how I'm able to do the show. She says she'll reschedule the phoner if I want her to. We call a cab, and I take my share of the dinner on a Christmas paper plate and Claire tells the driver I've got no choice but to eat it on the way. He knows better than to argue.

There's couscous all over the back seat when I get out, stuff the paper plate into the nearest bin, walk into the club and hand Felicity the magazine.

She's ready to tell me how things went with Richard Stubbs and the bananas – that's how she looks as I walk over, like someone with an adventure to report on – but the magazine is already opened to the right page when I hand it to her. Whatever she was about to say sticks in her throat when she sees the headline, and she opens the magazine out, stares at both pages.

'What?' she says. 'This is insane.' She's scanning the article, not reading properly. It's dark in here, but the headline and the break-out quotes and the picture seem to tell the story. 'How can they write this?'

And I have to tell her that it's true, much of it, though it didn't happen quite the way they think it did. I tell her what I can, here at the edge of a noisy club audience, and she doesn't seem to care at all that I've spent three days keeping the truth from her.

She pulls serviettes from a dispenser at the bar and wipes her eyes and says, 'You're making my make-up run, damn you.' And I laugh at that, as I'm supposed to, and she says, 'Oh, Meg, this is so sad.'

It's out now, my secret.

I have one drink and I get up and do my stuff. The day has worn me down but the audience brings me back enough, and the material is there as it always is. People might say I missed a few punchlines, I don't know, but mostly it goes the way it should. I notice Felicity's boyfriend, Adam, in the audience when I'm about halfway through, and that distracts me as much as anything.

He buys beers afterwards and no one seems to know what to say, so I tell them we should get a camera and the three of us should pose for a photo, one of those photos which would have me with my arms around both of them in a way that could only say Drunken Sex Romp.

He clinks his beer against mine and says, 'Works for me,' and Felicity tells him not to be so insensitive.

'I've been thinking,' she says. 'I don't know if the article's going to cause any problems over the weekend but, if there are any, let me handle them. Let me help with this. It might be totally okay, since you don't have any interviews scheduled, but if anything comes up I'll make sure I get in its way. I'll tell anyone to call Emma next week, and then you two can work out a plan.'

Three people from the audience move in on us before she's even finished speaking. They want to get programs signed, and they're treating her like a fan whose turn is up and who should be moved on. I push the rolled up *NW* into her bag and I tell her I want her to keep it, or get rid of it, but never give it back to me even if I ask for just one more look.

'I've read these magazines for years,' she says. 'I never thought about what it would be like if it was actually your life in there.'

Later, on the way back to the hotel, I work out what must have happened for the photo to have appeared. Gary took it in Calgary, I gave him my website address, he emailed the photo to the webmaster – as people do – and the webmaster routinely forwarded it to media. At which point, despite the esteem in which the webmaster holds me, the media usually decide to slip the email into the trash. Not this time. It's simple how these things happen. There's no need for conspiracy theories.

I want to read the article again when I'm back in my room, but I'm sure it's better that I can't. I'd get stuck gazing at it, at the horror of seeing my life dissected. I'd read it over and over until I'd find myself being able to quote whole paragraphs of it long into the future.

Murray said I was shutting him out. He said I was depressed, accused me of being depressed. That was his tone, accusatory, as if depression was another thing I was keeping to myself but giving him glimpses of when my guard was down. He said I was depressed and not admitting it to myself and I told him that was wrong, and also logically inconsistent with his idea that I was shutting him out. Or was I now shutting myself out too?

That was, I suppose, two years ago. Things can take a long time to fall apart, even once they've started to. Murray was putting in a lot of hours at work then, I got into kickboxing, my new TV idea came along. That these occurred at around the same time is no more than coincidence, I'm sure of it, but before then we'd been able to fix our problems, as far as I can recall.

I'd seen Cindy Crawford's arms on a magazine cover, toned new arms that looked like they meant business but didn't look bulked up. It was a great photo, a powerful photo. I don't even know what she'd been doing to get them, but I went to the gym and said I wouldn't mind Cindy Crawford's new arms and I ended up kickboxing.

It felt good, I felt good. I wanted to do more, the TV show idea was evolving. I started thinking more about my character and her physicality, how it worked for her, where it had come from. I needed to understand her better. It was a quiet process, an internal one, not one that I talked about. The dots don't join exactly that easily, but it was something like it.

No one was being shut out. But Murray would come home from his day's work and I'd have nothing to tell him about mine. My day had been fine, but I'd spent it in my head. I'd insist that I had nothing to tell him, though I probably sounded vague about it, and soon enough the smallest things would aggravate us both.

We fought about raisins once. He wanted some for a recipe but I didn't buy them because I thought we had some in the pantry. 'I wrote them on the list,' he said. 'I wrote it down because we didn't have them. I thought the plan was that whoever did the shopping got what was on the list.' But he would often put things on there without checking, and we had a pantry full of chick peas.

It was a small incident, and one that should have been a non-incident, but our life started to feel as though it was made up of conversations like that.

'You're overdoing it,' he said to me about my gym work. 'You can't blame the producers for getting ideas if you're training like Demi Moore for *GI Jane*.' And all I could say to that was 'You don't understand' because he didn't.

And I'd want to be on tour again, to get out of the house, out of my head, away from us not getting on. Emma would book some dates, and I'd go, though when the dates came around things had usually changed for the better. Murray and I would both wish I hadn't said Yes, and I'd miss the good parts of home every day I was away. I'd call him every night, and my days were busy enough that there were things I could tell him then, and he'd tell me his life was just the usual, longer hours in the office maybe since there was no reason for him to be at home on the days when Elli wasn't there.

So yes, there was, it turns out, a 'communication breakdown', as the magazine says. But it doesn't explain it, and it doesn't say that communication can break down even when both parties try as hard as people can to stop it, and that it's only long after that you can see where some of the unravelling began, a long time before.

Elliott met Murray, and they got on well. Murray cooked dinner once when Elliott was in Brisbane, and Elliott came over with a good bottle of merlot. He'd asked me beforehand what Murray liked, and Murray took a look at the label and went 'Hmmm', like someone who knew he'd quietly contrive to drink far more than his fair share.

During dinner we skirted around the issue of the consequences that would come if the show went as we hoped. We talked instead about the prospect of it meaning good work close to home, as though that would fix anything that needed it. But Murray and I had already been giving up privacy inch by inch and, if the plans worked, we'd start handing over yards of it.

We went to a counsellor whose name was Janis, spelt as in Joplin. Her staff happened to recognise me, so Murray and I spent the whole first session spinning out about confidentiality. It meant that our problem intruded on our solution from day one.

Janis had long straight hair that was naturally blonde, and the blue eyes to go with it, and a contained kind of smile that gave nothing away. She'd happily stay silent after one of us had spoken, which often led the person who had been talking to say more, and in doing that they would sometimes say more than they meant to. It might have been a tactic, but more often than not the final sentence was only a restatement of what had been said already, but more succinct, more direct and often inadvertently more likely to hurt. We each, once we had explained something, wanted Janis to go, 'Oh, now I get it,' and tell us the answer to our problem, and her silences made us wonder if we'd been helpful enough.

We sat in three office chairs, Murray swivelling and rocking in a distracting way, Janis quite still with her feet crossed at the ankles. I'm sure she can't be much more than thirty, but she looked younger, and sometimes it was as if a child was asking us the questions.

'Are you happy?' she said to me one day, quite directly. I suppose it's always a fair line of enquiry.

Most sessions involved the three of us, but Murray and I each had solo sessions with her too. I don't know what

I expected they'd be like, but it felt like she pushed me harder in some of them.

'How would you respond if I put it to you that you seemed to be resisting telling me some things? Maybe we could talk about your childhood, your family life, how your family communicates...'

Murray had, of course, already introduced the issue of me keeping things to myself, but that was weeks before and in his usual blunt way, and I'd fought him like a child about it, right there in front of Janis. We had an argument about a box of Garfields he had brought home once on a weekend between jobs. A box of plastic cartoon cats. 'You never told me you collected Garfields,' I practically screamed at him in Janis's office, as if I was accusing him of having an affair, when really it was the only example that would come to mind of him keeping anything to himself.

And Janis sat there, as still as ever, waiting for it to play itself out, and Murray said angrily, 'I never did collect Garfields. Someone gave me one once and it stayed on the desk and you know I'm not tidy. People came in and they saw it and gave me more of them. I was never collecting them. And I told you that. I told you that when I brought them home.'

So, we displayed the worst of our argument techniques to Janis, for the first time seriously and all to do with a box of Garfields that, over four years, had simply collected itself.

We laughed about it afterwards, of course, Murray and I. He promised he would never again accept a Garfield without first telling me. I assured him that we both knew I was in the wrong, and I told him he was at liberty to accept all the

Garfields his heart desired, with the exception of the ones that came with suckers for attaching them to car windows.

And I don't know what he's thinking now, with that article out there, if he knows about it yet. I don't know what he's thinking about us, or about what might have happened in Calgary with Rob Castle. What *did* happen in Calgary with Rob Castle. But it was a different story then, not the story in the article.

I looked happy in the photo in the magazine, happy with my arms around Jen and Rob Castle, and my hand on my first beer. I was making new friends, I was having a moment away from my life, that's all. And the events that followed were events my life allowed. It was over then with Murray, he'd told me that.

Banff – twelve days ago

WE HEADED WEST out of Calgary late in the morning in a minibus, with the mountains rising ahead of us from the edge of the brown plain. It was a cold clear day and we had the windows up, and the air was dense with halitosis, the breath of a load of battle-weary comedians damaged by drinking.

There had been a poker game till four in someone's room, and I've never been into that. No, I'm more likely to have sex with the wrong person, then spill my guts over a few beers the next evening before another night of low-quality sleep. At least I don't toss my per diems away on scotch and cards.

In Banff, I walked down Caribou Street towards Banff Avenue, struck by the scenery and the cold crisp air and determined to buy a disposable camera. I came across a fudge shop first though, and bought a large block of their gourmet Cointreau-chocolate blend. After a few bites it was too rich for me and I could barely swallow it, so I carried it in my pocket for days, to Vancouver at least. I bought a postcard for Elli, a scenic view of Banff in winter, and I sent it to her at Laura's. 'This place can get so cold it's insane,' I wrote. 'I'm wearing everything I've got, but I didn't bring anything for my nose. I have no idea how Canadian noses make it through winter.'

We had a night off that night, and we all ended up going to a poetry event at the Banff Centre for the Arts, where we were staying.

After each poet, there was a few minutes in which the audience could come and go from the auditorium, and I got the timing of a bathroom visit wrong and sat one poet out.

I got talking to a young guy who was involved with the catering, and bringing out dip and corn chips for the interval. His name was Toby – he wore a tag – and earlier on he'd shown me to my room when I'd become a little lost on my way there after checking in. I asked him if he was from Banff, and if he had been working at the Arts Centre long, and he told me no one was from Banff, it wasn't that kind of place. He was from Winnipeg himself, but people came here from all over. He was taking a break between college years to reassess his options, and Banff seemed as good a place to reassess them as any. It was a good place to put your life on hold.

He said he was looking forward to winter setting in, and he told me there's a saying that goes, 'If you can't get laid in Banff, you can't get laid.'

Setting aside the fact that some of us can get laid with relative ease in a prairie oil town, let alone the surely more obvious option of a ski resort, I asked him how he was going and he said, 'Well, not yet, but I've only been here a couple of months.'

This wasn't to be his night either. He was dorky and I wasn't sure he'd ever got laid in his life to date and, five hours later, after the pace of his drinking had gone badly wrong, I found him throwing up into a bin in the nightclub where he should have scored. He wasn't without charm, though he didn't know it himself yet. But I felt like his mother, detecting a nascent awkward charm in him and hoping for the best, and you can't learn about those things from your mother. He had blushed when he'd said the line about getting laid, and then laughed nervously, and those people don't get laid too easily.

The poetry had its moments. There was an Irish poet headlining, and he caught me unawares by reading a poem that made me feel Irish. I felt distinctly connected to what he read, and I hadn't expected that. From the way he had the moss growing on the rocks, to the feel of the sun and the air, to the tilt of the headstones in an abandoned island cemetery, I could see the pictures with perfect clarity. I wanted to tell him that afterwards, but there were too many people around him and I didn't know how to put it. I wanted to tell him that the rest of his audience might have caught the poetry, but I was sure I was the only one who really knew what he was saying. The only one who could see the gulls that he *hadn't* talked about, but that certainly flew over the cemetery, and who could see the exact shapes of the clouds, and the change in the colours of the ocean in winter.

Jen had driven to Banff in her car, and she stayed sober

and took us to the nightclub once all the poeting was done. The car was full and the others all men – Dave Stone from New Zealand, a Canadian comedian I hadn't met and a novelist from Toronto – so it's no surprise the turn the conversation took. One of the poets we'd seen had had large breasts, full lips and a quite beguiling smile and the second of her five poems wasn't awful, so in the car that came out from one of the boys in the back as a cagey, 'Well, I guess we'd all admit that that Megan was kind of talented . . .'

They had an urgent powerful need to talk about Megan's breasts, so they critiqued her poetry in detail, and sober Jen said, 'Oh you're all so clever. So metaphorical.' And the writer from Toronto, who was at that time shortlisted for two prestigious awards for his first novel, said, 'Quick, I need to write a limerick now. Can anyone give me two rhyming words for hooters?'

The club we went to was below street level and invisible from the outside. The temperature had fallen below freezing by then, and all of Banff seemed quiet when we got out of the car. Jen led the way and, when the heavy wooden door was opened for us, music was clearly pumping in there below ground level, and we walked down the stairs in hazy blueish light into a packed basement.

The club was driven by the line about getting laid in Banff, but it put an unhealthy sense of frenzy in the air. People were trying so hard to get laid they were paying far too much attention to one another for anybody to get anywhere. They were working on each other like mayflies, as if it were their last and only day in the world, and the species would not go on if they didn't get laid before the night was out. The five of us drank beers, or in Dave Stone's case water, several of us felt old, college students pressed against each other on the dance floor, but often not against the people they wanted to because that's how it goes in most countries, if not all.

We tumbled out onto the silent freezing street, and the night was done. On the way back up the hill to the Centre for the Arts, the Toronto novelist with the possible hooters limerick fell asleep in the car and Jen pulled over, put lipstick on his lips and drew circles of it on his cheeks, and the others tried not to rouse him by sniggering.

It was four-thirty then, or five, and I woke hours later during a slow dawn to see snow falling for the first time in thirty years. It fell like snow on a movie set, broad flakes drifting down, riding down the air with more grace than falling. I hadn't expected that. I thought it was a prank, being played on the out-of-towner from the subtropics, but then I saw that it was everywhere, off into the trees.

I walked alone in the cold air before breakfast, along the tracks by the river, seeing droppings that might have been from deer. Jen had offered me spare gloves two nights before, but I had forgotten to take them, so my hands stayed in my jacket pockets most of the time, one of them holding a map I'd picked up at reception. I knew this wasn't my world, and it would be a very bad place to get lost. I didn't know its rules, and probably never would. And I'd just had three of the most confusing days of my life and no one knew, not really.

Later that day we walked from Lake Louise up to Lake

Agnes, we had a snowball fight, I slipped on the ice and hurt my knee, and the puddles crunched under our boots on the way back to the bus. The temperature mid-afternoon had tilted from one side of freezing to the other.

Perth — Saturday

I'M ON A ROAD, face down, I can't move. I'm still deaf, there's no sound at all. My hand is being crushed by a boot. It's palm-up on the road with the boot on top of it and a man's weight bearing down, and gravel is being driven into the back of it. My head is twisted to one side, and I can see the boot, and the leg, and above that the bucking gun and the hooded head.

I wake, and I find that I'm twisted up in my sheets and lying on my hand. It's still dark, four-ten according to the bedside clock. I wish I could sort out the airconditioning in these places. I've had the temperature turned up too high and most of the bedding is on the floor.

I can't shake the dream. I'm better once I've checked the bathroom and the cupboards, and had a glass of water. I leave the lights on until it's bright enough not to need them.

It's early when the newspaper is left at the door. There are people awake in the hotel, and at work delivering papers and room-service meals. This is a good thought, the rhythms of the hotel going on as usual, as always. I'm about to drift back to sleep when the paper fixes itself in my mind. I'm standing at the door in the first moments of the new dream, opening the door and seeing the paper on the carpet, seeing it with its own 'Meg's Shock Break-up' piece all over the front page, quotes lifted from *NW* and anonymous sources, and a sidebar story about Rob Castle and his wife and three children in Thunder Bay, Ontario.

The image jerks me awake again, and I can't sleep until I've gone to the door and searched the whole paper and found myself exactly where I was supposed to be and nowhere else, in the magazine section that had the Thursday deadline. It's a liftout and it has a cover photo of me in red, feigning throwing a red cocktail, and on page three are the eleven hundred words, including the standard line about Murray that hasn't been true for a month. It was on a Tuesday that Murray told me it was over for the last time, and it's a Saturday now. Four weeks and four days later. That's more than a month. Murray is on a plane coming back from Shanghai today, but I don't know exactly when he gets home.

At breakfast in the CBD cafe, everyone's reading the Saturday *West Australian*, no one's reading *NW*. All week I'll be watching out for that magazine.

There's still an hour to go before I'm picked up for paintball. Is the *NW* article a big enough reason to call Murray? It's a change in circumstances, something new to deal with. But I expect he's in the air now, or about to be, and we'll both be back in Brisbane by Monday.

On the way to the Internet cafe, everything is just starting to open in the Hay Street Mall, shopfronts rolling up with a clatter, and the day is warm already. I don't know who will have seen the article so far, and I'm better off checking my email than sitting in my room wondering.

I had wanted Murray to come with me to Canada. We talked about it for a while, but it stopped being possible. His work stepped in and kept him home, or at least he worked out it was going to once the Hong Kong and Shanghai meetings went in his diary. 'I can't be out of the office for three weeks in a row,' he said, as if the company would have collapsed into insolvency if he'd tried it. But that wasn't so long ago, and I suspect he was already thinking of a life without me then.

There's only one email with the subject 'nw', and it's from Emma:

Hey Mega,
A couple of calls about the article. Nothing to worry about. A couple of people were just calling to say they hope you're okay, but that they didn't want to bother you directly. Nice. Felicity and I have been phone-tagging but we haven't talked yet. We can handle it for now, and you and I can talk more next week. You can call me any time this weekend of course. Do you want me to talk to Murray? He may be getting calls too, and he probably needs a plan. Let me know. I'm not sure that I know this Rob Castle guy, so we should probably sort out our position on that one. The three of you in the pic look like you're having a great night. Don't know if you'll get this before paintball, but slay 'em babe.
Em

Next, there's one from Elli, sent last night:

> emailing from home, buggery one,
> mum says to call when you get back to brisbane where it is
> dam hot. i am with dad on sunday so we will have movies
> and swimming i expect if it stays hot. i have bloody piano
> first thing saturday but. i am still no good at it.
> how is the tour? are you funny or just usual?
> e xxx

The last email I open – sitting between two offering me miraculous non-surgical breast enhancement – is from Dave Stone:

> Hey Meg,
> I think you're in Christchurch now? I hope it's all good and
> that the NZ hospitality is unstinting. I'm in LA, sleeping on
> a friend's floor. I'm beginning to wonder if I'm too old for
> it. My back's certainly too old for it. *The Lord of the Rings*
> DVD has scored me quite a few auditions, but most of the
> time I just have to strap on leather, pick up an axe and
> grunt. Is it just me? Or is there the tiniest possibility
> that people might be about to make some movies that
> could be seen as somewhat derivative? Well, must go
> and slay . . .
> Cheers
> Dave

I'm sure I'm still smirking at Elli's several attempts at swearing and Dave Stone's Middle Earth purgatory when I'm back in the hotel foyer. What was I thinking in Calgary? On any other tour I would have spent twice as much time with the Dave Stone equivalent, I would have been emailing Murray about my great new friend, and the great new friend would one day drift through Brisbane on a tour and end up crashing in our spare room after reminiscing till all hours. Instead, I was off scoring my magazine moment with Rob Castle.

I'll email Dave when I get back home. Somewhere, some day, we will again plunder canapés like Vikings, and we will reminisce about the simpler, better parts of our time in Alberta.

The minibus arrives, and Elliott King waves from the front passenger seat. He seems to be wearing one of those crumpled camouflage hats people go fishing in.

Nothing from the wave gives away any prior reading of *NW*. I'll have to tell everyone eventually, but it's still too early. I want him not to know yet, and I want to see that in his wave. I want to see that it's just another day for Elliott, another game about to be played.

Emma knows something's wrong, otherwise her email would have been headed something like 'what is this madness????' instead of 'nw'. But even imagining her fingers typing R O B C A S T L E is doing my head in at the moment. Some stories were definitely meant to stay in Canada and not come crashing in on my life back here.

My life back here – a day running around in the bush

with what looks like a busload of grubby boys. Where is Dave Stone and his axe when you need him?

The minibus door slides open. I am not supposed to be thinking of this as an ordeal, not supposed to be thinking of better company, or of Saturdays at home and driving Elli to bloody piano.

Ballystewart — 1972

MARK MACLEISH LEARNED piano because they had an old upright at home, and because his mother wanted him to. She said he would end up with long fingers that could span a lot of notes, and he would be the sort of boy who'd be glad he'd had some piano lessons. 'You'll go to the university,' she said, 'and that kind of thing goes down well there.'

One afternoon he did his practice while I finished my homework, and then we went outside and he showed me the bruise on his shoulder from the day before, from the first time he'd fired the old 303. 'You've got to have it right up against your shoulder,' he told me, 'or that's what it does. It's got quite a kick to it.'

His brother Paul went and got the rifle for me, just so that I could get the feel of it. He passed it over using one hand, I took it in two and I still nearly dropped it. It was far too heavy for me. But Mark said that was all right, and that he'd had to rest it on top of a gas cylinder before he'd had any chance of shooting it straight. I tried to line up the sights, but my arms shook and the rifle wobbled everywhere so

I handed it back. Paul said they'd get me something smaller some time. He knew I wanted a turn. I liked him for that. He was years older than us and already working on the farm, but he didn't cut us out of things.

In the weeks after Bloody Sunday, everyone knew it was going to get worse and we were all waiting for it. There was big talk from the farm lads, Paul in particular, and Danny who was around the same age and came from the village every day to work at the Macleishes'.

Winter was over, the fields were being worked, life went on mostly as usual. But, around us, the situation was changing. Everyone knows it changed in 1972, but for us it changed in a night.

Mark Macleish wasn't the same the next day. He arrived minutes before school was due to start, and on the way into the classroom he said, 'You have got to come round this afternoon. I can't tell you why, 'cause I'm sworn to secrecy.' And from the way he said it, I knew I had to go.

We told my mother we'd arranged it ages before and that Mrs Macleish was expecting me – which she was by then, since Mark had told her about it before he'd come to school. In the carpark they laughed about both forgetting the arrangement, and my mother drove home by herself with plans to come to the Macleishes' for me at six.

And Mark and I sat at the big table in the Macleishes' kitchen rushing through everything we had to do for school for the next day and, when his mother went out of the room, he said, 'You would not believe it. You would not believe what we've got under our barn.'

He had to tell me when it was just the two of us, because he wasn't allowed to get excited. That's what he'd been told. We had to pretend it wasn't there.

In the very middle of the night, he said, a lorry had turned up and he'd woken with the noise and the headlights shining in his window. He'd watched men – his father, Paul and two others who came on the lorry – unloading things. Boxes, guns. He had run downstairs right away and his father had told him he should go back into the house. Or he could help, if he did exactly what he was instructed to. He could carry a couple of boxes if he'd then go back to bed.

And his father had opened the hidden door to the huge cellar under the barn that had been there forever and used for distilling poteen and . . .

His mother came back in then. She made cups of tea and Mark said to me, 'So what are you writing for your "My Day at the Beach" story?' and I expect it sounded fake to all of us, even though it was genuinely part of the homework. His mother was doing the books for the farm that afternoon – her homework, she called it – and she took her tea and went back to them.

I'd always thought Mark had made up the cellar, since he was quite a teller of stories, and the stories always put him closer to danger or excitement than we ever actually were. A cellar for making illegal drink was an exciting prospect. I'd imagined a huge underground chemistry set when he'd talked about it, but I don't think I'd believed that the cellar was there at all till I saw it that afternoon.

When we could show that we'd done our homework,

Mr Macleish took us over to the barn. It was padlocked now, and he unlocked it, then used an inside bolt to close it once we'd gone through the doors.

'Now, you understand how this works?' he said to me quietly, putting the keys in his pocket. 'This is the biggest secret you've ever been let in on. Do you follow? This is one of those secrets that you never tell anyone, no matter what. And that means anyone. Your daddy doesn't want to know about this. So it's just between you and me and Mark.'

The barn light was a single uncovered bulb and I looked at our shadows on the stone floor and heard the pigs moving in the half-dark, snuffling and nosing around in their hay, and I told him I understood and could be trusted completely. He took the torch from where he'd tucked it into the pocket of his tweed jacket, he turned it on and said, 'Mark tells me you know the Gurkhas. Well, this might have been on its way to them.'

We knew the Gurkhas from Commandoes, the small but fearless Nepalese warriors with their famous kukri knives. The Gurkhas were legendary to readers of Commandoes.

The guns had come in on a fishing boat. They'd been taken from a container in England about to go to Nepal, then driven to the coast and brought in to Donaghadee by boat in the middle of the night.

'And here they are,' Mr Macleish said. 'In the last place anyone would expect.'

He lifted the trapdoor and led us down by the light of the torch. I could see boxes with writing on them, and the edges of the torch beam picked up metal here and there but mostly, beyond the steps, it was dark. Then he lit a lamp and the whole place lit up and all I could think of was Aladdin's cave. An Aladdin's cave of guns.

And Mark said 'Bloody hell' since he hadn't seen it all laid out before, and his father clipped him over the head, but just as a joke, and he told him, 'Don't you go using any of that bad language above ground. Your mother'll be right onto you.'

Mark laughed and then went quiet as we all stood there and took it in. We'd seen stories on TV about guns, Mark and I, and we'd handled one or two, but here was an entire arsenal all in one go. Guns being handed on by the British army to the Gurkhas, filling up the cellar under the Macleishes' barn, on their way to loyalist paramilitaries. Rows of 303s, Lee Enfields, with boxes of ammunition. And submachine guns, and two Brens with stands and, over in the corner, a bazooka.

'There's no ammo for this one yet,' Mr Macleish said, patting the bazooka, 'so it's just for show at the moment.' Then he picked up a handgun and held it in front of me and said, 'This'd be more your size. It's a Webley. It's a Mark IV, thirty-eight calibre.'

He let me take it right over to the light. Its grip was scored into little hard diamond shapes, with a screw going through a bigger diamond in the middle, and when you held it, you knew you had something special in your hand. There was an oval bit at the end of the grip where it met the metal of the gun, and it had 'Webley' written on it in raised letters, neat printing with the tail of the Y running all the way back to the W. I knew that Webleys broke in the middle, so I snapped it open, checked it was empty, and the cylindrical magazine made a series of smooth quiet clicks when I rotated it. I snapped it shut again, held it up with both hands and looked past the sight and into the dark on the far side of the cellar. I could keep this one still, still enough, even though it was quite heavy too.

Some of the guns were gone quite quickly, some stayed. Mr Macleish knew even more about them than we did. He told us he'd done national service in the fifties, using guns just like these when they were the best the army had, but Korea was over before he had the chance to get there. He gave Paul a go of a Sten one afternoon, after he'd found a silencer. He'd said he couldn't try it till then. Single-shot might have been okay, since the farm was on the edge of the woods and people would think it was a fox or something, and not be bothered about the legalities. But there was no real point in trying a Sten if you couldn't use it as a sub-machine gun.

He lectured Paul about how he had to do it, but Paul just wanted to have a go. Mr Macleish told him we weren't gangsters, there'd be none of that shooting from the hip rubbish. And no thrashing around, since his turn would be up in seconds that way, and it wasn't how you were supposed to do it. You had to fire bursts of two to three shots only, and use them to walk your fire to the target.

Paul gave it a try, and Mark and I stood well back and behind Mr Macleish. Paul never paid enough attention to instructions and he'd already done a gearbox in the tractor because of it, so we weren't going to take any chances. But he did all right. And the silencer didn't make it silent, but it wasn't noisy either, certainly not like you'd expect a submachine gun to be.

Then Mr Macleish handed me the Webley, and he took three bullets from his pocket and told me he'd give them to me one at a time. He told me to keep steady, and to use both hands and keep both eyes open. He said there would be a kick, but I'd be okay.

I missed the can with the first bullet, and we all laughed since I wasn't too close, but I hit it with the next two.

There was never one clear moment when it turned serious – perhaps it was the afternoon in the cellar, perhaps shooting at the cans, perhaps not. Each step seemed small, and also exciting, and the natural successor to the step before. We were eight, we'd read about these things, here they were and we were getting our chance. We'd read Commandoes, we'd played at being commandoes but we couldn't get caps for our cap guns any more and now, once in a while with Mr Macleish, we could use the real thing instead.

I wondered where the bullets went, into the dirt in the potato field. I wondered if, one day, someone might dig there and find them, and we'd all be in terrible trouble. They'd tell my parents, for a start.

I picked up the three empty cartridges, and the last one still felt warm. I gave them back to Mr Macleish and he put them in his pocket and said, 'Good girl.'

Perth – Saturday

WE TRAVEL NORTH and inland, through the suburbs. There are twelve of us, nine men and three women, and I'm sitting next to Terri, a location scout who has been working with Elliott somewhere outside the city for the past two days. They've been searching for beaches that have the features their script calls for, and a place that can look like a fishing town that's down on its luck.

'I'm probably only here because you need a minimum of twelve,' she says, 'but I thought I might as well come when Elliott asked me. You never know what these things are like unless you give them a go.'

She sits with a water bottle between her knees and tells me that she saw in the paper this morning that I'd been busy lately. She asks about Canada, and says she's always wanted to go there, particularly to the Rockies and to that very grand old hotel that's in either Montreal or Quebec City.

There are fewer houses now, and more dry bush. Elliott has the radio tuned to a commercial station with a playlist that owes a lot to the soundtrack of *The Big Chill*. He keeps turning around and telling anyone he makes eye contact with how great this is going to be, like someone trying to create nostalgia from scratch, and too early in the process. The two men from the network head office in Sydney are sitting behind him, but most if not all of the others are locals – the Perth station general manager, a sports reporter, the producer of a local travel and lifestyle show.

I remember how quiet I was in the car when my mother picked me up from the Macleishes' after my first turn with the Webley. Not quiet but silent, actively not speaking in case the new secret came out, sitting saying nothing and remembering how the gun had felt to fire. 'What's got into you?' she said, since we usually talked a lot. 'Are they tiring you out with all that homework?' And I told her that was it exactly and she should get them to give me less, and she messed my hair around with her hand and laughed and said, 'Next you'll be telling me they're sending you home from school with specific instructions to watch more television.' I had wanted to keep the empty cartridges, to take them home and hide them in my room, but I knew that wasn't possible.

I had wanted them because they could remind me always of where I stood, and what I was part of. I could have hidden them in plenty of places. And they were mine really, since I'd fired the bullets.

Mr Macleish had seemed proud of me for hitting the target twice, and for knowing not to leave the spent cartridges lying on the ground. 'But I'm sure your ma's always been one for tidiness,' he said. 'She's always nicely presented.' It was the only time I can ever recall him mentioning her.

221

Close to twenty years later, when the movie *JFK* came out, my mother said to me, 'Do you know what Mark Macleish's father said about all that when it happened? When Kennedy got shot? It must have been the day after, and I said how terrible I thought it was and he said, "But sure he was only a Catholic." And that was it for him. "Only a Catholic."'

We turn off the road and drive through an open gate. There's bush on either side of us, but it thins out after a couple of minutes, and we come to a large dirt carpark with open land beyond it. There are maybe ten cars and another minibus there already, and a row of demountable buildings marking the far side of the parking area. A man waves to us and starts walking over. He's wearing a black T-shirt, camouflage pants and a black Oakland Raiders cap over buzz-cut hair.

The first thing he says to us, in a rousing kind of way, is, 'So, is everybody ready to have fun?'

He must be twenty or so, and up close he looks less like someone in a militia and more like a student on a weekend job. He introduces himself as Trent, and says it's up to him to show us the ropes. In the distance, a whistle blows three times, and a group of male voices cheers.

Trent leads us to one of the demountables, where he takes us through the rules. He uses words like 'tagging', 'opponents' and 'markers', instead of 'shooting', 'enemies' and 'guns'. He says paintball is 'like a living chess game', probably knowing that he's saying it to a roomful of people who are mostly half-listening and fantasising already about leaping into enemy bunkers and blasting the bejesus out of each other. All the way here on the bus, not one person thought to liken it to chess. Not that Elliott would have made it easy.

The analogy is hardly helped when Trent drags a boxful of camouflage overalls from the corner of the room.

'These are optional,' he says as he starts handing them out, 'but most people like to wear them, more because you can get dirty out there than anything else. But don't be worried if your own clothes get tagged, because we use a biodegradable dye, rather than a paint, and it comes out easily. There's also a pair of gloves for everyone and some personal protection equipment that you have to have on before you can go out on the course.' He lifts another box onto the table in front of him. 'And in here we have the mask–goggle system that we use for face and eye protection.' He pulls one out and shows it around. 'As you can probably tell, it's adapted from something similar that's used for motocross, but it has enhanced visibility without compromising on safety.'

As soon as he's got his overalls on, Elliott starts being irritating and saying he wants to get out there shooting people. He looks like a gardener, but he starts talking in a way that I think is supposed to be Arnold Schwarzenegger. A couple of people laugh politely. If he moves on to say he loves the smell of napalm in the morning, I will probably kill him.

The room feels different now, with everyone in their camouflage. The padded vest I'm wearing flattens my chest and bulks me up. Outside I can hear noises, someone running through nearby bush, the rapid-fire gas discharges of shooting.

Trent puts two markers on the table, an Automag Semi and a Tippmann pump-action. He explains the different ways they work, and Elliott picks up the Tippmann.

He holds it waist high, pointing it out in front of him, and he says 'Just like a Tommy gun' and he puts on a stupid scowling face and goes 'eh-eh-eh-eh-eh-eh' in a fake machine-gun noise, raking the room with pretend bullets and shaking the gun in his hands as he does it.

I grab the barrel as it's about to swing my way. He looks at me as if I've spoiled his fun, and I find myself saying 'Except for not being like a Tommy gun at all' and some of the others go 'ooooh', as if I'm about to start a fight. Elliott stops pushing against me, but I can't let go of the barrel, not yet. The room goes quiet. 'It's nowhere near as shapely as a Tommy gun. It's got that ugly functional thing happening, more like an Uzi, or a Sten. Not that the Sten was brilliantly functional. Anyway, it's more like an industrial glue dispenser than a gun.'

The others come back at that with a louder longer 'ooooh', and Elliott smirks at me and lowers the barrel.

'Didn't I tell you?' he says to the rest of them. 'Didn't I tell you how good she'd be at this stuff?'

But we don't choose the Tippmann. We choose the Automag Semi. It can fire eight shots a second, and that's more like what Elliott had in mind. Trent takes us to the firing range for some practice shots, and he says, 'This is also where we execute people who shoot referees.'

He gives us each a large bulbous black paintball hopper

which fits on top of the marker and feeds paintballs down into it for firing. Once that's attached it doesn't look like a gun at all. Elliott blasts from the hip and a couple of others do too. Paintballs spray around, bursting in the dirt and against trees and sometimes on the targets. The targets are black silhouettes of people.

I get the feel of the trigger and I lift my gun and look along the barrel under the hopper. There's a row of eight targets, standing still and waiting for it, black silhouettes against a white background. There are paintballs buzzing in the air around me and splattering against everything in front of us. I take aim at a gum tree over to the right, and fire a single shot. There's almost no recoil, and the paintball seems to dip a little and goes slightly to the left of where I'd expected. I take another shot, and it's almost corrected, a couple more and I have the feel of it.

Trent leads us to the first course, and we divide into teams of six. We're fighting for a village, he tells us, but it turns out to be more an arrangement of high corrugated-iron fences, with gaps and some holes cut for windows and doors. There's no time to get a sense of the layout, so no real chance to plan how to handle it. Elliott takes his team down one end and I'm with the others.

Someone says 'What do you reckon we should do?' and I tell them I'm pretty sure Elliott's going to go mad. We should fan out in good defensive positions and let them attack.

I check my equipment. I take a slow breath in and out. My heart rate's up already.

The whistle blows, the game starts. There's whooping

from the far side of the village as Elliott and his team charge into action. They appear in the distance around a wall, in a clump and running bent over. We should hold our fire, but of course we don't. The shooting starts, and they don't scatter quickly enough. They return fire, and keep running our way. I'm crouched on one knee at the edge of a sheet of corrugated iron, and paintballs start clanging everywhere.

I fire a burst of a couple of shots and they go wide to the left. Another couple of shots and I'm closer, and the next burst collects someone in the chest. I aim to the right as he falls, and I fire again. Dye splatters from the next guy's visor.

I roll back fully into cover as two of the others start shooting at me. There's a crack in the sheeting further along, and I lie down and fire through it. Three of them make cover, and the shooting stops.

It's quiet for a moment, then I can hear them running in the dry grass behind the fencing. They're coming to our right. I signal to the others, pointing that way. They're circling us. I signal to listen, and to move quietly.

They burst out of a doorway firing, most of their shots slapping into metal, and the first of them is hit so many times he recoils against the wall and red dye splatters all across his front and he drops to the ground shouting out, 'You've got me already.'

We take out the other two at the same time, and lose only one of our own. The whistle blows to end the game, but my heart's still racing. We've got them, all six of them, I counted as they were hit, it's over. I wipe my palms on my overalls.

The others are laughing, pushing back their masks. Terri reaches a hand down to the sports reporter, who is still on the ground. He pulls himself up in a B-movie wounded-soldier way and leans back against the wall.

'That really hurts, you know,' he says. 'When you get hit by about twenty of them at once. How did I get to be the one coming out of the doorway first?'

A gust of wind blows through the village and rustles the grass. Trent hands around a bottle of water. Elliott tries to brush dye from his overalls with his hand, but only spreads it around. The band from his mask has pressed his dark wavy hair flat, and there's sweat running down his neck.

'New teams,' he says indignantly, looking mainly at me. 'You used a strategy.'

I remind him that it's a living chess game, not a day out for rampaging maniacs, and that draws a third 'ooooh' from some of the others.

He takes me aside on the way to the next course and says, emphatically, 'I love what you're doing. Love it.'

The second game is 'Woodland Sniper', and it sends one person alone into the trees to evade capture for twenty minutes, while sniping at pursuers. The first two times we do it, it lasts about five minutes. The sniper claims a couple, then starts shooting crazily as they're encircled and brought down.

I'm sent out third, and I go far into the bush and up a small rise. I have good cover, and can only be attacked from the front and one side. At first I've still got the chess-game analogy in my mind, but then I see them advancing in a line, moving from tree to tree, eleven people unrecognisable in their camouflage and masks. There's no shooting, just the sound of them brushing past bushes and low branches, moving in and out of shadows. They're not even talking. I'm their target, and they're coming my way.

Like the first two snipers, I suppose, my nerves start to fray.

I want to run, to see if there is better cover further back. But they'd see me, they'd get me. They're crouching, running between trees, closing in, and I can never see them all at once. I try to get lower, but they'll find me anyway. I can't be small enough, I can't hide.

Their line breaks up as they get closer. They're almost upon me. I have no choice but to shoot now.

I take out one, two, and the others go to ground. But I keep shooting, hitting trees, and they're onto me, returning fire. Firing through the bushes all around me and moving again, coming forwards. I'm firing almost blind, staying low and firing. I hit another one, but it won't be enough. I'm feeling sick, and hot.

I manage to get six of them, or seven, before they storm my position.

'Eighteen minutes,' Trent says. 'That's as close as we'll get, I reckon.'

He gives us sandwiches and bottles of soft drink, and we sit around in the patchy shade at the edge of the course. I wipe my visor against my overalls to get the dye off. I drink, but I'm not hungry. I'd be happy to go back to the city now. I'd prefer that.

For the third game we're on the same course, with two teams each fighting to claim the enemy's flag. Our tactics quickly go wrong, and I get separated from the others. I'm down on the ground behind a log when two of the enemy come past. I can see their boots but nothing more. They're talking, whispering to each other. I can't hear what they're saying. Until they're gone I don't even breathe.

Shots are fired, one or two hit a tree, more than that I don't know. I get up on my knees and then run to the next piece of cover when it's all clear. There's a long burst of fire in the distance, another in reply.

My heart rate is up again, I can feel it.

I run to another tree. To the left, in the distance, the two who passed me before are searching. I don't know who they are with their masks on. They're going from tree to tree, holding their guns waist-high and ready, sweeping their guns in front of them, ready to fire.

It's not like the first game, not any more. In the first game they just charged at us, shooting for the sake of it.

I run harder but there are more of them than just those two, and they could be anywhere. The treetops bend in the wind and the light comes through and the shadows move. They're closing in on me again, I know they are. And I could be the last. I could be the last of my team, and maybe they're all after me now, sweeping through the trees.

I go faster, but it's getting hard to breathe in this vest. It's constricting me, I'm getting dizzy. There could be one of them behind any tree, behind anything. I'm making too much noise. I know I'm going to be caught, and they're going to shoot me. I keep running, dodging around bushes, pointing my gun at shadows. There's something red on the ground in front of me. I see its eyes and its teeth and I jump over it, trip and fall. I look back and it's a tree root, bulging up out of the ground. I thought it was a fox, just for a second there, but dead already.

I pick up my gun and I run again. I want to be out of here, out of the trees. I can do better if I'm out of the trees.

I jump over a branch and between two bushes to a patch of clear ground, and someone in camouflage turns and brings their gun up to fire but I fire first. But my gun's jammed. I'm upon them already, our guns clatter together, their shot goes wide. I kick, stomach high. Breath grunts out of him – it's a man – and he falls to his knees and drops the flag. I swing my gun at him like an axe at a tree, two-handed, and his head snaps back when it hits, his visor split down into his face, into his right cheek. He flops to the ground and lies on his back looking up at me. It's Elliott, Elliott King.

His eye blinks and blinks as blood inks it in darkly. There's noise all around us. I'm standing over him, my gun in my hand. I'm stuck. I can't read his expression at all, but that's the blood. It should be fear with him in that position, he should be unable to feel anything but fear, but that's not why we came here today. I want this to stop.

Paintballs hit my back like fists.

I settle for some more laps later, since I'll go crazy if I stay in my room until the show, and I don't feel like drinking.

I swim freestyle, up and down, ten long strokes a lap, ten long hard-working strokes till my muscles burn and can pull me no further.

Elliott was taken to the nearest medical centre at high speed, a tea towel and a wad of bandage clamped to his face by Trent's gloved hand, a sheaf of incident report forms in a folder beside them. The rest of us drove back into Perth on the bus.

And the bush gave way to suburbs and then the city, and I reminded myself that I have a job to do tonight, an audience ahead of me with expectations. There's plenty to think about, to focus on. It was hard, though, to put that blinking blood-filled eye out of my head, and the sharp cracking sound that came when I hit him, when he was on his knees.

Elliott explained that he had tripped while running with the flag, and had struck his head when he fell. He wanted to walk back to the carpark but his knees went wobbly on the way and he had to be helped.

I have no idea how I'm going to describe this to Emma when the time comes. He should have picked golf. Not that I play, but I would happily have caddied. I wouldn't have beaten anyone up if we'd played golf. Or mini-golf. I'm always up for that, and happy to play whether I win or lose.

When I'm out of the pool, I call Elliott and get his voicemail. I apologise, again, and I tell him I'd like to buy him breakfast in the morning, if he'll let me.

Back in my room, there are messages from Claire and Felicity, checking how I am today and saying I should call if I want to. 'Everything's under control,' Felicity says. 'I hope you managed to shoot a few of those TV people.'

When we next talk, Emma will ask how paintball went and I'll say 'I whacked Elliott in the face with a gun' and she'll say 'I'm sure it was an accident' and I'll have to say No.

I whacked him in the face because the moment called for it, inexplicably, and that's just how it was. My gun jammed. Elliott had the flag. Something like that.

Tomorrow night I'll be on a plane home. There's one more show to get through, and the canoe race, and a dinner. Murray will be in Brisbane now, I suppose, ordering takeaway and hoping for good sleep before his day with Elli tomorrow. A good sleep in an otherwise empty bed.

Christchurch — five days ago

In Vancouver I ate raspberries from the Granville Island markets. I bought a punnet for four dollars and I hadn't eaten such fresh raspberries since I'd left Northern Ireland, not that I could recall. And the people I worked with were as nice as they'd been on my previous visit, but they said I looked tired and they'd heard we'd had a big week in Calgary and Banff.

I could have done without the Rob Castle posters as I walked around the island. He'd been there in August, and August was long ago.

They were right — I was tired and I was losing the capacity to hide it. The hotel gym was an exercise bike almost rusted through in some places and a stepper gone lame on one side, so I caught the ferry and ran around Stanley Park, breathing in the cool, wet, temperate air among the big trees. And the temperature fell quickly as the light went, but the run didn't shake the listlessness, and I faked it for my show as best I could and the next day I left Canada for New Zealand.

Christchurch brought me closer to home, and to realising

properly that home, when I arrived, would not be the place I had left.

On the last of my three nights there, I went to a fan's house for dinner. Her name was Jill and she had seen my short-lived TV show when it screened in New Zealand, as well as some of my regular guest appearances before then on cable. 'I got $2.42 for that,' I told her when I replied to her first email a year ago, 'so I'm glad someone was watching.'

That email had invited me to her husband David's birthday, since it was his fortieth and she wanted to line up some kind of surprise. It couldn't be me that weekend, but I'd made it now, weeks before his forty-first, and David had a roast under way and he put a glass of wine in my hand as soon as I walked in.

The house was built for a colder country than home, with somewhere to put your boots just inside the door and fireplaces everywhere. They had two children, a girl aged eight and a boy aged six, and the house was warm and full of Lego, colouring-in pencils and story books. They had a roster magneted to the fridge – soccer, ballet, piano – and two very fluffy cats with a birthday the day after mine. I don't know if the house always felt the way it did then, but that night it felt perfect. I wanted to tell the kids how lucky they were, but there's never any point in that, so I read them a story instead when the time came for them to go to bed.

I found myself late in the evening talking to Jill and David about how New Zealand wines are among the best in the world, the very best, as though that was half an excuse for drinking so much, and they looked at me slipping lower in the seat, jet-lagged and drunk and dull-witted and they said, 'You must have an interesting life.' And a bunch of interview anecdotes circled in my head and nearly made me cry.

Forty minutes later, back in my room at the hotel next to the one once stayed in by Bill Clinton, I washed some clothes in the bath, I took a last look at the cold empty square, I imagined the porch light going out at Jill and David's and I fell asleep missing them already. And I dreamed, of course, because I do that often when I'm jet-lagged and I've been drinking.

And I woke and flew on, to the next country, where I broke my tooth and slept again, at the wrong time, over the desert. Still dreaming, with nothing any clearer.

'Why did your family move to Australia?' Of course they asked that. We had a long talk about our lives, and it's a part of mine.

I told them the six-line version of the story, and that I'd been their daughter's age at the time, perhaps a few months older, and Jill said, 'Well, you'd remember quite a lot then. You would have done, what, three years of school there? Assuming it's the same kind of system.'

Ballystewart — 1972

'MY DAY AT THE BEACH' was typical of our school story topics. They never gave us much to go on.

We had a beach just near us, but one you would hardly choose to go to. It was all stones and thick black bladdery weed, and somehow we all got the idea that it wasn't the kind of beach that was meant to be in the stories. The teacher was looking for sand, buckets and spades, an interesting bleached starfish or sea urchin. She held up a picture book with that kind of beach scene on the cover and said we could use it for inspiration if we had no ideas.

I did my best. I started with the beach in the picture, though I don't think I'd ever been to one like it, and I had sandcastles being built and plenty of fun going on before I brought in the squadron of Spitfires and the bullets kicked up the sand and smashed down the sandcastles and killed some people, left them lying there in shapes you wouldn't lie in. Not like sleeping, definitely dead. So I came up with plenty to write about, what with the shot people and the blood in the sand, and the description of the planes, which I knew quite well.

I thought I'd done the job, and done it to quite a high standard, and the teacher called it 'vivid' after she'd read it from beginning to end, but then she said, 'Now try a different kind of day. Maybe there's a girl who finds something in a rockpool – a fish, a lost piece of jewellery. Maybe she's a girl your age. That could be quite a story.'

So I thought about it, and I came up with one idea to do with the jewellery and pirates, but then I decided my girl would be a fighter in the French Resistance being tailed by the Gestapo. And, just when the Gestapo think they've got her, just when they've chased her down and got her cornered on this beach, she finds a grenade in a rock pool and blows them to bits. That way I still got to use some of the best parts of the first story, the parts about the blood, as well as the idea about a girl finding something in a rock pool.

And the teacher thought about it for a while and said, 'That's good writing. It'd be interesting to try something less dramatic some time. A description of a sea anemone could be nice.'

But I couldn't see it. And I had no idea what a sea anemone was, anyway.

My school report that term said, 'Margaret has a very active imagination, and she writes well.'

The French Resistance figured in quite a few Commando comics. They wore berets, they rode bikes, they kept their guns hidden. Commando comics were always clear in the way they defined different groups of people.

Mark Macleish said we were like the Resistance, not in every way since we didn't have the Vichy French and the Germans to deal with, but I knew what he was saying. We had no uniforms, the guns were hidden.

In one Commando comic, the Resistance took a baker's lorry and attacked a Gestapo headquarters and killed an officer. There were dreadful consequences, but they had to do it. In another, the Germans strung two of them up from the blades of a windmill, so maybe they were Dutch Resistance that time. In Commando comics you would only get windmills in Holland, even though there had once been one in the next village down the peninsula from Ballystewart. I never felt the same about windmills after reading that story.

The other thing I remember about the Resistance is that they were often betrayed. They had some of the bravest fighters of all, but also some of the worst traitors.

We had a housekeeper, Mrs Tannock, who came in a couple of days a week. Once, when I was drinking milk and eating toast and my mother wasn't there, she said to me that my father was like a fine English gentleman. I knew that, didn't I? That people thought well of him, and knew he believed in everything he should, but he wasn't really part of all this.

'There are some things your mummy and daddy wouldn't understand,' she said, 'and I think you know what they are. And I think you know how to keep secrets. You're one of us, so we know you'll keep them.'

My father wasn't English – he was never English – but I knew what she meant by 'fine English gentleman'. My father had had another life somewhere else, my only life had been in Ballystewart. I had to be 'one of us' because it's what I was. It was the only place in the world that meant home to me. It was a natural thing, to take the Webley when it was offered, and natural for Mr Macleish to offer it to me. I finished my toast and I finished my milk and I told her I knew, and that she was right. I was good with secrets.

That was almost the whole conversation. My mother came back into the room not long after, but Mrs Tannock and I were already talking about school, and the conversation about secrets would have had no detail to it anyway, however long we might have talked. I assumed the details, then and since, and no doubt accurately.

I nearly blew it once though, maybe more than once.

We read about the guns that were under the Macleishes' barn. There were books in the school library that had information about them, and we would read them at lunchtime on wet days. There was a lot I didn't understand. The Sten has forty-seven parts, two of them machined and the rest stamped or pressed. But what did that mean?

One afternoon after school we had a plumber in and he was doing something with a pipe under the sink in the bathroom, so I asked him what the difference was between machined and stamped and pressed. Some of the important parts of the Sten were metal tubing, so he seemed like someone who might know.

My mother walked in as he showed me his spanner. He pointed out the mark that ran long the edges of it like a seam, and the lettering on one face of it. He was starting to tell me about the different ways metal is handled in order to make things. My mother had brought him a mug of tea. I told her we were doing the Industrial Revolution at school – which we honestly were – but if my question had been about the Industrial Revolution I would have asked her, and she knew it.

Two months later we were gone.

I might have dropped some clues, that might have been one of them. To this day I don't know. Her answers about us leaving have always been more general – my father's job offer, the fact that her skills were sought after in Australia then too, and it was a better place to bring up a child. A better place. That's a very general way of putting it, but it's how it's always been put.

The children's TV programming was interrupted one afternoon with a newsflash about a bomb. It might have been at a place called the Abercorn, but it could be that that's not it at all. The name's in my head, though. I was watching a cartoon when they broke for the news, and it had the typical footage of splintered timber and fallen masonry, but this time more casualties than usual. They might have let this one off without a warning.

I was there with my milk and toast and suddenly my mother was in the doorway and saying 'What's going on?'

And I told her, 'The plastic bags are for the bits of bodies,' since I took her question to be specific and that's the part of the story she'd walked in on, police and emergency workers sorting through rubble and bagging remains.

Then I remember footage of a woman – who I now realise was a teenage girl – with blood running out of her hair and down her face. She was saying that she was looking for her friend but she couldn't find her. She kept wiping at the blood, as if it was rain, and looking around with only her missing friend on her mind.

She said, 'We weren't supposed to be here, but I made us come.'

The way I remember it, it wasn't long after that that Paul Macleish suggested a trip to Belfast. Take a look around, visit a few people. Mark asked him who we would go with, and he said, 'I can drive a tractor, so I can drive a van. I've been doing it at night you know, lately.'

I don't know how old he was. I thought he was a man. Maybe he was just sixteen, thinking about it now. Maybe not even that. I don't know.

Perth – Sunday

Elliott, a sumptuous serve of the full buffet breakfast in front of him, is talking animatedly, saying I was 'fucking brilliant' and he hardly felt a thing anyway.

'Maybe we should have owned up to it,' he says. 'There's a life ban for that, for hitting someone with the gun. Trent told me. I asked him. Imagine that, a life ban. Imagine how that'd work for us.'

He has three stitches in his right cheek and the early stages of a black eye. And, for anyone of note who can't be here, he already has the photos to prove it. We might not have owned up to it yesterday, but there has been some fresh thought given to the subject overnight, and not to anything as small as admitting it at the time, out on the course. Elliott is loving the idea of going very public, exactly when it might do us the most good.

I could hardly speak when we pulled him up from the ground yesterday, and I don't think I was any help. He was stunned at first, perhaps simply physically, but I don't suppose what had happened made a lot of sense. Trent lifted his mask off cautiously and Elliott blinked his good eye and tried to focus, and he started telling his story about falling, perhaps because the real story seemed too implausible, maybe even to himself at first. It was a blur and I hit him hard, and in the head. I don't know yet if other people saw it or if they didn't. No one talked on the bus as if they did, and a full minute might have passed before I took the shots in the back, but I can't be certain.

Two tables away, three comedians are eating breakfast by the plateful, going back for thirds of pancakes. I've never been so antisocial at a festival, never in my life. One of them was on the opening night program with me, and I haven't spoken to him since.

Elliott is waving a big piece of sausage on a fork.

'The eye hardly opens,' he says, as if I'm unaware and it's news we'll both love. 'I'm not faking that. I emailed the pictures to Sydney this morning. The guys are on their way home now and I know they'll be stoked. And the bruising'll probably only get uglier over the next day or so. The doctor said it won't scar much, but it might scar a bit. And if anyone asks me I can go, "That's where Meg Riddoch hit me with a gun." How excellent is that? Decked, by a girl, with a gun. And you're the girl. Hilarious.' So I've become Elliott King's favourite war story, and all I did was snap in the heat of the moment and hit him with a toy. 'You were like a fucking soldier out there,' he says. 'Like the SAS. We're going to have to feminise you so you can play the part.'

'Go easy on that face,' I tell him. 'Grin any wider and you'll snap a stitch.'

I can't go hitting people. It's not what I should do. I don't know what was on my mind at the time. It was a kind of panic attack, perhaps. I was on my way out of there, not going for the flag.

The waiter is asking if I'd like a second latte. Elliott says he'll have another, sure, he'd love another, and he's scooping up omelette and filling his mouth.

I put the idea of tumble turns back in my head, and the mystery of my inability to line the end of the pool up from any distance away. I can see my hand, breaking the glassy surface of the water, bubbles bursting away from it, but the wall is too hazy for me to measure how far it is, every time, until I'm upon it. Is it something in the water? My goggles?

'The buzz about this show will be so big when we put the photos out there,' Elliott says, his next mouthful of omelette still not all swallowed. 'Maybe we'll do it just before we go into production, or maybe right before it runs.' He stops. He's thinking about magazines, his best victim shot next to a story about my dark side, and its impending release. 'Hey, I heard about that *NW* piece last night. Was that all bullshit or . . .'

The look he gives me says he can go sensitive right now if I need him to, and we can't have that so I tell him, 'Pretty much. I guess I'll be home tomorrow so I'll find out, won't I?'

'Good,' he says, his knife and fork in the air for a moment above his plate. 'Well, I hope it's okay. Really.'

Suddenly he's let the exuberance slip and he's just a battered guy who seems to mean what he says. In a conversation in which everything gets said twice and loudly and at length, he tells me once and quietly that he hopes my life is okay, really, and there's a pause.

I suspect he knows it isn't okay, but he's telling me that he's noticed and he won't push. He's aware, if I want him to be. It's the better parts of Elliott that I often forget. He's more observant, more decent, than I usually give him credit for. I need to remember that's the case, throughout this wild hunger for bacon and sausages and omelette, and whenever we're bickering about subtlety, weapons and the contract clauses pertaining thereto. He was won over by the original idea, and genuinely so, and he responded exactly the way I needed him to. He's not just a guy who'd love to get his face split open for a photo, or to prove he was dealing with the right person.

But that'll be our angle. I'll be some mad-dog gym junkie with an anger management problem, and that's why I'm right for the part. That's how I get to reinvent myself, move on from stand-up. How I get to do this series, working day after day within driving range of home.

'I'm sorry about smashing you in the face,' I tell him, since the conversation's gone quiet and that's made it a good time. And I'm thinking of home again, so it's best to get us talking about something else. 'That all pushed some buttons out there, more than I would have expected. I'm not good with that stuff.'

'It's okay.'

'It's not, really. I would prefer not to have hit you. But it's a long story and my life has been a little out-of-the-ordinary lately. Perhaps I should have kept it to just the kick to the solar plexus, or maybe slugged you with my non-weapon hand.'

He laughs, and says, 'It's really okay. The kick hurt more, actually. I was pretty winded from it, so the face wasn't a big deal.'

'I'm not a violent person.'

'Meg, this is a good news story as far as I'm concerned, plain and simple. So stop being dumb about it, sort out those buttons that got pushed and let's go to work.' He smiles an asymmetrical smile, half his face going with it, the other half too swollen. 'We've got to establish you in this new type of role. My face will work for us. And I never thought a face like mine would get me anywhere professionally, so there you go.'

He has a laugh at his own joke, and himself, and he reaches for a piece of bread to mop up the tomato juice on his plate. He takes on every meal like a Tudor king at a banquet. I've noticed that about him, and it's one of the many things that could make a person doubt his capacity for subtlety. I could see him happily taking to a quail with his bare hands, if there had been one on the smorgasbord table.

'Anyway,' he says, 'face aside, you were awesome yesterday. Everybody thought so. And I want to make this show physical, but keep it smart. We like the idea that she's a physical force, but she holds that back unless she's in a really tight corner. You were tactical yesterday, low to the ground, a small target. I watched you out there. You are this person. I'm more convinced than ever.' He folds the slice of bread in two, and stops just before eating it. 'And nice photo in this morning's paper, by the way. The one with the sick kid. Very nice. Sensitive, yeah?'

This time I walk to the Barrack Street Jetty, since I know how close it is. The mall and the streets are quiet, and the shops look as though they open later on Sunday. There's no sign of business starting.

I'm not sure that my paddling muscles are quite prepared for the task ahead.

I can see two marquees on the parkland next to the river, and smaller tents selling food and drinks. A crowd is gathering, and serious boats – rowing fours and eights – are gliding up and down on the water. I'd forgotten we were part of an all-day event.

I realise that the shock effect of the *NW* article has worn off. It's out there now, and that's how it is. It still feels bad that truths so close can be public and circulating in however many thousands of copies of a magazine, but I'm over the lurch that came with the first glimpse of my name on the front cover, and the shudder that followed it when I saw the boozy Rob Castle photo inside.

We don't get to keep all our secrets, and I wasn't going to keep this one forever. People were going to find out about Murray, even if they never found out about Calgary. I didn't expect to hide the break-up, or plan to, but I did hope for more control, and some time to myself first to collect my thoughts. I would have put a statement out, within a month I'm sure, and it would largely have gone ignored. I would have done it just so that it was on the record, and I would have been happiest if they had ignored it. I don't want it to be news, but it would have been better to have put my version out there first. I needed to be home for that, though, and to talk it through with Murray.

There's no reason for people to know about Calgary, or care. It's not really part of my story. It's just an incident now, no more. I don't know what I thought about it that night, or what I hoped for. I was lonely, I know that, and wanting to be less alone. And Calgary seemed, for me, like a place where things might be done without consequences. I owed no one any different behaviour by then, I let events take their course, and at the end of it I felt both better and worse than I had before.

At the smaller of the two marquees, one of the race organisers gives me a name tag to wear around my neck, and a carry bag with a water bottle, a towel and sunscreen.

'Actually,' she says, 'it might better if we keep all that here for you until after the race, but you might want the sunscreen and I'll get you a hat.'

The VIP tent is mostly full of corporate sponsors, middle-ranking executives from a chemicals manufacturer, a transport company and a bank, hanging around in their usual groups in baggy shorts and deck shoes, drinking beer from large plastic cups. Some of them look my way and recognise or half-recognise me, and I've never known quite what to do when that happens. People assume that anyone who does stand-up is an uncomplicated extrovert, unless their act is specifically about being dysfunctional and strange. I'm sure I'm seen as an extrovert, with more than her share of loud opinions, and that means it's assumed that I'll walk up to any group of people anywhere, shake hands and get talking.

The woman who almost gave me the carry bag – I now see that she's wearing a name tag that says Judy Luckett – comes over my way, straightening out a hat that she's pulled from a box under her table. For the second time in about three minutes she asks me how I'm going, and then she says she should find me someone to talk to, and who would I like? What kind of person?

Her two-way radio crackles, and a man's voice tells her that the first minibus for the celebrities has arrived in the carpark.

So Judy Luckett shrugs and says, 'Well, there we go then. No time to talk. Come with me.'

Celebrities are found in and around the tent by name-tagged organisers and we clump together on the way to the bus. My partner Anthony isn't there, but someone else with a two-way says that he'll meet us over at the canoes with his camera crew.

Soon we're travelling along Riverside Drive heading upstream, and I'm sitting next to Pia Miranda, with Mal Meninga and Joe Bugner in front of us, one each side of the aisle. I should appreciate moments like this, gliding through traffic in bizarre company – a twenty-something film star, a rugby league legend, a big guy who once went the distance in the ring with Ali. And all of us setting out together to canoe.

You can never tell how many years you might get of this, how long your name is on the list before it stops appearing any more. Each event gives you another story you can tell when you're washed up and it's all over, or when you've given it away and made less public choices. And I read far too many trashy magazines to turn a chance like this down.

Pia is Joe Bugner's canoe partner, and she's surely no more than a third his size. She says she's trained by studying the canoe scene from *Shallow Hal* in detail, and doesn't expect her paddle to touch the water much. She tells me she came along to one of my Sydney shows earlier in the year, so I find myself talking about how talented I think she is. It comes out sounding like a very Hollywood way to respond, even though I mean every word of it.

Joe turns around and says, 'What is this? A love-in? Don't listen to her, Pia. I want to see some aggro.' He punches his fist into the palm of his other hand, and tells me Pia is their team's secret weapon and I shouldn't think I'll get anywhere by sucking up.

Mal says his partner's an author, so none of us rates his chances too highly.

The other minibus, though it left second, arrives before us at the canoes, and its paddlers are all standing at the water's edge when we get there. There's a Perth Glory soccer player, local TV and radio presenters and a comedy duo who will need to be split up to have any hope of avoiding disgrace. Anyone unpartnered will surely be running a mile from the one with the silly hat.

Anthony comes over and gives me a hug, and says, 'Hi, darl. Thought I'd put in a few more laps by myself beforehand, just to make sure I'm in tip-top shape.'

His crew closes in and films the hug, so I tell him practice is a fine thing as long as he hasn't peaked too early, and the guy on the camera lets it run for a few more seconds and then says, 'That's great, but could we get you to do it again and we'll come round the other side?'

'Ah, the beauty of television,' Anthony says, with a wry smile. 'You get to be spontaneous over and over again. Now, big hugs.'

I've seen the wry smile before, on the couple of occasions when I've watched his show. It's usually directed towards a piece of particularly artless work done by one of the amateur renovators, while they're trying to turn a friend's lounge room into something less drab.

Anthony, when he's leading a renovation, loves a bold theme and bright colours. I've seen him go retro, I've seen him go Aztec, I've seen him go nautical, with a room painted half dark blue and half light blue, with the dark blue finishing in waist-high wave crests, and lifebelts used to 'create a porthole effect over the windows'. After the show had been running for two years they did an episode of follow-ups, and Anthony visited house after house from the first series. Almost every wall had been painted magnolia again, or cream, and all the old pictures were back in place. But he's not a man given to much self-doubt, and he decided his best response was to lament the unadventurous tastes of the nation.

We put our life-jackets on and clamber into the canoes.

'We're a motley old crew, aren't we?' Anthony says, as we paddle out with the other seven boats. 'I mean the lot of us, not just you and me. I wonder if they'll squeeze any footage of the real rowers into the news tonight, or if it'll just be all of us making fools of ourselves.'

A lot of manoeuvring around goes on, and several boats drift downstream. Anthony and I hold back behind the start line, but eventually the organisers give up and fire the gun with at least four boats well ahead of us.

We give it our best shot, though we're coming from far behind. We make up some ground in the first two hundred metres, then Anthony's technique becomes a little ragged. He scoops water into the boat and grunts with each stroke. He swaps sides with the paddle because his arms are about to fail, then he wants to swap back again and his paddle slips from his grip and hits the back of my right hand with some force, splitting the skin.

'Shit, sorry,' he says, though he can't see what's happened. 'I hope that didn't land on anything precious.'

The paddle clatters from the side of the canoe and into the water. I work hard to stop us being last, swapping my paddling from one side to the other. Anthony, suddenly purposeless at the front of the boat, sweeps his arms out like wings and loudly declares that he's king of the world.

Mal Meninga wins it, partnered by some skinny guy I don't know who's flailing away and drenching him as they cross the line. Pia and Joe finish second, I think. We come about sixth out of eight, with Anthony air-breaststroking us over the line and a race caller on a PA system declaring that our controversial tactics have been, at best, only partially successful. Thousands of people laugh and cheer. That's how it sounds, and there's nothing to do but stow the paddle, and take a bow towards the riverbank. The comedian and the hopeless boy designer have undoubtedly done their job.

I paddle us over to the jetty, where Anthony's camera crew is waiting to film our wrap-up of the race. They stand us next to each other, framed by the crowd and the river, and I'm still out of breath when we start. Anthony explains that we ran into a significant technical problem out on the water, and I agree and put it down to the failure of the organisers to fit each craft with a spare paddle.

'Exactly,' he says. 'Exactly. In the heat of the moment, you can forget to grip.'

'And, really, if it hadn't been for that...' They move in on me for a close-up. 'If it hadn't been for that, I think we would have been looking at a podium finish, but what can you say? Rowing was the winner on the day.'

We end there, and I have a feeling I've just made the remark that will close the six o'clock news.

Meanwhile, out of shot, there's blood running from my hand down two fingers and dripping onto the grass.

Anthony sees it then, for the first time, and he almost shrieks. 'You're not going to tell me I did that? Oh, darl, Christ, I've brutalised you with my paddle.'

That's when I notice that Felicity and Adam have walked over this way from the tents. She's wearing a sun dress and he's carrying a picnic basket, and they'd been hanging back while the camera was rolling.

'What a week,' Felicity says. 'First the tooth, and now this...'

I hold the hand up, spread my fingers out, and take a look at it. 'In the wars, as my mother would say.'

'Do you think it needs stitches?'

I touch the wound, and I can feel a sharp edge. This is what the paddle has hit, and the skin has split between them.

I lie about the glass when it comes out. I had enough time on the way to the medical centre to get the lie ready, so it's quite convincing. It's glass from a car windscreen, years ago, that much is true and undeniable. In cross-section it's a hexagon or an octagon, one of those shapes you make when you shatter windscreen glass.

'From a while ago?' the doctor says. 'From a car accident a while ago? Is that what these other scars are too? Let's hope it's the last bit. You could think about an ultrasound at some stage to see if there are any more. Do you want to keep it?'

He drops it into a plastic specimen jar, and starts suturing.

'You'd be surprised how long foreign bodies can stay in there before causing trouble for no good reason,' he says, drawing the edges of the wound together as he ties the first knot. 'I did my residency in a war vets' hospital and I can remember one old guy who had to have shrapnel removed from his buttock about seventy years after the Somme, because it was starting to irritate his sciatic nerve.'

I look at the piece of glass, and it's fresh but for the blood, kept fresh all these years inside my hand. But its time was up. It's been surfacing for days, this piece, pointing and starting to hurt. It's amazing what the hand can hide away. There's not much of it, and where's the room, with all the fine workings for fingers? But every so often it's done this, delivered up a piece.

Four times now, I think, since the glass blew in there on a city road, on a rainy day, in another world, when I was young.

Ballystewart — 1972

I'D SAID TO my mother that I was going to play with Mark and Sammy in the woods, so she thought I must have fallen out of a tree when Mr Macleish brought me home with my hand bandaged.

'It was my own stupid fault,' I told her. 'I fell on some windscreen glass in the McKendrys' field.'

'Honestly,' she said, 'is it safe to let you out?'

But she wasn't too worried. She could see I was all right. I might have had a bandage, but she could see four fingers and a thumb, and all of them moving. It must have been a weekend, and I'd been taken to the Macleishes' in the morning. My parents were going out somewhere for the day, I can't remember where.

'They came back to our house when she hurt her hand,' Mr Macleish said, 'so we thought the best thing to do was take her to Newtownards and get it sorted out. She bumped her head as well, so we thought we'd better get her seen to. Everything's all right with that, though.'

My mother thanked him for going to the trouble of

looking after me, and she took a closer look at my bandaged hand and said, 'Margaret Riddoch, could you not see yourself liking dolls just a wee bit more?'

She shook her head, and smiled and put her hand on my shoulder. She took me inside, made me something to eat and said, 'Let's not turn the television on this afternoon. Let's listen to music instead.'

We played Cliff Richard, and sang along. My heart was still racing, my head was still sore, I couldn't eat much. My whole body ached in bed that night, and I lay awake, listening for cars above the ringing in my ears.

When we moved to Australia, we lived in a suburb where the cars drove past all night. We slept with the windows open, with screens on them, and the noise of bats and possums came in from the mango tree outside my room. There was so much noise, so much life out there in the dark, that it took some adjusting to. I was used to silence at night, or perhaps just the sound of trees, sighing as the wind went through them.

I didn't know how to make new friends when I got to Australia, since I'd only ever had one set of friends and I'd built that up from scratch. We shared things by the time I left Ballystewart, my friends and me – interests, secrets, a small but intense amount of history even though we were only eight.

I didn't fit in in Australia. I was the foreign kid, obviously, but I was more foreign than they knew. I didn't realise till now how much I was the odd one out. Back then it was everyone else at school who was odd, as far as I could see. I'd been dropped into a crazy country and I had to make the best of it. It's all a blur now – a blur of 'Sesame Street', Coco Pops, fights at school, my mother telling me I'd never make friends if I kept going round hitting people, and did I not want to make friends? And I did, of course I did. I wanted them to stop calling me the foreign kid, I wanted them to stop frustrating me with how little they understood, I wanted to find out if there was more to them – the kind of stuff that might come out if you hit them a few times – but I also wanted to make friends.

So I learned hopscotch, and knuckles, though I didn't like them much. I learned a new accent. I learned to swim in my first summer holidays, though I was never much good at butterfly, backstroke or turns. I won a prize for most improved time over twenty-five metres breaststroke. I waged war with boys across three gardens at once, commando-style.

One night in my twenties, my mother said, 'We always thought when you were nine that you'd be a lesbian. We'd fully adjusted, you know. All that short hair, that toughness, playing with boys.'

So, there were two things at least that my mother wasn't clear on: me, and how sexual orientation works.

In Ballystewart, it was the boys who happened to be close to home. From there, it wasn't so much that we found common ground, but more that we invented it together. We took what we had and what we saw and we kept ourselves busy and, in time, that amounts to something.

In Brisbane, it was the boys who seemed to be interested that I'd seen soldiers on the streets. I came from a place that was in the news because of bombings and shootings, and the most normal thing for me that year was to take a few of my new friends and teach them some of what I knew. How to crawl without being seen, how to ambush, how to signal. And I'd say things like, 'I can strip a Sten gun in the dark. I can kill, you know.'

I'd be scared when I said it, but I knew it left them awestruck in the right kind of way, and ready to take orders. And I made it clear that there was secrecy required, and they swore to observe it. And I never told them much anyway, just what they needed to know, and only general information at that. The scars on my hand were still pink then, though they were fading.

Within a year or two, we'd all moved on to other things. Football and cricket for them, David Cassidy for me, mainly. A few of the girls in the class were big on 'The Partridge Family', and I wanted flares and then Susan Dey hair, since that looked very grown-up. And I thought if I mastered that look David Cassidy and I might drive around in a bus and he'd think I was great, and I never got round to addressing the issue that they were brother and sister.

In the dream with David Cassidy I had no scars, and he thought my hands were beautiful, and told me so.

'It was my own stupid fault. It was my own stupid fault.' I'd practised the line in the car that day, with my hand bandaged up and throbbing, and my head ringing and blood in my hair as well. Mr Macleish said it was the best way.

And he also said 'Soldiers never tell', and we were all proud when he talked that way. So I've never told. Never.

'It was my own stupid fault.' It sounded too grown up, almost, but it worked when I practised it, and I liked him for trusting me with a line he'd use himself.

He'd been angry before we got in the car, though. Not with me or Mark, but with Paul. 'What were you thinking?' he said to him, with the anger just kept in. 'What were you thinking? You idiot. How could you think it'd be anything but trouble? Right now of all times. And in the van, too. Are you never going to learn?'

He took the keys and he locked them away after that. They'd hung on a hook inside the door before then, and Paul could just take them from there. Not any more.

We shouldn't have been in Belfast that day. We should have gone to the woods, but that was never the real plan. Paul took us to Belfast because he'd heard there would be trouble and he said you should never back down in the face of trouble. So we should go.

There was a show on, an agricultural show. There were diggers and harvesters, and brighter newer equipment than I'd ever seen before.

I remember the van we drove in to get there, but not much of the trip to Belfast. We bought a big serve of chips wrapped up in paper, and ate them with vinegar and salt. I remember being pushed in a crowd, pushed out of the exhibition and onto the street. Paul's hand was on my shoulder but he was looking straight ahead. 'It's on,' he said. Something like that. 'I think it's on.' And he looked scared.

I remember his look now with complete clarity, as if that was the moment we'd lost the afternoon. And we were hurrying and the person behind me was kicking my shoes, bumping me in the back.

It's clear, but it's a picture I sometimes can't trust. I was eight, I was a kid in a crowd, I can't know the whole story.

The bang split the air like a punch to the chest, that's how it seemed. I don't know where we were by then. It's a moment I can't see. I can feel its percussion, in a hazy unforgettable way, how the world shook like a beaten blanket, and some things are certain after that, too. How hard the road felt, and cold. How fast my heart beat against it. The weight of being pressed down against the road, the inability to move other than to turn my head. The sight I saw with my one open eye then, the man towering over me in camouflage, the black hood over his head, the loose bottom edge of the hood shaking and shaking as he kept firing and kept firing. Emptying that Tommy gun and spilling cartridges down onto the road not far from where I lay, close enough that I could feel them land hot in my hair once or twice.

Perth – Sunday

I stuck with the story, the one about the accident in the McKendrys' field. I could see it, it was more plausible, it was more complete, and I had a duty to stick with it. I rehearsed it in the car and afterwards, and I can picture it all still, as good as a memory. When I look at the scars on my hands, it's the first thing I see. The ground rushing up at me as I fall from the top of something in the McKendrys' field. And I landed on the grass with my hand trying to break my fall, but my head hit the ground anyway and picked up some glass, too. And we climbed back over the fence and crossed the ploughed field to the Macleishes'.

I took what actually happened and I made it go away. I don't know if I even meant to, and I don't know if I could have done it, or would have done it, if we'd stayed in Ballystewart. There, it was something to be kept secret, but to be kept as a shared secret – in Brisbane it felt different. It was mine alone, it was a secret no one would ever come looking for, and it was wrong for my new life. It didn't fit. I looked around me, at my new life and the things that made it up and, when I did that, I saw that it simply couldn't have happened. It was a horrible bad dream that had stopped making sense, and that I had to make go away.

I don't know if it was quite that deliberate, but I do know that, at some level, I needed somehow to find a way to live, and there were things that had happened that could not be part of my story.

I'd had a life that had made complete sense to me, however much it shouldn't have, and it's as if, in the middle of it, someone had grabbed me by the heels and dragged me out backwards. I didn't live through it to the end. Nothing ended. Abruptly, one life was done and another underway and I was still eight but in a new land, with the wrong accent and the wrong skills and the wrong life led, with a lot of business started, none finished. But no one thinks of an eight-year-old – an English-speaking British eight-year-old – and the unmet necessity of closure.

So I took the past and I shut it out and I shut it out and I kept shutting it out, and at the worst and shakiest of times it can be lurking there for me. And at great times too, occasionally. It's not predictable.

So, the Thompson gunner isn't lifted from a Warren Zevon song or too many comics. I looked up and I saw him. But it's better, most of the time, not to believe in him at all.

I don't know if he hit anyone or anything with those bullets, or if by that point it was mainly about firing them. The full story would include that – some information about the target, and whether he hit it or not. And why they blew something up, but still stayed to shoot. But I never got to ask. I never got to know the full story. We were gone not long after, I was left with these fragments, all secret and best denied. Blocked and blocked and added to and compressed by layers of news stories and pictures, clouded by being over-remembered and by being buried, and by surfacing patchworked in my sleep. I can make no inventory of the facts, just the lingering signs that something happened, some time.

Here's what I have from when the bomb went off. A minor hearing loss, but at a very particular level, and not one of much day-to-day use. A tattoo of road dirt across my scalp, tiny flecks of bitumen deep in the skin and there to stay. The fragments of glass in my hand, and the small scars left by them going in, and out.

Something landed on my head. A bag, a briefcase, maybe carried by the man who fell across my back. It hit me hard, probably hit my forehead into the road, knocked me out maybe, jumbled a lot of things, but it stopped it all being as bad as it might have been.

And that's all I have to help me make sense of it, and it doesn't make sense. You don't get to make sense of these things. You end up injured in a way that would require more contortions than you could have managed, even when you were young and supple, and nothing lets you work it out. There's no slow-motion view of it, no camera angles, nothing. One moment you're scared and being pushed, in the next all that's gone. The gaps stay gaps, though your inclination is to fill them with something, and that leaves you doubting the rest.

You try to see more than you did, or could, and you can talk yourself into seeing it. You work it, and work it, and fight against it and dream about it, and the Thompson gunner sometimes speaks and sometimes doesn't have a hood and sometimes steps on your hand, and what's true any more? You were blown deaf by the bomb for a while, probably, but there's a version of it where you can't hear the gun or the screaming and yet the cartridges land before your eyes with the pure sound of wind chimes, and that can't have happened, even though they're hollow when they're spent and it's a noise they might make.

But I do have scars, today's new glass, and the absolute lack of any honest memory of the injury that was once, in a lie, put down to the windscreen glass in the McKendrys' field. Some things stay true.

My mother had by then stopped being surprised by me coming home injured after time spent with my friends. Not that it was a common occurrence, but it wasn't exactly rare either, for any of us. In the year or two before, I'd had the usual cuts and bruises, but I'd also had a nail go right through my foot when running around among the McKendrys' trucks, a greenstick forearm fracture when I'd fallen from one of the apple trees in our garden, and probably more. I didn't have the best grasp of consequences, perhaps.

My mother decided to see me as an 'active child'. That's how she put it to her friends. 'If there's trouble brewing, Meg'll be in the thick of it,' she said, and I was annoyed about that since it wasn't how I saw the situation at all. We never stopped talking about how I had to be more careful, and learn my limits. But at the same time she would say that I had a sense of adventure and a great imagination, and that they were assets and I could do anything if I put my mind to it.

I have no idea where it was that I saw the doctor that day. It might have been somewhere else in Belfast, it might have been Newtownards, it might have been neither. It might have been a hospital, or somewhere smaller. It was probably a hospital, the doctor was probably young, though I wouldn't have known it. There were a lot of injured people, I think, and I would have been among the less important. He picked at my hand and scalp with an instrument, picked away looking for bits of glass. There was an antiseptic smell. I was lying down on something, but I was a long way off the ground. Paul Macleish had a cut on the cheek, and a big piece of glass in his shoulder. I saw it come out. There was a commotion then, in the corridor, and the doctor was called away. I can't remember if anything happened to the others, but maybe it didn't.

There was a leg on the road. I remember that too, from when they picked me up. I thought it was a man under a car but it was just a leg, dressed like the leg of a farmer, in for the show and minding his own business.

But there's wreckage and clamour at times like that, and you're never too sure what you've seen. You're lifted up half-wondering if the leg was there at all, half-knowing they'll be back later to put it in a bag.

And you're carried to the hospital, and fixed, and you move away from there and put together a life in the new country, from new parts as much as possible, but you end up accepting that you have learned a vigilance that you can't forget.

There are some things that will never be safe for me – the unattended bag, anything in the middle of a road, the empty carpark. I can deal with them – all of them, and without difficulty – but dealing with them is my second thought. My first is always the thing that will never happen. That it means a bomb.

There won't be a bomb in a Coke can on the road outside home, and I can run it flat if I choose to and my aim is right. There won't be a bomb in the shopping centre carpark. I won't stick my key in the door of the car or in the ignition and set anything off.

But of course I can see how it would go, the ball of flame and smoke pressed flat by the low ceiling, bursting out from me and my car, the jolt of the blast smashing windscreens all over and knocking people to the concrete in various states of damage.

No one else thinks about these things, as far as I'm aware. I do, and I have to. That's how I am. They're a normal built-in part of me. Keeping them in mind has become as innocuous as a habit, and I'm fifty times more fucked up than I thought.

Felicity sits next to me on the minibus, worried about my hand and whether or not it should be elevated, telling me I honestly don't have to perform tonight if I don't feel up to it.

Today Murray, back from Shanghai, will have been moving boxes out of our flat. He's taken a new place nearby. It's a temporary thing, he told me, till something more permanent gets sorted out, something still in the same part of town though, since it's close to Laura's and that's better for Elli.

All the way to the sponsors' showcase, that's what's in my head. Murray packing clothes, books, who knows what? Who knows what would count as a short-term need? A carton of wine, with the bottles separated by underpants and socks, a shirt or two shoved on top, his non-travelling toothbrush dropped vertically into a corner – maybe that one box would do him for the moment.

There are fairy lights in the trees outside the venue, a gallery and restaurant in East Perth, and the guests are moving inside as we arrive. I sit at my designated table for eight, with two lawyers and an accountant and four people too many chairs away to work out, and we're served a porcini mushroom tartlet and then salmon and then a trio of sorbets, and I drink a lot less than usual because I've had more than enough to drink this past month.

I explain that I'm on strong medication for my hand, so I shouldn't really drink at all and, if I seem a little vague, I hope they'll forgive me. They laugh, because I'm a comedian, or because of the way I said it. They tell me they think it's great for Perth, great that there's a festival like this. Two of them give me business cards, and another says he didn't think to bring any and then he looks through his wallet just in case.

I have something planned for my turn at the microphone, and it starts with a clear reveal of the bandaged hand – perhaps I'll adjust the microphone with it – and the line 'This hasn't been the easiest of weeks for me.' Then I'll tell them they don't know the half of it. They think I just made a dick of myself canoeing today. They haven't seen my spectacular new porcelain tooth. Then on from that anecdote to Elliott, the accident at paintball, and the three stitches he has in his cheek to match the three in my hand from the canoeing. Honestly, what are they thinking? They seem to be turning this comedy festival thing into an extreme sport, and I hope they're proud of themselves.

'You're not looking well,' Felicity says. 'And I don't want to sound like your mother, but have you eaten any of the dinner?' She's claimed the seat to my right, now that the accountant is up talking to someone. She's sitting side-on, facing me, frowning. 'You're scheduled to be on in ten minutes, but we could . . .'

'I'll be fine,' I tell her. 'I'll be fine. I'm just going to go for a walk and think it all through.'

Outside, the evening breeze has picked up. It's rippling the surface of the river and it feels cool on my face. My napkin's in my hand. I pushed my chair back and strode away and forgot to put it down. I start crying again. It just wells up from somewhere.

I sit on a rock on the bank and put my face into the napkin. Breath jerks in and out of me, and there's nothing I can do to stop it. I cry till the wetness comes through to my hands.

'It's okay,' Felicity says. She's standing behind me, on the path. 'We've got someone else ready to go on. I've told people you've reacted badly to the drugs. That was the line, wasn't it?'

'But I've got a plan,' I tell her. 'It's new material. Things from this week.'

'Don't make a liar of me. I've got your bags and, the way I've told it, we're off to the medical centre to see if you're fit to fly.'

She waits to see if I'm going to fight her, but I don't. She calls a cab. The side of the restaurant facing the water is all glass and people are back in their seats, ready to be entertained. When I stand up, a business card falls out of the napkin and cartwheels along the path in the breeze.

Felicity starts to move after it, and I stop her and say, 'You're already my hero. I don't need the card.'

She sticks with me all the way to the check-in counter at the airport. I ask her if she thinks I can't handle it myself, and she says she's sure my chances would be at least fifty–fifty.

I want to say something meaningful, but every thought I have sounds clumsy and better off not turned into words.

'Call me,' is the best I can manage, 'if you're ever in Brisbane. We could go out for a drink. I could stop lurching from crisis to crisis, you could stop saving me . . .'

We spent half the past week together, and I don't remember asking her anything about her life or what she's hoping for.

'Call you?' she says. 'Sure. I will. That'd be good.'

'Or email me at least, in the meantime. Who knows when we'll be in the same place, or where it might be? I really owe you, you know, for the past few days.'

'Don't hurt yourself on the plane,' she says, and smiles. 'It's a long trip.' She hugs me. 'If you cry I'll cry, so don't.'

As my carry-on bag passes through the scanner and I'm emptying my pockets, I look around and see her going through the doors and towards the cab rank. I would have cried if I'd said any more. She was right about that, judging that it could happen all too easily.

In the Qantas Club I realise how little food I ate at the dinner, and I get myself a bowl of pumpkin soup and a glass of mineral water. I sit in front of a TV that's set to Fox Sports, and I watch two clay-courters slugging it out in a tennis tournament somewhere in Europe.

I've never pulled out of an event before. Never.

I find Claire's number and I call her and thank her again for seeing me through my craziest day. For giving me ice-cream, letting me cook, hearing me out, as far out as I wanted to go.

'Yes, well, I did rather make it up as I went along,' she says. 'How are you going now? Are you okay?'

They're calling the flight. I tell her I'm fine.

On the plane, the flight attendant takes my bag and says she'll put it in the overhead locker for me. She asks if my hand injury is from the canoe race, and says they played the paddle-dropping bit on the news several times in slow-motion. I don't tell her about the glass.

I've been true to my word, my word that I gave when

I was eight and everything in the world seemed to be riding on it. How could I tell Murray now, or my parents, about the glass in my hand, how I feel when I see things lying in the road? Where would I begin? It should be over. It should have been over long ago. No more glass, or dreams, or ideas that don't apply. New memories have come along and been cast on top, and they work like a whole story most of the time, but not all of it.

My doll's house came out here to Brisbane, then I got the Partridge Family bus for my ninth or tenth birthday. I passed it on to Elli, and to her it was just a bus and there I was, with a five-year-old, doing my damnedest to explain the Partridge Family.

'Maybe when she's a bit older,' Murray said. 'Contemporary five-year-olds aren't always great at grasping the cultural significance of the seventies.'

And when he said that, I thought about being young and how I had gone about grasping the significance of things, and I remembered old houses, tall clocks, display cabinets of knick-knacks – though I had been more like seven then, and the knick-knacks were from the thirties or earlier. But there was a sense in those places that if something was behind glass it was significant, and that's where your grasp of significance starts – with other people's meanings and how they get them across.

Murray has a cricket bat of his grandfather's that's too heavy to use, as well as his two World War One service medals. He has a book of poetry that his father studied at school, mainly by memorising. He has three mismatched horseshoes from the property his other grandparents lived on until the sixties. He has a Bible someone gave him on a forgotten occasion, and which he kept because it was the only book he ever had that zipped up, and it had gold along the edges of the pages. Murray has a picture of the cart he built at the age of nine, taken earlier on the very afternoon that he stacked it and broke the front axle and took the skin from his forearms on the bitumen road.

In the photo, the mood is clear. There's pride in the construction and excitement about the ride to come, no hint, of course, that the afternoon would end the way it did.

'But you've got to be a kid,' he said, when we'd known each other a while and he showed me the photo. 'You've got to feel invincible and sometimes come a cropper.'

And he showed me scars on his arms, which were next to invisible, and the blueish hints of pigment below the skin where flecks of bitumen had gone, and stayed.

But I told him nothing, showed him nothing. There's a past I started keeping from him that very day, him and his cart story, and once you start keeping it, your choice is made.

'You're getting my full story,' he said in one clear moment of anger, or at least anguish, 'and I'm not getting that from you, I don't think.'

And he looked at the floor, and Janis the counsellor looked at me, and I said, 'I don't know what you want. I'm not going to make up stories because you haven't heard enough. People are different. That's what this is.'

It was meant as observation, not as a catalyst. We could

observe difference, and accommodate it. That's how I meant it. But it was a big one for Murray – Murray whose self-disclosure was absolute and who, if pushed, would say that he found any other way dishonest. So I'd set us on the track to a conclusion, just by rounding off my response.

It's well into night now, and this is the notorious red-eye flight – out of Perth late, into Melbourne a few hours afterwards, at dawn. I chose, two months ago, to take it just this once, since it was the very soonest I could be home. My life was only weeks away from changing then, and I can't believe I didn't know.

I should sleep, but I don't want to sleep.

Ballystewart — 1972

I CAN'T PLACE it in time, that trip to Belfast. Not on a calendar, since that's not how life worked for me then. There were school times, and school holidays. Short days, and long days. Time for planting, time when things grew, harvest. There was a time when the people who fell from boats at sea would not last long at all, and that was winter. I read that in the bank, next to the lifeboat.

But it was probably spring when we went into Belfast that day, and I know it was June when we left, and not much happened in between.

Books arrived and told me about Australia and how different it was, and I had to adjust to the idea of leaving everything I knew behind. 'It's very sunny in Australia,' my father said one drizzly Sunday, while we waited for the weather to clear for our walk in the woods. 'Sometimes people don't even wear shoes.' I didn't know how those two things were related, or why the second was good, but he seemed very positive about the prospect.

Perhaps it was a matter of a few weeks between the bomb

in Belfast and us leaving. I think I can remember a ninth birthday party with a magician when my hand was still bandaged. It was inside at someone's house on another cloudy afternoon. And there was also a day when the sun shone and we did walk in the woods and I collected flowers for keeping in a flower press, so that I'd have something to take with me from the only place I knew. No one explained quarantine laws to me, and the flower press made it through customs unnoticed. I still have it, with its layers of spring flowers and leaves, brown and flat. I can still remember putting some of them in there when they had some bulk, then refitting the top and tightening the wing nuts at the corners.

There was another roadblock too, the same people standing there with a few rifles and a handgun, waving the traffic to a stop, making a show of looking in the boots of people's cars.

And a trip to Belfast, another trip to Belfast in the van. This time, at night. My mother did my hair in Heidi plaits before I left for the Macleishes'. It was a style that she quite liked, though my thick unruly hair didn't make it easy. I was sleeping over, which was something we did quite often at each other's houses. But this time, in the middle of the night, I remember someone waking me and soon we were in the van and on our way to Belfast. Paul was driving, and his friend Danny was in the front with him, talking tough, which is what he did. The rest of us were in the back, with the bags.

But that was before the other trip in the van to Belfast, not after. It was before.

Brisbane — Monday

It was before, that's the thing. It was a time when there seemed to be people killed every few days in shootings and bombings, and a lot of it was put down to retribution for previous attacks. Tit-for-tat killings, they were called. They were always on the news, and one would lead to more and they didn't stop. And the night trip to Belfast was somewhere in the middle of that, and before the trip with the bomb and the Thompson gunner.

The sky is clear as we come over the fields and into Melbourne. I'm not awake and not asleep either. In the Qantas Club I make coffee, I press the wrong button and get a long black, I eat a plate of fruit. I sit with my back to the wall and people come and go, most of them travelling with work. I listen to them talk, lining up their days, making calls. There are newspapers, but I can't read them.

I can remember the smell of the van, farm smells, and the way everything jolted and clattered around when we hit a bump in the road, and how there was nothing to hold onto in the back.

It's almost as if the smell is in the plane on the way to Brisbane, it's so real to me. They serve us breakfast, but I've had my fruit. They show us the early news, housing approvals for the last quarter, Tiger Woods putting to win a golf tournament.

I have a window seat, which leaves me feeling stuck, but I can look out at the world down below, at the mountains and the brown, drought-stricken fields.

We lived in a peaceful farming area. My parents always said that, and it was true. Much of the province was relatively unaffected by conflict, or seemed like it, and life went on in a lot of respects as it had before. There were real seasons, and they had a bearing on our lives. I have sycamore seeds in my flower press, collected before that final spring, I think. They were too fat for the flower press really, the seed parts of them anyway, but they had the most interesting shape so I had to have them.

I call Janis's rooms as soon as I'm off the plane. My plan is to say that something's come up, but I can feel my voice going, or my breath going wrong, as if I've breathed in too much before calling. My lungs feel stuck full with air and I can't move it in or out.

'Do you want to come in today?' a voice says, when I'm stranded with my request half-made. 'Do you want to make an appointment? We have a cancellation mid-morning, if you'd like that. If you can get in here in about forty minutes.'

I go into the toilets and I sit in a cubicle until I can fix my breathing. I read every word of the tampon ad on the back of the door. I count, and breathe slowly in and out, and I remember Elli reading the condom ad in a cubicle at this same airport.

There's still a crowd around the baggage carousel when I get there, and my suitcase is out and doing laps.

Outside the terminal, the air is warm and thick and humid, carrying the usual smell of spent fuel and the nearby wetlands. I queue for a cab and give the cabbie Janis's Wickham Terrace address as we pull away from the kerb. He's not a talker, and I'm grateful. We glide down the airport road, swinging in and out of the curves on the lazy suspension. There has been rain while I've been gone. The grass is now lush by the roadside and it was brown when I left. The early summer storms have come.

A plane takes off beside us, the road curves and then curves again, the cabbie fiddles with a knob, trying to tune in properly to the radio station that's crackling away playing Steely Dan.

'Bloody thing,' he says. 'It's not my car.'

We loop past industrial buildings and the wharves to Kingsford-Smith Drive and the Inner City Bypass. There is hardly a cloud above the city today, and little traffic now that peak hour has passed. I'm home, but it's not enough like home. I know it all well – the steel and glass of the city centre, the timber and tin of the old houses, the tall trees in Newstead Park – but the light is harsh today and nothing looks entirely like itself, and I feel sad.

Janis is still with her previous client when I arrive.

'You've hurt your hand,' the receptionist says, and I tell

her that's what celebrity canoeing does to you, if you're partnered with some dweebie guy who's known for the best mosaics on TV, and some idiot goes and puts a paddle in his hand.

I wish I could remember her name, but I can't. She's not always here, but I know we've met before. I push my suitcase into the corner and she gets me a glass of water and says I should sit. I tell her that I've been sitting on planes, sitting for hours, and I'd rather stand, if that's okay. She nods and gets me more water. There's a plant in the corner and I ask her what it is and she says she doesn't know. I tell her I like the look of it and she says it's probably artificial. She doesn't know for sure, but she never goes near it so she hopes they're not expecting her to water it. She laughs.

I'm feeling slimy and unclean and tired from the flight and I realise I must look far from my best, so I explain that I've just flown overnight from Perth via Melbourne and that it feels wrong and unfair to have jet lag without having left your own country.

And she says 'Oh, jet lag' as though it might account for a lot at times like these.

I ask if there's a bathroom, and I go and wash my face. I take my time, and Janis is waiting when I get back.

'Hi,' she says with a smile. 'Come on in.'

And I say Hi to her and ask her how she's been, and it's not so bad. It's familiar. I walk into her room and she shuts the door behind us.

There's a picture of a boat on the opposite wall and all of a sudden it seems to shudder and she says, 'Take a seat, take a seat.' She gives me the calm smile therapists give you before you tip your life all over them, and she says, 'So, how have things been for you? You've been away for a few weeks, haven't you? There have probably been a few times during that that haven't been easy.'

And I say 'Yeah' and I start to tell her my tooth story, and I'm racing through it but she's onto me, giving a polite half-laugh and saying that as long as I found a good dentist the worst of that episode is hopefully behind me.

So I tell her, 'I met this guy in Canada, and it's so complicated, but he has a wife and three kids in Thunder Bay, Ontario, so not that complicated in the end. And of course, I wasn't looking for anything like that, not that it amounted to much, but Murray and I had reached our conclusion by then.' She's nodding, nodding and waiting for this to go somewhere. I'm talking too fast, and the timing of my breathing is all confused. 'It was just an incident, hardly life-changing. Anyway, anyway, okay, there's one or two other things, I have to admit that. I hit a guy in the face with a paintball gun and it *was* deliberate.'

'Could I just stop you for a second,' she says in a voice that sounds half-speed, so slow it's hard for me to stick with it. 'Could I ask what happened to the wrist that you've got the bandage on?'

'Well, sure, that's part of it. Not part of it directly, but it got hit by a canoe paddle, and I'm getting there. I'm getting to that bit.' I have things I want to say and she shouldn't interrupt me. It's hard to get them right. 'Remember those times, remember those times when Murray told us that stupid story about the cart and the bent axle? Did he tell us that one in here? Do you remember it? And how I didn't tell the same sort of thing, the same sort of story? And that was a difference. Which was the bit I said, just that it was a difference . . .'

And she says, 'Slower. You're losing me. Just take your time and tell me what you need to tell me.'

'Yes, it's from a long time ago. And it's a secret, a sworn secret, you have to understand that. Lives depended on it once. Or there was a chance they might have. I don't know.'

She has a jug on the desk, and she refills my water glass, which I'm still holding tightly in both hands. She pushes the box of tissues over. She nods, but doesn't speak.

'All right. It's a complicated story. There was glass in this hand, there still might be more, but I don't think so . . .'

And I'm afraid telling her, afraid telling her one word of these things that I'd promised I'd keep to myself. Everything would be okay if I kept the secrets, that's what I knew. And it was okay, or next to okay, ever since. Though it was a terrible effort sometimes, and very tiring. Dreams came along and got mixed in, and things can lose their certainty, but stay just as vivid when they come back at you. And you call it a dream, a bad dream, a recurring nightmare, but you can hear it, smell it, taste it because you did it. Because you were there. And it never figures in other people's stories of that time – your parents' stories, told with authority – because they weren't there, not that day, not that night.

And you never tell them because you said you never would, and because you flew away with them to start a new life, without them knowing what you'd done. Time passes, and why would you change that? Why would you bring anguish upon them, and guilt they don't need to feel? They can't be faulted, and you can't let them down.

My mother said it was bad dreams, then and later, when I'd wake up shouting in the middle of the night. And it *was* bad dreams, but here's where they came from.

I tell her. I tell Janis about the Macleishes and the arsenal under their barn. I tell her how it felt the first time I fired the Webley at targets in the field. I tell her I'd got the story wrong in parts, remembered the wrong worst bit. The wrong trip to Belfast.

Belfast – 1972

We're in the van and it's dark and bumpy, but I've got a torch in my pocket – just a little one my mother gave me for any bathroom visits in the middle of the night. Not that it's a room that's hard to find at the Macleishes' house. It's two doors down on the right from the one I get to sleep in.

The torch is like a pen and it has a clip on it. It's in my pocket and I take it out and turn it on and Paul says, 'What are you doing back there?' but not in a bad way. He's just asking.

The light shines on my hand in a circle, with fuzzy edges. I can see other people's faces, just. I turn it off and put it away.

There's the smell of a cigarette from the front, from Danny not Paul, and in the back the smell of dogs and earth. I'm on a sack and the floor's hard. The sack's empty and it slips and slides. It's a potato sack, probably. There's a bag poking into my side.

We ate a bird for dinner, and it looked more like a bird than chickens do. I know chickens are birds just as much, but you buy them half-ready. This one wasn't a chicken, it came from the woods, it had a pellet in its neck from the shotgun. There were some other pellets too but Mrs Macleish had got them out by then. Mark found the one in its neck and she told him, 'Don't be such a fool with all your noise about lead poisoning, just eat what's in front of you.'

I got my hair done in plaits before going to the Macleishes'. I don't like it that way much, but some people do. Actually, I quite like it sometimes, but mainly it's good for keeping your hair off your face, which is good if you mean business.

So, Paul has this plan, and we've been practising for it. And we've put ideas in too, Mark and me, and they've made the plan better, so now it's ours as well. I don't know who the other people are, the people in Belfast, but Paul does and you can't know everything. You know what you need to know and you follow orders. And when it came to the plan, he listened to Mark and me because we know strategy. Cover the exits, work out your escape routes, set it up as a trap, things like that. And it wouldn't have worked with just him and Danny, but it would work with us.

He said it was boring, driving guns around hidden in the back of the van. He said it was good the first time, since you didn't know what would happen. But nothing happened and, if you knew the right roads, nothing would. He said, 'I'm good for more than that, and I'm going to show them. We're going to show them we can do anything. I'm sick of being their donkey, just carrying things around.'

There are more lights above us outside now. It's a city road. More stopping and starting, not so many bumps.

'It's here,' Danny says, 'Yeah, that's the one.'

We turn, and then turn again and drive slowly down a quieter street. I'm just getting settled when we make another turn, this time a left into a street with no lights, a back street. Paul stops the engine and the van rolls down the hill, with only the sound of gravel and the road pressing under the wheels, and then the squeak of brakes as we stop.

I shine my torch into the bag, and the Sten is sitting next to its magazine and silencer, and the Webley and the other guns are in there too. Mark goes to get the Sten ready, but his hands are shaking and he's rattling the silencer around when the back door opens and Paul's there, looking at him like he's an idiot.

Paul points at me and I take the gun and fit the silencer in one go, and then he pulls the Webley out of the bag and gives it to Mark instead. Mark's not happy, but he doesn't say anything. He wants the Sten, but Paul gets to decide. And Paul points to me, points to the Sten. I get to keep it.

Then we're out of the van and signalling, doing what we've trained to do. It's cold outside. It'd be warm in bed, warm in the spare room at the Macleishes'. From the window in that room you can see the fields and the corner of the barn, and the woods in the distance. And the bed is huge and high, and no one could be too big for it. I should be in that bed now. It's very late. I hope they don't miss us. I've done my homework though, that beach story for the second time.

Danny and Sammy are off – I can hear their feet going at a quick walk, boots on the laneway, then around the corner.

Then nothing happens, it's all quiet. There's traffic on

a road some way beyond the houses, but not here. I'm waiting, I'm cold, the moon is out. The house in front of us is white, but the door is dark. It might be black or dark blue, or it might be dark green like ours. I'm ready, I'm ready, I've found a wall just the right height to lean on, next to the back gate. I know all about these men, all about them, all I need to. Paul has told us the plan, and what we have to do.

There's a bang around the front of the house, another bang, shouting, then the back door's flung open and they run out into the moonlight, two men. That's what we're here for and I line them up. It's too easy, and I fire. A burst, another burst and I hit the front one in the chest or the shoulder and I see his face properly and I'm thinking you look like my uncle, a bit like my uncle, but you are a bad man, a Catholic IRA man and bad, and you'll be down my lane with guns if I don't get you first, I know you will, I know you will. I've seen the news and I can use this gun.

And the Sten pulls and jumps around and it's hard to steady. The silencer makes it click instead of banging, and there's more noise made at the other end with the bullets hitting things, a window, the door, the wall. And the second man is thrown back and he hits the door frame, and a piece flies off it as though he's hit it that hard. The bullets go right through these people. The magazine empties, thirty-two bullets if it was fully loaded, thirty-two bullets across their middles, enough of them hitting that the misses are just as well or the mess would be trouble. They'll need a new coat of whitewash on that wall as it is.

And there are hands under my arms pulling me away,

but I've learned all this so they shouldn't. I have the gun and we have to kill these people. I can change the clip on a dark moonless night and keep firing, so they shouldn't take my Sten even though the job's done. There might always be another, another of the bastards not dead yet in some bad bit of shadow in there with a Sten of his own, or in his big saloon car coming up my lane, any night, any night for the rest of my days.

When I'm big I'll be better at this. When I'm big I'll be strong. I'll make myself strong. I'll be ready then, if they come for me. As ready as a person can be. As ready as a soldier, always.

Brisbane — Monday

'So that's it. That's the whole story, as much as I can think of.'

I wait a while for Janis to talk, and she says, 'Right.'

'And we might have been ambushed the other time, at the show, or just unlucky. Mr Macleish said he reckoned they could have seen the van that night, someone probably had, so they went for us when we took it back to Belfast. And that might be wrong, but it might be right. In which case, the guy with the Tommy gun was after us. In fact, after me. So, you see, if that's where the dreams come from it's not irrational, not paranoid. It's not strange at all. Another reason not to have talked about the dreams without getting into the whole story. And that didn't feel possible. And I haven't been depressed. I know you both think I have, but it wears you down, all this. That's all.'

I'm turned at an angle in the seat, my forehead on my arm, face down on the desk blotter. I've run out of energy. I'm crying a warm damp patch into the absorbent paper. Murray's hand is on my head, on my hair, patting, resting there.

He leans down near me, puts his chin on my shoulder. 'We'll get through this,' he says.

And I find myself saying, 'Yes, that'd be good.' My mouth, lips and face are all tingling. 'I'm going to be sick. Damn that airline food.'

Murray laughs, I think. That's better. I wanted to hear that. Janis grabs the bin out from under her desk. I put it in my lap and wrap my arms around it, and lean on the edge of it with my chin.

'Some people would recycle that paper,' I tell her, and the airconditioning is cool on the sweat on my face, and this wave of nausea subsides. 'I can do better. Airline food's such an easy target. And it's improved from the way it was years ago, mostly.'

I'm staring down into the bin. It's rectangular, and I'm staring at an angle where two sides meet. It's like my first memory, my face squared up in the corner of my pram under the laburnum tree full of yellow flowers, back when nothing had gone wrong and I had no secrets.

I have no secrets now, for the first time in thirty years.

Though it hasn't gone, the weight of them has shifted. Maybe they don't have the hold on me that they once did, now that they're not kept in my head.

I'm through one telling of my story, and I'm still here. And Murray's still here. I'll have to talk to my parents too, but perhaps I can now.

'You were eight,' Janis says. 'Eight years old. Whatever happened that night, you didn't make it happen.' There's another pause. Murray doesn't contradict her. 'We'll get you through this,' she says.

And Murray says, 'Yeah, we will.'

Acknowledgements

FIRST, for canoe races, conversation, fundraising anthologies and, in some cases, some very timely observations, I'd like to thank the handful of people whose names are attached to characters who make cameo appearances in the novel. I'd also like to thank the people I've met and friends I've made in places like Calgary, Vancouver, Christchurch and Perth, while I've been on tour with books or attending writers' festivals. You have made my experience of all those places so positive that I have since bored my friends at home by recounting details at length, and probably repeatedly.

I'm also grateful to the people who – to borrow briefly from Meg's insights on page eight – look after me in my role as a 'special idiot, someone who had some kind of gift but who could not be expected to show any sense or remember what they were there for'. Author care isn't always easy, and for providing the right kinds of it at just the right times, I'd like to thank, among others, Fiona and Pippa at Curtis Brown, Clare and Kirsten at Penguin, Liz at Sunny Garden, and Rachel for discussion, debate and sizeable numbered lists of questions that were a crucial part of me getting the most out of this story.

And I'd like to thank Sarah, family and friends for making life work in the important places where author care doesn't apply.